A Shudder in Time

John G. Powell

Dedication

I dedicate this book to my sons, John Robert Powell and Michael Glenn Powell. They share my fondness for science fiction, for them dating back at least to the original *Star Wars* movie. Mine dates to Robert Heinlein and Ray Bradbury. The boys were very young when *Star Wars* came to the theaters, but we sat through that film two and one-half times. In a drive-in! We left only because the boys were having a hard time keeping their eyes open. And their mother was making certain comments regarding our intelligence. Fond memories.

Prolog

"The future ain't what it used to be."
~ Yogi Berra

After reading Jim Drake's experience, which is retold in the following pages, you will probably think about this in a different way.

Forward

Perhaps this should be called a disclaimer, since its primary purpose is to certify that all the names used in this recounting are fictitious. If the real names of the participants were to be divulged, especially the scientists, the career of every one would be destroyed utterly. After all, who would want their name or their company or their institution associated with researchers who claim such events as these are fact? That's why you'll never read of this in a professional publication. Additionally, the testing and measurements were not done in the laboratories cited, although they could have been.

Chapter 1

Out of Nowhere

The murmur of the Dodger Stadium crowd danced all around the edges of Jim's awareness. Thousands of voices blended into a meaningless babble that possessed enough power to arouse an excitement in him, a sense of anticipation. A sort of adrenaline-like tingling energizing his body. It was always like this for him at a ball game, part of what made it fun. He looked at Trina hoping to share the moment, but she seemed to be making an effort to detach herself from the hubbub that was stimulating him. He surveyed the people seated near them, and they seemed nonchalant. Not Jim.

He turned toward the field to watch the first pitch, and did a double take at a girl making her way down the row in front of them, looking for her seat. Her blouse was stretched to the limit over a chest that was... he realized he was ogling and quickly looked back to the field, careful not to glance at Trina, hoping she hadn't noticed him noticing.

Ball two.

Trina leaned over to him, her breath warm and moist in his ear, a smirk flavoring the words as she said, "Do you suppose they're natural?"

Jim took a sip of beer, sat it down between his legs, then turned to his wife. "Honey, I noticed but I wasn't interested." He realized that wouldn't quite cover his blunder. "It was just... God, what normal male wouldn't look? I mean, her breastwork is sort of, well, it's formidable."

Trina almost never let her insecurity seep out into the open and she did not now, although Jim sensed it was there, covered by the underscore of nonchalance coloring her words. "Formidable? I never would have thought of using that word. Maybe I can find a place for it in my new book. The murderer is a well-endowed young woman with an unfaithful husband."

He just smiled. He knew from experience that any comment could and would be used against him. He glanced at the scoreboard. Two balls and two strikes. He had missed two pitches. He turned back to Trina, hoping it was over so he could watch the game.

"And breastwork?" Trina grinned in genuine amusement in spite of herself. He guessed it was the author in her coming out. "What an interesting vocabulary, sweetheart." She leaned closer. "It's going to be a strain all afternoon, isn't it?"

So she was pissed. He'd thought so. As he began trying to come up with a suitable response, he was spared the need. The crack of a bat shattered the interlude and the crowd erupted in a roar. The ball sliced over the dugout, arrowing back toward them. Jim jumped up along with everyone else hoping for a chance to snag it. His excitement made it seem as if the ball was moving in slow motion. There was nothing but the ball and the surging growl of the crowd. The ball and the roar. White ball against blue sky. The roar. The ball. He could see the seams, the stitching circling slowly, slowly. A big white circle that filled the sky. A zero. a Japanese Zero, for Christ sake! Coming right at him! He could hear the engine, an enraged roar behind the blur of propeller. It kept coming. Closer. Engine screaming.

Machine guns erupted. Belched fire. Orange flames stabbed from the wings. Bullets shredded the air. Smacked into the ground a hundred yards in front of him, tearing a path toward him through the sand and lava. Clattering guns, roaring engine, streaming tracers. A cacophony of terror. Fear filled the world. Chaos. Splattering rock.

"Get down, you idiot!"

Adrian grabbed him, yanked him down.

Bullets pulverized the side of the shallow rampart he had been standing in front of. Tore the ground. Sand and lava pelted his helmet, stung his arms and neck.

The Zero pulled out if its dive and passed thirty feet overhead, engine roaring in outrage. It banked, seeking other prey.

"What the hell's the matter with you, Osborne?"

"I... I..." Philip cowered down with his head against the side of the pitiful little barrier that separated them from the inland jungle but left them exposed on the ocean side. The side where the plane had come from. The sand pushed his helmet back, and he felt sharp grit grinding into his forehead.

"Christ, don't you remember what happened to McGilvery?"

"God!" The image was immediate and stark: blood splattering, red and pink flesh. Guts and organs. All over him, all over the ground. All over. Just twenty yards back toward the water. Just minutes ago.

"What the hell were you thinking, Philip?"

"I don't know. I... It seemed like I was somewhere else."

"Well, you damn near were. In heaven or hell."

"Where's Leon?" Philip raised his head to look for his friend, but everyone was crouched behind whatever barrier they had found or dug. Hiding. Sweating. Cursing or praying.

"Captain's got him on the radio trying to find out where the hell our flyboys are. Radio man was killed." Adrian rolled onto his side, then pointed out over the ocean. "Guess he doesn't need to ask. They're busy."

Philip twisted to look. There were maybe fifty planes in a dog fight. "We upset a hornet's nest. Our guys can't even get here." There were at least as many Zeros as Mustangs, and some of each were going down, leaving filthy gray smoke trails that dirtied the sky as the fallen heroes corkscrewed toward the waiting arms of the somber, immutable ocean. The dogfight was a pantomime of hell, a ballet of death. Philip felt involved yet disconnected from the emotions, the terror that had to be reigning in those cockpits.

But hell dwelled down here too. Philip squirmed around so he could look inland to the jungle maybe fifty yards away. Black-green foliage, hanging fronds, trees sulking in their own gloom making everything dark. Deep shadows, dark green and darker green cut by bright slashes of sunlight. Figures moved, but whether it was leaves and shadows or Japs he could not decide. Patterns formed and faded and twisted. Shadowy places writhed and slithered. The air, thick and heavy, seemed to cling to the echoes of horror resounding across the deadened land, over the bodies littering the beach.

The ragged sound of distant machine gun fire pummeled him from the airplanes, salvos of savagery stabbing out from the roar and whine of fighter engines, sounds of life and death for the men above. Sounds of anguish and escape and failure, of killing or survival as the dogfight tumbled through the sky. Close yet remote. Intimate yet disconnected from here. And the chest deep booms from the big guns on the battleships and destroyers lurking farther out. But Philip couldn't see where the shells were landing. That must be some distance beyond the silent, ominous border of the jungle.

One patch of leafy concealment reminded Philip of the ungainly, tatter-leafed banana tree his mother nurtured in the back yard, hoping each year to get more than a few misshapen bananas from it, and the large patch of bamboo next to it, canes growing shoulder-to-shoulder from a mad tangle of roots. That was where he and his brother used to play war, hiding from each other. Play war? God, what naïve innocence. War was sure as hell no game. It was friend's bodies ripped apart leaving a pile of bloody pieces on the beach. Lots of bodies on the sand, many without life.

He had a sudden image of Mom tending her chickens, reaching under the brooding hens to gather eggs, all the birds in the hen house cack-cacking. Then he thought of her teary eyes and proud face when he left to join up, and a surge of anguish filled him. He was not able to help much with expenses now. He wondered how his parents would make it with the rationing. The little two-bedroom house. The driveway, two dirt tracks with grass in the middle. He had planned to paint the outside of the house this summer, fresh white paint, and build that trellis his mother wanted. That seemed so alien now. So distant. So irrelevant.

"All right men, we're moving. Up to that line of lava. Keep low. Don't run in a straight line. Go!" The Captain, a dozen or so men down from Philip, thrust himself up in the trench. Jabbed with his arms. The remnants of the company, the half that was left after the landing, staggered to their feet. "Go! Go! Go!"

Then the gates of Hell clattered open. Their own machine gunners opened fire in a strident, hammering cacophony, raking the slumbering jungle, shredding bushes, leaves.

Then enemy fire erupted. Muzzle flashes licked out, fiery tongues probing for prey. The jungle came alive. Some of those shadows were Japs. A lot of them were. More machine-gun fire, jagged sonic eruptions that retched hatred, this time from the enemy lines, and more rifle fire. He and Adrian scrambled out of the tiny trench with the others, loaded down with ammo and gear, M1 ready. They began running bent-over toward the trees which now seemed to have a Jap behind each one. Thank God for the new semi-automatic Garand instead of the old bolt action Springfields. But he didn't fire. He couldn't tell what was what. Shadows among shadows. Dancing killers, waving branches, green-black confusion. Firing everywhere.

A bullet plowed the dirt near his foot, and the earth puked an eruption of sand. But he still had no target. A muzzle flash, and he saw one. Aimed. And it was gone. Into the green-black shadows. Rifle held half between hip and shoulder, he fired a round anyway, blinded with confusion and noise and fear.

Adrian grunted beside him, stumbled, fell. Blood burst from a tear in his pant leg. Philip stopped, dropped to his knees, crawled back and reached for Adrian's leg, for a pressure point as life pulsed out onto the ground. He took Adrian's hand, pressed his thumb over the artery. "Push. Hold pressure here."

"Get the hell out of here. The medics will get to me."

"Keep pushing here or you'll bleed to death."

"They need you up there. I'm okay."

"Shut the hell up!" Philip unbuckled Adrian's trouser belt, threaded it out of a couple of loops and yanked it out the rest of the way. Shoved it under and around the leg. Threaded the end back through the buckle, took up most of the slack. Unsheathed Adrian's bayonet and stuck it under the loop, sharp edges up and down. Twisted. Half a circle. Removed Adrian's hand from the artery. Blood spurted. He twisted more, a full circle. One and a half turns. The gushing finally stopped. Almost. "Here, hold on to this." God, he must have lost a quart or more. Adrian's lower leg was soaked, the ground was covered, Philip's arms were coated, his hands sticky. Philip looked back, spotted a Medic. "Medic! Over here!"

The Medic looked, nodded, and began crab-crawling their way, abandoning a man sprawled motionless on the ground.

Philip lay down near Adrian as he waited for the medic. Here on the ground, in a slight depression, the firing seemed more distant. The war seemed to have slowed, moved farther away. Philip raised up on one elbow and looked at Adrian. The strained tendons and muscles that at first had protruded from his face and neck had flowed back, leaving smooth skin. The fear in his eyes was now softened by the bland haze of shock. Philip squeezed Adrian's wrist, the one holding the bayonet, and Adrian managed a grim smile and put his free hand on Philip's. "Keep your fool head down."

Philip gazed into the now peaceful face—not a mask of oncoming death, but of relief, of coming escape from the hell of Truk Island, escape to the swaying fronds of Hawaii and the VA Hospital. Philip felt relief too, and gratitude. And envy.

"I got him." The medic slithered into the depression and put his hand on the bayonet. "Good work, private."

"So long, Adrian."

Adrian nodded, but there was a sadness in his eyes. "Write me when you get a chance, my friend."

Philip scrambled to his feet and stood bent over, wiping his hands on his pants so he could handle his rifle better.

"Give my parents a call when you get a chance. Tell 'em I'm fine."

A bullet slapped the ground near them, flung gravel. Philip hit the ground. Scanned the jungle over his sights from a prone position. Another bullet ripped the ground to his right, but this time he saw the sniper. He lined up his sights and throttled the trigger. Barely felt the recoil. An impersonal figure in dark clothing jerked and his weapon flailed skyward as if someone had yanked him from behind. A stain bloomed on his chest like a black rose. A slash of sun illuminated his body, and he became a real person. He crumbled in slow motion, a pantomime of agony, of fleeing life-force as death descended, plucking a soul.

"Jesus!" Philip gasped a breath. Another one. He relaxed his grip on the rifle; looked down at the ground two inches from his face. "I'm sorry, God." He noticed little rocks and grains of sand and crushed bits of sea shell, all in sharp relief. All created by God. The enemy he didn't even know had also been created by God. Did he have worrying parents too? He musts have. Now it was over. "I'm sorry," he said again. "Please forgive me."

He took another deep breath, and scrambled to his feet. Ran bent-over in a zigzag pattern. Sweat blinded his right eye, and he closed it. He could feel the jungle now, seething with fear and hate. And the sharp odor of gunpowder mixed with the steamy, sticky air. He still had ten yards to go. Didn't know if... a mortar shell exploded in front of him. Debris flew into the sky like a burst from a Fourth-of-July rocket. Like stars exploding.

His world went red. Then black.

Perturb. The word seemed to float in darkness.

The sound of battle slipped into the distance and evaporated. The blackness melted and became gentle, silver-soft. The lighting was uniform, shadowless, as if he were inside a pearl. And in a sense they were in a pearl, or an egg. An egg transporting a bit of humanity through...

Zeleece, sitting next to him in this immense eggshell, yanked on his arm and squeezed it in a clutch of fear. Something was scaring her, her face a taught mask. Then Talaan felt it too.

A shifting of the universe. He looked at the other passengers.

Reality defocused as atoms and molecules briefly lost coherence, as mesons and quarks became uncertain in their pairings. The strong and weak nuclear forces unwrapped into other configurations, attended other dimensions, then returned. All this subatomic activity took place at intervals of femtoseconds, of course, and for durations much shorter still, yet the cumulative effects were noticeable and unsettling.

Fear welled within him.

"Talaan , look at the stars!" Panic rattled Zeleece's voice.

Talaan looked out the virtual viewport where Zeleece was pointing—their seats were cheap, a hundred meters or more from the hull of the starshuttle. They were massed with twenty thousand other standard fares.

The stars were stark points and appeared perfectly normal.

Then they moved! Shifted, as if gathering then dispersing! But stars can't do that. Now they locked into place, and things seemed normal.

But suddenly the universe shrugged again. Rippled. Became fuzzy and smeared. "Zang!" Talaan said. "We've got big trouble, Zeleece."

The smudges that had been stars began wavering into and out of existence. Space itself dissolved, then precipitated back, to black and stars and galaxies. Talaan started to relax a little, but then everything shuddered again and crumbled into gray chaos, vacillated between real and not, between normal spacetime and the quantum uncertainty of alterspace.

The universe was undecided. The ship was undecided.

"God, Talaan! The ship isn't locking into realspace." Her eyes were wide, seeking assurance in the depths of his. Begging for salvation.

But all he could say was, "I know." He patted her hand. A pathetic little gesture. He looked from her to the holographic viewport. It was true. There was no lock. They were sideslipping along the hyperdimensional brink of real spacetime.

"I hate this shit," Zeleece said. "This piece of junk barge is probably a thousand years old. No more of this economy crap, Talaan."

"The captain better override, dive back in on manual," he said.

"If he can."

Then the stars locked in. He could feel deceleration, a feature of realspace. They were back, in solid. Talaan heard himself let his breath out, then felt the release of tension in his chest and stomach as he took in a fresh breath.

"Never again." Zeleece tugged on his arm for emphasis. "Never again will you or anyone else get me to travel on one of these decrepit old scows, I don't care how much cheaper it is." She yanked his arm again.

Perturb.

"Jim, are you okay?"

Trina pulled on his arm once more.

Jim took a breath. Fought the panic. Tried to get oriented. He flicked his eyes right then left real quick without moving his head. He was at the ballpark. He felt the body heat of the guy next to him.

Jesus Christ! What the hell had happened?

"Are you okay?" Trina said again.

"Yeah." He kept his eyes down. What the fuck had happened? Where was Zeleece? The war? Adrian? The starship? How did... who—

"It's a home run," the guy next to him shouted as he stood up.

Jim sat still, rolled his eyes up to look at the people. They seemed real. The girl in front jumped up and down, breasts threatening to explode from her blouse. He buried his face in his hands, could feel the pressure of his fingers, and his fingers felt his head, and it was solid.

What the hell happened? Where had he been? How... Jesus! It was like... he had *been* there. Wherever there was. *He had been those people.* That was the... that was the most... he saw the beer between his feet. Sitting on hard concrete. He tapped his foot. It was there all right, the concrete. He reached down, picked up the cup and had a drink. It was beer. Stale. It didn't taste good, but it was real. He set it back down.

"What's wrong, Jim?" Trina sat down and took his hand.

"Nothing." He kept his eyes averted because he knew that what she would see was wildness. And panic. He couldn't let her see that.

"Look at me," she said.

"Why?" He studied his shoes. There was no blood on them. No sand.

"Jim, look at me."

He looked.

"God, Jim!" Her face paled. "What's wrong?"

"Nothing." He wrenched his eyes from hers to the ball field. "What just happened?"

"Anderson hit a home run. What's wrong with you? You look like you just witnessed your own death."

"Who gives a... I mean, that's not what I meant." He turned to her. "Did an airplane just fly over here real low?"

Trina raised an eyebrow. "An airplane?" Her brown eyes were big and serious. "No. At least I didn't notice one."

"Well, I did, and... It wasn't one of ours, Trina."

"What do you mean?"

"It was a Japanese Zero. Firing bullets."

"A Japanese Zero? I don't think there are any of those around anymore. It was firing? Jim, what are you talking about? That's crazy."

"Yeah. I must be."

She smiled a crooked little smile that flickered with uncertainty, trying to decide how worried to be, or not. "Did you doze off? Did your mind just fantasize?"

"No." There was only one explanation. He'd gone crazy. Left reality. He pressed his thumbnail into his finger. He could feel the pressure, the hurt, and it was real. But so had been the bullets. And the blood. They were real, and the sand. The wavering, dissolving universe, it had scared the crap out of him, because he had understood what was happening. And Zeleece. She was soft and fun and real and he loved her. He knew who he was, and he was Talaan. He had a history. He shook his head no. "No, that wasn't me."

"What?"

"This wasn't... It was..." He stopped. What was it? What could he say? That it had been life? But how could it have been?

"What?" Trina was intent. She pulled his head around so it was facing her.

"I don't know. Nothing."

Trina felt his forehead. "Honey, try to relax. Have you got one of your headaches? Don't drink any more beer."

"No. I don't know. Maybe. Yeah, probably that's it. Blood vessels exploded in my brain."

"I'll go get you some coffee. Caffeine helps those headaches." She got up and he pulled his legs back so she could work her way past him. She smiled primly at the men next to them. "Excuse me please, gentlemen."

The two men got up and moved into the aisle for her.

"Are you all right?" the one next to Jim asked as they sat back down. "You look kinda pale."

"Yeah. I'll be okay. I just had some sort of a spell." The last thing Jim wanted to do was talk. He turned away. Then in a surge of fear he looked up and checked for planes. He listened intently as he surveyed the sky inch by inch, but the only sounds were from the game. The home plate umpire, the crowd, the announcer. A radio someone had tuned to the game, and a vendor selling ice cream the next section over. The sky was empty. He wished Trina was back. Looked out at the scoreboard without seeing it. Nothing mattered. He didn't trust his senses.

The inning was over, and everyone shifted in their seats. He wondered what inning it was without caring. First? Second? He glanced down at his beer, but didn't want it. Where the hell had that fighter come from? He looked at his hands. But he knew before he looked that there was no blood. He'd looked before. Besides, hallucinations don't leave residue. And what about Zeleece? His girlfriend, with the stripe of chrome hair across her scalp? They were getting pretty serious.

Then Trina was back. The two men got up again to let her in. She handed a coffee cup to him, then sat down. He gulped half of it. It had an unpleasant taste, like the coffee maker was dirty, and it wasn't very hot.

She looked at him intently. " I think we should leave."

"Yeah."

"I'm sorry," Trina said to the two men. "Would you excuse us one more time?"

Jim stood up and felt a little disoriented, but quickly regained his balance.

The men mumbled something about no problem as they hefted their weight aloft once again.

"Thanks," Jim said without looking at them.

As they left the stadium Trina said, "I'm driving." She held out her hand.

He fished the keys from his pocket and dropped them into her palm, which she closed without a word. She didn't like to drive the Porsche, didn't like stick shifts and refused to use the paddle shifters. But after they got to the car and she started it, she found reverse with no problem.

Truk Island? Where the hell was Truk Island? He remembered hearing of it on the History Channel. At least that had happened, a landing there during World War II, way back in the forties.

But not to him. He wasn't born then!

And realspace? Starshuttle? Zeleece and Talaan? Where did that come from? That sure as hell wasn't some buried memory. But when he was Talaan he knew Zeleece and her family, and knew Talaan's history and his parents. They were his, Talaan's, parents. His and his older brother's. Man-oh-man. He really was going crazy. He must be. But the weird thing was, he was at home there. He had a history, knew who he was and where he'd been yesterday and last year and back to childhood and school and his toys as a kid. In both lives. With all the details filled in.

He leaned his head back and looked over at Trina. She was concentrating on driving, on shifting gears. He stared at her long, dark auburn hair, the recesses plaited with highlights and dusky shadows, shifting patterns, caves of jungle darkness and deep-space blackness. Panic surged, threatened to explode. "Jesus!" he whispered under his breath.

His mind was spinning, churning, racing. His emotions seemed ready to explode. What the hell was going on with him? He glanced at Trina, but she was intent on driving, convinced he had a vascular headache and needed silence. Thank God. There was no way he could deal with questions.

The quiet wouldn't last, but for now he could struggle in isolation with thoughts that rampaged and tumbled despite his efforts to shut them off. He tried to reason but what had happened was beyond reason. He tried over and over to bury the insanity with logic—this could not happen; it was a dream; he imagined it; it was plain stupid; his beer was drugged. But his mind knew better as it kept leaping across centuries, and identities, and impossible situations. Yet underneath each image, every remembrance, he found insanity leering at him, prowling and gaining strength.

Chapter 2

It's all in your head

He realized they were home with a mixture of relief and dread. Trina executed a smooth downshift and turned into the driveway, paused for the door to open, then pulled into the garage. They entered the house as the overhead door grumbled closed, shutting out the night and the world. The real world, he thought sarcastically.

Trina handed him the car keys, and he chucked them on the antique Biedermeier table on his way to the family room. He absently noticed them skid across the veneer pattern, the Austrian shellac finish. He hated that table, especially after learning how beautiful the Biedermeier style could be, which this one wasn't. Damn waste of money.

"Don't be scratching that up with your stupid keys." Trina picked them up and placed them in a porcelain dish sitting atop a doily on the table, then rubbed her finger over the spot where they had landed.

He frowned, but refrained from saying she was more worried about the damn table than him. Screw it. He needed to numb himself, not worry about that kind of crap. Then it occurred to him. His anger had completely removed his preoccupation with insanity. His thoughts were normal. For the first time. "Thanks," he said.

Trina looked at him in bewilderment. He turned away and strode to the bar, not interested in explaining. He grabbed a glass and shoved it against the lever on the ice maker. Watched cubes clatter in and form a jumbled heap. He sloshed Jack Daniels up to the brim, slurped a little of the whiskey, jabbed the cubes a couple of times with his finger, then headed for the couch and plopped down.

Trina stood in the open area between the family room and kitchen, one shoulder against the wall, arms folded. "What are you doing? Alcohol makes your headaches worse. You need caffeine." Her voice was accusing, saying without saying, 'I can make it better if you let me, but if you don't let me you'll suffer.'

Jim held his hand up in a stop signal and took a long, slow sip of bourbon. He swallowed and sat the glass down on the coffee table, making sure to use a coaster, and leaned back as the liquor lit a path to his stomach. When his throat relaxed, he said, "I don't have a headache." Talk was good. This sparring was good. It was keeping his mind right here.

Trina glared at his whiskey glass, then at him, and shook her head. "I was going to make you some strong coffee, but I guess you don't want it."

"No." He searched his mind for any bits insanity. Found none.

"Can I get you anything?" she persisted.

"No." Stop trying to fix it, was what he really wanted to say. This is my problem and I'll solve it myself, is what he didn't say. How could he tell her anything that made sense? How could he make her understand? How do you explain going nuts to someone who has never gone nuts? And if he did talk about it, she'd think she could fix it, pestering him with all kinds of stupid ideas.

She gave an angry shrug. "I'm going to put on my slippers. Want me to bring yours down?"

"No."

She flounced around and went up the stairs.

"No thanks," he said.

He took another slug of whiskey, then closed his eyes. How had he been transplanted to another place and time? It hadn't been at all like a dream. He had *lived* the experiences, and he couldn't go back and change them like he sometimes did in a dream. He had literally become those people. He knew everything about them. History, family, friends, circumstances leading up to the moment. Everything. He knew that as Philip he was afraid of heights and that was why he had put off painting the house. He could picture Captain Mancer on the ship telling them at the last minute that they were landing on Truk Island. He knew how Zeleece loved changing her hair style, and making love in weird places. He remembered everything, and that really scared the hell out of him because it made even less sense.

Maybe it had been a fantasy. Maybe that's all it was. But if it was, how did he have a history in those other lives? It should be fuzzy. Or nonexistent. Yet everything was crystal clear. He knew the personality of each of them based on past experiences. Successes and failures and friendships and relationships and school and work and fun and tragedies. Family and friend's marriages and deaths and birthdays and trips to the beach. He remembered every one of them. He couldn't have fantasized all that stuff right in the middle of a baseball game. Could he? Right in the middle of a crowd?

Could he?

Wait a minute! What he had done here, while he was there? How much time had elapsed—here? He thought back, and figured he'd been on Truk Island between ten and twenty minutes. And on the starship maybe five. So that was fifteen, twenty minutes, maybe as much as thirty. If he knew what inning it was when he came back, he'd have an estimate of whether twenty minutes or so had passed, or basically no time at all.

But wouldn't Trina have noticed if he'd been—somewhere else that long? Unless he was sitting there acting normal, paying attention to the game. Answering when she spoke to him. Could he have been living two lives? He hadn't remembered this one at all, as far as he could recall.

That struck him like a blow. Jim Drake did not exist in Philip's or Talaan's minds to the best of his recollection. The only person that existed was the one he was living. Or imagining. But he remembered them. Panic surged anew and he looked around at his surroundings, and they were normal. He settled back, took a deep breath and tried to relax. But his mind began remembering again. He stopped it. Damn! What was next? An aluminum foil hat to pick up signals from new alien friends?

He concentrated on the room, on the hundred thousand dollars-plus in furniture and accessories in just this room. He'd earned it, paid for it with his own efforts. He paid his own way, solved his own problems. And he'd always been able to control the persona he presented to others. He could put on the front the situation called for. And he never, ever showed fear. But now, goddamn it, he was afraid. Like a little kid.

He took another drink, drained the glass. He got up, went to the bar, and refilled it. He was just sitting down when Trina came back. She was wearing big fuzzy pink slippers, but somehow that did not diminish her grace. They actually matched her coral ear rings, which he did not think she'd had on earlier. But he couldn't remember for sure.

"All right, Jim," she said as she glided over to the couch, "what is it? What's wrong with you?" She glanced at his glass. "Judging from your medication, it's not a cluster headache."

Anger flashed and he blurted, "I was in goddamn World War II on the front lines, being shot at." Damn, he hadn't intended to say that. What an idiot! Where was that control he was so proud of?

Shock shuttled across Trina's face, and questions, but all that was quickly replaced by disbelief. Then it hardened into anger. "What an incredibly stupid thing to say. First it was a Japanese Zero over the grandstands, now it's a soldier on the front lines. I think maybe you need a few more drinks, sweetheart. Why don't I just bring the bottle over?"

"Trina, that's why I haven't been able to talk about it. It's crazy. It doesn't make sense. You and everyone else saw a fly ball coming toward us. I saw a Japanese Zero. It was shooting. Real bullets. On Truk Island."

"Truk Island?" A swirl of emotions from anger to puzzlement tangled up her face. Then, and what really hurt Jim's pride, it settled into disgust. But as he began to feel defensive her emotion morphed to pity and bewilderment. She sat down tentatively, automatically, on the edge of the couch. "Let's start over," she said.

"I was a soldier."

"Jim." She cast a raised eye on his glass. "How many of those have you had?"

"Dammit, I'm telling you. My brain short-circuited, and that's what happened. It was not my imagination. It was as real as you and me. I was there, Trina. On Truk Island. I was actually, physically there as a soldier. And I'm not drunk."

"How—have you been fooling around with psychedelics of some kind? She twisted so she was facing him directly, still only half sitting on the couch, one pink-slippered foot extended out for support.

Jim reached over and picked up his glass, but Trina put her hand over his. She took the glass from him and set it down on her end of the coffee table after moving the coaster over.

"God, I wish. I wish I'd been under the influence. Then I'd have an easy answer. But how in the hell do you explain being transported into another existence? There *is* no explanation. It doesn't make sense. But it happened."

"You've got part of it right. You're not making sense. Let's try again. Jim, start over."

He took a deep breath and tried. "I know it's crazy, and maybe that's the whole answer right there, but my experience was that I literally became someone else. I've been trying to figure it out and I can't, and it scares the living crap out of me. All of a sudden I wasn't at the ballgame. I was in a trench and..."

"Stop!" Her lips formed an angry line. Diamond-drill eyes bored into his, and she said, "Stop talking nonsense, or we've got a serious problem."

He wrenched his eyes from hers and started to reach for his glass, thought better of it, and took her hand in one of his. "We already have a serious problem, or at least I do. I was watching that fly ball like you and everyone else, and it transformed into a Japanese Zero. A plane firing at me. And just that fast," he snapped his fingers, "I was a man named Philip Osborne in a trench on Truk Island in the Pacific. My company had just landed, and about half of us had been killed or wounded. We were dug in between the beach and the jungle, and that Zero came in from over the ocean with guns blazing."

Trina scowled and said, "Didn't you realize it wasn't real? That you were hallucinating or something?"

"That's the problem. It *was* real. It wasn't like I saw silver aliens land in center field. If that had happened, I'd be aware of you, and point to the aliens and ask why you didn't see them. But you weren't there. The ball park wasn't there. *I was in the South Pacific.* I could smell it, I could taste it, I could feel it. Jim Drake did not exist."

Her accusing glare melted into uncertainty. "Well, I don't believe any or that."

"I knew the people I was with, Trina. I had a history—I mean the person I was in that life, Philip Osborne, he had a history. I remembered my family—his family. I knew everything in my life leading up to that day. And I'd never heard of Jim Drake as far as I know." He turned his hand palm up and looked at it. "The only thing is, there's no blood on me. My friend got hit, and I helped him. But I didn't bring back any blood."

"God!" The life that normally glittered in her eyes had long fled, leaving just a dead swamp of helplessness to search his face, to seek answers, reasons. The corners of her mouth tightened and drooped as she shook her head slowly.

"Trina, maybe you can help. I need to know, what was I doing all that time? I mean, what was I doing here? How long was I... there?"

She closed her eyes, as if gathering strength, then took a deep breath and said, "You seemed to be watching the game. For about an inning, I guess. You were really intent. You didn't say a word, didn't even answer me when I said something. That's when I began wondering if something was wrong."

"Something was wrong, all right." He tapped his head. "Jim Drake wasn't home."

"Jim, you're scaring me."

"Scaring *you*? It's scaring the *shit* out of me."

"What... what can we do?"

"Nothing. I don't even want even talk about it anymore." He didn't dare tell her about the starshuttle. That would *really* make her not believe him. Hell, he didn't believe it himself, and he was the one that it happened to. He looked at his glass, wanting to take another drink.

"Try and remember what triggered you coming back to reality. In case it ever happens again." Her face seemed to have aged, overcome with anxiety and uncertainty. With the need for assurance. For some way to fix it.

He studied her, trying to decide how to handle it. How to avoid talking about the starshuttle. "Well, I..." He started to make up a story, but realized the truth was going to come out sooner or later. If he lied, it would be even harder for her to believe him later, so he told her. "I didn't come back here from Truk Island. I think I was killed or wounded by a mortar shell. Things went black, then white."

"My Lord! Have you been reading one of those near-death-experience books where they enter a tunnel or follow a white light? Maybe that's what happened. Maybe that..."

"No. I didn't want to tell you this, because if you think World War II sounds like I went crazy, this will cinch it. It wasn't a tunnel to God I experienced, Trina. This was a starship. There was a weird sensation, like a spoken word that just materialized in my head, then sort of a tugging feeling, and I found myself in a starship."

Trina's eyes flared and her mouth opened as if to yell at him, then she regained control. "A starship," she said in a voice so patently monotone he knew she was trying her hardest not to show emotion. Not to get up and yell or slap him or something. After several silent attempts, words finally found their way out, very softly. "You found yourself in a starship."

"That's why everything was white. The starship was white inside."

"I see. A white starship." She spoke so quietly he barely heard her.

He knew she was fighting to control herself, maybe fighting panic. Or fury, maybe afraid of what his reaction might be if she exploded. Was she afraid of him? Probably. He was a certified lunatic. But now he had to follow through. "I was a man named Talaan."

She closed her eyes. "Jim."

"The starship was having trouble reentering real spacetime."

"Real spacetime?" Her eyes were still closed. "Oh. Real spacetime."

"That's where we are right now. This universe. This, here and now," he patted the couch, "is real spacetime."

"Jim!" She opened her eyes. "Where do you suppose the ship had been if it wasn't here, in real spacetime?" She sat very stiff, very erect.

Jim shrugged. "An alternate universe in higher dimensions where it can short-circuit space and time in this one. Where it can circle around behind the laws of relativity. But we, me and my girlfriend Zeleece, we understood enough of that science to know we were having a hard time materializing in the real universe."

Trina's face hardened. "Zeleece. You had a fantasy lover."

"Well, yeah. But Jeez, Trina. It wasn't me. Talaan was thinking about getting engaged to her. Jim Drake didn't exist. He hadn't existed for thousands of years."

"Now it's beginning to make a little more sense. Are you having an affair with someone?"

Jim felt a surge of anger and lashed out. "You know, this is why I never want to talk to you about feelings or inner thoughts." He waved his arm in an arc. "You go out of your way to find something to be upset about, or feel betrayed over. I can't just tell you the way things are without you twisting it into something against you."

She seemed ready to cry. "Talk about your feelings? I haven't heard one thing about your feelings. You give me this outlandish story about Japanese Zeros and space ships and expect me to believe it, then accuse me of being the one with a problem."

"You took a couple too many psychology classes in college. Now you're imagining all sorts of things. You always do. And it's always the worst of all possibilities."

"I'm imagining things? *I'm* imagining things?" She shuddered in a silent sob. "God, Jim, listen to yourself."

"I suffered something that scares the hell out of me," he jabbed his arm toward her office, "and I don't need you turning it into some cheesy affair in your novel."

"Then how *do* you explain it?" She was looking away, taking short breaths.

"I don't." He looked down, shook his head. "I don't," he said quietly. He couldn't remember ever feeling this inadequate. "I don't," he whispered. He closed his eyes, fighting back tears, and said, "The only possible explanation I can come up with is, I went crazy. I completely lost touch with reality. There was no warning. It happened instantly. And I'm scared, Trina. I'm really scared."

She reached for his hand. "You're serious, aren't you? You really believe that starship stuff."

"Yes." He kept his eyes downward. "It was real."

"You really are scared."

He looked at her through tear-film and saw that her eyes were glistening too. He said, "Yeah, baby. I am. I'm telling you what happened, and it didn't have anything to do with any affair. I'm not having one."

Trina dropped her gaze, then looked back up and said, "I just, I want everything to be normal. I want our life to be, I want to know what happened to you, and why. We need to fix it."

"Sometimes you... never mind. I want that too."

"I, I don't know what to do. How to deal with this. I almost wish it was an affair. I could figure out how to cope with that. But I have no idea how to handle this."

"Me either."

"I asked you a minute ago, what brought back to here and now? You didn't answer me."

"I think you did. You pulling on my arm and calling me."

Her eyebrows shot up in a surge of hope. "Really? That's good."

"It is?"

"Yes. You were really here, you just thought you were there."

"I guess. Yeah. At least at that moment. Or maybe I was coming back anyway." He leaned over for his glass.

Trina opened her mouth to object, but closed it with a patronizing little smile. He took a drink and started to put the glass back, but she took it from him and had a long one herself. As she lowered the glass, her head and shoulders shuddered. "I don't know why you like this stuff." She sat the glass back on the coaster.

"I need to numb myself."

"I guess I can understand that." Her eyes roved over his, over his face, silently imploring him to come up with a solution, with reassurance, with an answer even while knowing he had none. She desperately needed things to return to normal. She started to reach out to his face, then stopped with her hand in midair, and let it drop to her lap. She opened her mouth to say something, and stopped. Then her eyes brightened slightly and she said, "I'm going to call Dr. Weagins."

She started to get up, but Jim held her hand. "What's he going to do? There's nothing wrong now. I'm normal."

"I don't know, I'm not a doctor. But we *have* to find out what's going on. I mean, what if it happens again?" She turned to get up. "I'm calling him."

He held on. "Don't bother him at home with a medical matter that doesn't exist any longer. You don't do that to friends who happen to be doctors. Maybe I'll call him at his office tomorrow."

"Jim..."

"I need a shrink more than a medical doctor."

Words erupted from her in a staccato cadence. Hard, metallic words. "You're not crazy." It was not an opinion, it was a demand. She would not allow it. "Don't even think that." She actually had a crinkle above her nose, Trina's version of a frown, something she almost never allowed to happen.

"If I am, then they could fix it. Maybe a lobotomy. Medicate me until my personality melts into a puddle."

"This is no time for your stupid so-called jokes."

"Yeah, it is. It's keeping me sane. At least for the moment."

"Jim! Stop!" she yelled. She scooted closer to him and put her arm across his chest, and said in a lower voice, "Stop it. You're not going crazy. I won't let you."

He put his arm around her. She seemed so tiny and fragile, and he wished he could insulate her from his problem. They sat in silence until he said softly, "I love you, Trina."

She mumbled, her face buried in his shoulder, "I love you too." Her arm tightened around him.

They hadn't sat like this for a long time, and it was nice. He felt a calmness begin to replace his fear of madness, and an isolation or distance from his typical frantic busyness, the constant seeking to grow his business. He took a deep breath and let his gaze wander over her head to the oil painting leaning against the wall, the one she bought last week at a Butterfield & Butterfield auction. She paid forty-five thousand dollars for it, spending all the money from her book royalties and then some. He had accused her of being extravagant, but he had to admit it was a captivating piece.

He relaxed a little more in the unexpected calmness of the moment, deliberately directing his thoughts toward appreciating her esthetics, her counterpoint to his intensity, and her moderating influence. Trina, in fact, had been the one to introduce him to art. She had gently prodded him away from his arrogance and contempt, and tickled his curiosity until it sprouted tendrils of its own. He now, at least sometimes, sought the nuances in art, the emotion. The beauty, the sadness, the horror—the horror of war and blood and body parts and... he burned the thought before he went there.

He forced his attention back to the painting, an oil by the Mexican artist Roberto Montenegro. The influence of Montenegro's time spent with Picasso was evident. Jim studied the abstract blend of geometric shapes—dark triangles and rhomboids of almost-black reds and greens and yellows—shapes that formed a curtain of tragedy behind the slender, somewhat surreal harlequin. A talented, sad dancer. The masked figure, probably a male, waif-thin yet not young exuded competence—the dance must be second nature to him and require no conscious effort—but his life was unhappy almost beyond bearing. Jim let himself sink into the heroic tragedy that was the dancer, into the transcendental effect it created, the emotions it radiated. And realized that all those emotions were supplied by him. By his perception. It was his interpretation, and the emotions were his. He supplied every bit of reality it had. To someone else the meaning and the emotions would be different. The reality of the painting's message was a creation of a person's own mind.

Was that what had happened? Had he created a living canvas in his own mind? It had been so real! What could have caused him to create World War II, and then some far future? What stresses, what distortions of reality could cause that? What quirks in his life? Maybe he needed to slow down. Maybe he needed a change, a chance to become carefree once again. He realized he hadn't been relaxed or carefree for a long, long time. "You know," he said, "maybe I need a change in my life. A vacation."

"Yes!" She sat upright, suddenly alight. "That's it! Stress and overwork could be the causes of your hallucinations. Psychological problems aren't just caused by drugs or mental illness, you know. That's got to be it! Yes! You've been working too hard and too many hours for years. That's the problem."

"Maybe." He had been working ten, twelve, sometimes sixteen hours a day. He was tired, actually exhausted, and had been for, jeez, he couldn't remember. Years. But this experience had been so real. An actual life. How could it have been an hallucination? On the other hand, maybe that's what hallucinations were. Maybe she was right. "Could be," he said aloud to himself with a nod, and felt a slight relaxing within himself.

Trina was sparkling. "I know that's it. A vacation's exactly what you need. Let's go to Hawaii." Her eyes danced. "Let's go for two whole weeks. We haven't been there in years." She ran her hand over his cheek. "We haven't had a real vacation since you started your business, what, seven years ago? You've been working nonstop ever since. Let's leave next week."

This wasn't like her, leaping into something spur-of-the-moment. She always had to plan, consider alternatives, make schedules and notes. But here she was ready to pack her bags. This was more like him than her.

She opened her mouth to say something else when he said, "Whoa. Slow down. I've got to get that big government job pretty well finished first. Another week or two."

"Oh. Yes, I suppose you do. Then we'll go?" She pulled on his chin, turning his head so they were looking each other squarely in the eyes. "Promise? Can I make reservations?"

Jim had to smile in spite of himself. "Yeah. Go ahead." He loved her being spontaneous and vivacious like this. It had been a long time. Maybe he'd drug her down along with himself. And he hadn't even realized it about either of them.

Trina said, "Let's spend five days each on Oahu, Maui, and the Big Island. Rent a car on each."

He noticed his fears and worries had faded into the background as he opened himself to the riotous colors of her excitement. Drawn in by her enthusiasm, he dove in himself and said, "I think three days on Maui is enough. I'd rather spend a couple extra days on Hawaii."

"You're right. That's an interesting island to explore. Maybe just three or four on Oahu, too."

"Let's do it right. Book us first class air and some fancy hotels. And see if you can get us into the Volcano House on the Big Island for one night. It's not plush, but it sure is unique."

"I've heard about that. It's right on the edge of that big caldera, isn't it?"

"Yeah. Kilauea. I was there years ago, but never spent the night. But boy did they have some great sashimi set out on the table for everyone to sample."

She took his hand in both of hers and shook it up and down. "This is so exciting! I bet it's exactly what you need."

He looked in her eyes and saw hope, and felt the need to share it. "You could be right. I think maybe you are." He almost smiled. "Yeah."

"I want one more promise."

"I'm not going to the doctor."

Her eyes flickered wide, but ever so briefly before she regained control. "Yes, you are. Dr. Weagins. Call him first thing in the morning, before you leave the house."

"There's nothing to find."

Her grip on his hand tightened. "Jim..."

"No."

She released his hand and put her little fists on her hips as she looked directly into his eyes, chin up. He knew he wasn't going to win this one. She actually looked ruthless, even dangerous. He had rarely seen that look on her, and found it interesting. "You are going to call the doctor," she said, "if I have stand in front of the door with a gun."

"The last month or so you've been going to the shooting range every week. What's up with that?"

She didn't bat an eye. "Self defense." Her stare was hard and unblinking. Then, like a mask slipping away, he could see the killer leave.

He said, "Defense from who? What happened to that mothering instinct of yours?"

A shimmer of mirth enlivened her face, and she said, "My mothering instinct, as you call it, went out the window with your brains." Then she caught her breath when she realized what she had said. "Oh, my Lord!"

He ignored it, and returned to his goal of distracting her. "You were always afraid of guns."

"Since I'm writing about them, my literary agent suggested I learn about them." She tilted her head slightly toward him. "I'll have to thank her."

"Don't let it become an autobiography."

"You wouldn't like that," she said, and smiled a conspiratorial little smile, as if letting him in on a secret that would be revealed in the last chapter.

He laughed a little, and that flooded him with additional relief. It made his experience seem even more remote, almost as if it had happened to someone else. He made an effort to prolong the feeling. "Is that why you write under your maiden name, so you can plot murder with anonymity?"

She raised one eyebrow. "You expect me to use my married name?" The tiniest curl of satisfaction touched the corners of her mouth as she said, "Katherine Anatrina Spaneas sounds much more literate and mysterious than Trina Drake, even you'll have to admit that. Trina Drake? Come on. Trina Drake sounds like the author is a small, sexually ambiguous duck."

He couldn't help but laugh, and said, "Thanks for your concern. I go insane, and you crack jokes."

A shade of irritation rumbled from deep within her. "You're the one who started trying to make jokes, you jerk! You told me it was keeping you sane. But you're not insane, and that's that!"

Dismissal and denial had always been her tools for confronting personal problems, for maintaining a polite distance from the smudges and scabs in their life.

She raised her chin defiantly. "And quit trying to change the subject. You *are* going to call the doctor first thing in the morning."

Well, that had sure worked well. No sense arguing when she got this attitude. It was easier to just agree. Deal with it in the morning. He gave up and said, "All right, all right. So come here. Let's be sure tonight is real." He reached for her and she scooted over close to him, melded against him willingly, her arm reaching and pulling his head to her.

"Don't scare me like that anymore, Jim."

Their lips met, parted, met again.

"Never." She felt just right against him. This was real.

"Want me to get a boob job ?" Her breath was warm against his ear.

"No. I like you the way you are." He rubbed, felt the nipples under her clothes.

"Your eyes were bugging out at the ball game. If she hadn't been so phony and slutty, I might have been jealous. And that would have made me *real* mad." She played with his ear, the way she did when she was aroused. "Just the same, It's a good thing I was there."

"Honey, if you had breasts like that, that's the only part of you men would notice. You're too beautiful and elegant for that. You're intelligent and graceful and classy. Why mess with that? You've got way more to offer." He kissed her soft lips.

"You lying con artist. Carry me away on your star ship."

Chapter 3

Reality has multiple faces

Jim had always admired Dr. Weagins's hair. It reminded him of sun bouncing off ripe wheat. Honey poured out on a plate. His eyebrows were the same, and his eyelashes, a gentle color. His voice was golden too, a perfect match. The doctor looked up from a computer over his wire-framed glasses, pale blue eyes that complemented his hair. "Your blood tests and vital signs are all within the normal range, Jim. I don't see anything physically wrong with you other than that your blood pressure is a little high."

A black shroud of despair descended and enveloped him. So. He was crazy. That's all that was left. He searched the doctor's eyes for any sign of hope, then looked down at his hands in his lap and said, "That's what I figured. There's nothing you can do. I went crazy, and that's that. And who knows when it might happen again." He looked up at the doctor in total defeat.

Dr. Weagins shook his head. "That's not necessarily true, Jim. At first, based on my limited knowledge, it sounded to me like schizophrenia. But after considering all the facts you described, I don't think that's what it is. On the other hand, if it is that or something similar there are treatments that can be of considerable benefit. Regardless, I'm going to try and get you to a specialist, Doctor Marquand. He's an absolutely brilliant man, with an office right here in this building. He may be able to come up with answers for you."

"A specialist, huh? You mean a psychiatrist, Seymour?" Jim and the doctor had been friends for years, and it was hard to remember to call him Dr. Weagins in the office. Not that it mattered.

"Yes, he is a psychiatrist. One of the best in the world. I'm also referring you for an MRI scan to see if there's anything physical in your brain that might have caused it. I want the scan done immediately. I've checked just about everything else I can think of."

"Yeah. Maybe later this week."

"No. Right now. There's no way to know if that will ever happen again, but if it does, say when you're driving, the results could be disastrous. I had my office call over, and the lab had a cancellation. They can take you this morning if you hurry. Hopefully, Dr. Marquand will be able to look at the pictures." The doctor looked at his watch and said, "I know that he only sees patients on Wednesdays, so this being Monday I'm hoping he'll be free to drop by the MRI lab. But you need to get right over there."

"Shit, Doctor Weagins, I have a company to run."

"Shit, Mr. Drake, you need to find out what went wrong up here." Dr. Weagins tapped his head. "Or you might end up without a company to worry about. Aliens may take it over." He chuckled and his eyes glimmered. Jim had to laugh too. The doctor quickly got serious again, and continued, "If there's something physical it will probably happen again and may get worse. We need to know right away, Jim."

"If this Marquack is such a great doctor, how come he doesn't have an office full of patients?"

"Mar-QUAAN, smarty." Seymour paused and almost chuckled, but not quite. He went on, "His name is Aubert Marquand. He has a PhD as well as an MD, and spends most of his time doing research. He does a lot of work at UCLA and back in Pittsburgh, and travels around the world giving talks and presenting papers at psychiatric conventions."

"Does he just see enough patients to afford his research and travels?"

"No, no. Research grants pay for all that. To tell you the truth, I'm not sure why he sees patients at all. He says it's to keep in touch with the human side of psychiatry. I know that he just takes cases of special interest to him. I also know I'm going to have to call a favor to get him to see you."

"What makes you think he'll take an interest in me whether he owes you a favor or not?"

"I'm not a psychiatrist, but based on what you've told me your case is… well, I think it'll interest him."

"I'll be a challenge, huh? That's about what Trina says."

Dr. Weagins nodded. "I suspect most wives say that. I know Eva does."

"Yeah, I've heard the two of them talking."

Doctor Weagins smiled.

This chit-chat was requiring a real effort. Earlier this morning when he woke up and had his shower, yesterday had seemed remote. It was almost as if he had been a bystander, an uninvolved observer of an event that happened to someone else. Like maybe it hadn't even happened. Now though, with confirmation that it might be psychological or even physical, his sense of vulnerability and helplessness returned. A brain tumor made sense, resulting in a mind capable of flying across space and time without warning. It drove home that this was totally out of his control. He looked out the window and said, as much to himself as the doctor, "How long before I become a whimpering mess huddled in the corner?"

"Jim, that's not like you. Pull yourself together. We don't know if there's a damn thing wrong. This may have been a one-time anomaly, some misfiring synapses caused by a fluke electrochemical imbalance, or God knows what. But we must find out if there is anything physical. If we find something we'll probably be able to treat it. That's why I want you to get to the MRI lab, and why I want Doctor Marquand to interpret the results."

"Okay. I need to call my office first though, and let them know that I'll be a while."

"Jim, you have to go right now. They're holding a place open for you, but the schedule is tight. Call your office while you're walking over there, and tell them you'll be another couple of hours."

"Seymour, you're almost as bossy as Trina."

"Glad you're back to normal, Jim."

When Jim entered the MRI lab the technician glared at him and made a show of looking at her watch. He ignored the gesture, little inclined to try to placate her. He didn't have the time or the energy.

She would not be ignored, though. "Mr. Drake, I want you to know I wouldn't have accepted you this late if that kooky Dr. Marquand hadn't called my supervisor and demanded it. Now thanks to him, I'm going to be behind schedule all day."

"Dr. Marquand called?"

Instead of answering, she aimed a muscular arm toward a table with a white plastic bowl on it. "Get rid of all your metal. Rings, watch, change and so on. And take off your shirt."

"Is Dr. Marquand coming over?"

She glowered. "How should I know? You never know what that nut's going to do. You don't have a pacemaker, do you?" she asked with her back to him, as her heavy black shoes thunked on her way back to her desk.

"No." He began removing his shirt.

"Any implants or prosthetics? Pins in your neck, a plate in your head, anything like that?" She was fussing with paperwork on her desk, not looking at him.

"No." He glanced around for a hook to hang his shirt on but saw none, so he laid it on a chair.

The woman strode from her desk over to him. "Sign this release. And this form. And fill out this one." She thrust a clipboard at him.

"Will I feel anything?" Jim tipped his head toward the hulking machine he had avoided looking at it. He didn't like the idea of being shoved inside that contraption. He hated to feel trapped. It looked claustrophobic. He wasn't claustrophobic. Well, maybe he was. He usually stayed away from places like that.

"No. Get busy with the form."

He sat down on the hard plastic chair and began filling out the form, which was mostly just a matter of giving his name and address and checking twenty or so boxes. As he did, he wondered if this woman was always this unfriendly. If she had any friends. But she must. She couldn't be like this all the time, to everyone. He wondered if she'd ever had a lover. Male or female? Not that it mattered. But he had a hard time imagining being sexually attracted her. The poor thing's most remarkable feature was her scowl. And her sturdy legs. They'd hold up a piano, he thought with an inward smile, then immediately felt guilty for being so insensitive and judgmental. He signed the form, then the other two, and handed them to her.

"All right. Over there." She thrust an arm to her right. Jim stood up and headed that way without responding. He had no reason to talk and did not want to, although for some reason he was actually beginning to feel sorry for her.

"Lie down on your back." She jabbed a finger toward a table on tracks that led into the machine.

The MRI machine was a gray metal box taller than he was with a gaping mouth. A ponderous beast squatting in the corner of the room waiting to be fed. And he was the meal. The trolley tracks under his bed penetrated its clinical white guts. He could imagine a ceremonial sacrifice to appease the machine. He lay down on the narrow platform anyway. There was no alternative. Maybe he'd close his eyes.

"Shoulders flat."

Jim wriggled into a flat position on what seemed like a slab in the morgue ready to roll him into a vault pending identification of his personalities. And the determination if any of them were dangerous.

"Put these on. The machine is very noisy." She handed him a pair of ugly green ear muffs.

He put them on. Wondered why music wasn't provided. But if it had been and this woman had chosen it, it would probably be a Sousa march. Or one of Brahms' depressing chamber pieces that Trina had drug him to hear when the Los Angeles Chamber Orchestra was playing at UCLA's Royce Hall. Thanks to her he had learned to appreciate most classical music, even the occasional chamber piece, but not stuff his new friend here would play.

"Put your hands here." She placed his hands on his upper thighs, then leaned over him, her face directly above his. "This is going to take a while, and you must not move. I repeat. Do not move." With the ear muffs on her voice seemed disembodied and distant, which was agreeable. She checked the position of his earmuffs, tugged and jiggled them roughly, then disappeared from view.

The platform began moving, drawing him into the maw of the MRI, into the shadowless white cylinder that drilled through the innards of the beast. The opening seemed just wide enough to clear his shoulders. Good thing he wasn't very claustrophobic, he repeated to convince himself. He closed his eyes anyway. He flinched with the loud bang, opened his eyes and promptly closed them. Then a second bang. Another and another and another. Like a drop forge in a foundry. It sounded as if the damn machine was going to disintegrate. Collapse on him. Crush him. He wished he had ear plugs as well as the muffs. How long was this going to last? She had said a long time. He started to open his eyes then decided that would not be good.

After a moment and without warning the racket subsided and became a distant thumping and rumbling, and like everyone else he moved a little in his seat to relax, realizing how tensed he had been.

Zeleece turned to him and said, "Talaan, why are these little interplanetary hoppers so noisy on liftoff? It's not like we're going extrasystem or something."

Talaan leaned his head over and nibbled on her ear and said, as she shrugged her shoulder and giggled, "It would cost money to make them quiet. And reduce the payload by a couple of passengers. You wouldn't want Starlift shareholders to suffer that hardship, would you?"

Talaan glanced at the woman sitting in the seat facing them, and Zeleece followed his gaze. Her hair was beautiful, the color of a ruby. It even had the sheen and facets of the gemstone, glistening with her every move. Her eyes were extraordinarily large, a startling aqua, but whether these features were natural or the result of cellular manipulation it was impossible to tell. More intriguing was a protrusion across her forehead near the hairline—she was a cytogen, he realized, altered for some specific enhancement. This was the first time he had seen one.

"I love your hair," Zeleece said.

Zeleece's was still chrome, one strip about five centimeters high across her head. She had kept it like that for almost four months now, a record for her. Talaan liked it, and it occurred to him that maybe that was why she still had it, although being concerned with someone else's opinion was not one of her traits.

"Thank you," said the lady.

Talaan instinctively liked her. "My name is Talaan," he said, "and this is Zeleece."

"Nice to meet you both. I'm Brenicia."

"Brenicia," Zeleece repeated carefully, stretching and savoring the syllables. "What a lovely name."

Brenicia had an easy smile and seemed comfortable with them. "Why are you two going to Ektar?" She focused on Zeleece. "Not that there's anywhere else for him to take you in the Delphia system, except for Delphia itself." Her voice was lilting, melodic, for some reason reminding Talaan of wind chimes in a garden back on Earth. Her sentences pulsed with a random cadence and had inflections and rolls like a brook flowing over rounded stones, burbling into little pools. It indicated she was from one of the colony planets in a star system that had been settled several centuries ago, and that had rejoined the rest of society after a couple hundred years of near isolation. Maybe Eighty-Two Eridani, now commonly referred to as Eratitoo. Or maybe Eta Cassiopeia.

"I'm on a routine service call, and Zeleece here is my companion, as you probably guessed. We're going to Ektar because some of the mining robots there are evolving a communal instinct, and that's causing them to spend more and more time with one another, reducing their efficiency.

I've been assigned to give them some neurotronic psycho updates to reduce that tendency."

Zeleece scowled. "I'd like to give them a program tweak to help them develop more of that, not less. I think we should encourage their evolution into social, independent beings. If we did I bet some day they would emerge as a civilization in their own right."

"Yeah, maybe, but this is what I'm paid to do." Talaan hated this assignment, but didn't dare let Zeleece know or she'd devise some scheme to do exactly what she said. And if she did and his company found out, and he didn't get fired, he'd get reassigned. Probably way to hell out somewhere servicing huge machinery on a series of icy, black, airless moons.

"You're a paid murderer," Zeleece said with fire in her eye.

Talaan had to agree, but only inwardly. To change the subject he said, "How about you, Brenicia? Why are you going to such a desolate planet as Ektar?"

"I'm a cytogenic cognate, as you can see." She pointed to the bump on her forehead. "I'm going to try to establish diplomatic relations with that intelligent plant species you may have heard of. The Talal'a."

"Oh, yes!" Zeleece leaned forward. "The Talal'a. Thinking plants. That just intrigues the shit out of me." She flashed wide, expectant eyes at Talaan, then back to the woman. "I'd love to see them. I wish I was going with you, instead of him." She poked her thumb toward Talaan as she continued, "I took a couple of courses in xenobiology back in college, and that would be a dream assignment if I was working in the field - which I'm not. Maybe I should try to get into it. The Talal'a, they are on the forbidden continent of, what's it called? Cashla?"

"Kasla'a. We don't like the term forbidden, even though the continent is strictly off-limits. We prefer to call it a closed ecological zone. Forbidden has a perverse appeal to some people. If something is forbidden it becomes a challenge that draws poachers and others who might harm the species or their environment."

"Yeah," said Talaan, "I imagine living samples of those would be worth a fortune to some individuals."

"That's why we have fully monitored sentry shields around the entire continent."

"How do you know the plants are sentient?" Talaan asked.

"Oh, they're more than sentient. Their abilities far exceed having a sense of themselves and their surroundings," Brenicia said.

"I guess I misused the word. What I mean is, how do you know they can think?"

"For one thing, they utilize an electropathic function to communicate. They electromagnetically alert one another to danger, then act in concert and take action, such as bending aside to form a path to minimize harm to themselves."

Zeleece scooted forward in her chair. "Do they actually talk to each other? Can you talk to them?"

"Yes, researchers have engaged in rudimentary electromagnetic communication with them. I hope to extend that to personal communication with my enhanced abilities." She tapped her forehead.

"Zang!" Zeleece scooted to the edge of her seat. "That would be incredible."

Brenicia continued, "They also seem to meld with the perceptive organs of others in the group to sense things at a distance. In a way, to be present at a remote location. Or at all locations at once, because when one of them senses something they all do. That's another part of what I'm going to investigate."

Zeleece scooted back in her chair and looked at Talaan. "I just love this shit," she repeated. She leaned against him and wiggled her shoulder against his. "Maybe that's the field I'll change into for my thesis. What's it called," she asked Benicia, "xenosociology? Xenoethnology?"

The woman leaned her head back and closed her eyes. "It's both. And more. Whatever you call it, it's a very long road to get there." She suddenly seemed older, and said after a sigh, "And a difficult one, I warn you. A great deal must be sacrificed. But I think it'll all be worth it."

Zeleece looked mischievously at Talaan, leaned toward his ear and whispered, "Would some bulges on my forehead make me more interesting, my lover?"

"Yeah, I think so."

Zeleece tittered and squirmed. She ran her hand lightly across his chest. "I bet I could add some on you." She drew her finger over his cheek, then slowly kissed the spot she had rubbed.

"You already have."

"See what a natural I am?" she said softly.

"I've known that from our first date."

"Yes, you have." Zeleece leaned back into her own seat and asked a laughing Brenicia, "How did the first settlers realize the Talal'a weren't just another plant species?"

Brenicia turned serious, but her eyes were sparkling as she said, "What would you think if some chest-high plants emitted shrieks when you started to walk through them? And then bent aside, forming a path for you?"

"Zang! I'd go nova," Talaan said.

Zeleece scowled at him. "Anyone with a wit of intelligence would stop, back up, and say, 'I'm terribly sorry. I didn't recognize you. My name's Zeleece. What's yours?'"

"Yeah, sure." He paused pointedly. "After you stopped screaming."

She poked at him with an elbow, but missed as Talaan twisted away toward the far side of his seat. He continued, "I'd have to grab you by your heels to pull you back down from the trees."

Brenicia chuckled and said, "Reading between the lines, that's pretty much what the first encounter amounted to."

Talaan could almost picture it.

Zeleece said, "Shrieking plants. That really would be eerie." She was alive with enthusiasm.

"Technically, they're not plants," Brenicia said. "They're monopods. They are animals that ingest much of their nourishment through the soil."

"Do they have a mouth? They must have, if they can talk."

"They don't have a mouth as we know it, but obviously they do have some mechanism to make audible sounds. On the other hand, we don't know if they are physiologically capable of verbal speech."

Zeleece leaned back in her seat. "That will make your job of communicating with them sort of difficult. I mean our job—the rest of us. You have the enhancements, but we would have to use someone like you, or instruments."

"Probably."

Talaan scratched his head. "How was this electropathic function discovered in the first place? I couldn't imagine having the intuition to set up equipment and scan the electromagnetic spectrum and check out a dozen or more possible modulation schemes."

"I don't think anyone would," said Brenicia. "It was discovered by accident when an odd interference was noticed in the original discoverer's communicators."

Talaan was getting more interested by the moment. "So no one's actually communicated with them. Conversationally, I mean."

"No. Some researchers have used rudimentary yes-no, good-bad signals, and they were even able to pick up an audible complement. I hope to be able to extend that."

"Zang!" Zeleece's eyes were dancing from one of them to the other. "I wanna do that too."

"If they can talk," Talaan said, "then they can reason. They would definitely have intelligence."

"Yes," Benicia said. "What's more, if they possess that sort of intelligence it would be a collaborative, synergetic intelligence utilizing this electropathic function to achieve a group oneness, a group mind. If that's true than each individual mind would not have to be so powerful."

"That could be very powerful. Actually computer-like."

Brenicia shook her head. "I don't think it goes that far. On the other hand, we know very little about them. That's why I'm so excited about my job."

"Me too," Zeleece said. She looked at Talaan. "Wouldn't it be awful to be anchored to one spot?"

Brenicia said, "There is some indirect evidence they can move, and in fact do from time to time for reasons that are not clear. Perhaps when their location becomes too harsh from drought, or because of nutrient depletion."

"Another thing they could use is hands and fingers," said Zeleece.

"They do have claw-like appendages. We don't know, but they may be able grasp things."

Talaan wagged his finger in a 'no' motion. "Don't let Zeleece show them what to do with those appendages. Their first movements would be, well, inappropriate for young audiences."

"Okay, mister. We'll see how you like it tonight when these babies don't make any movements at all." Zeleece shook her hands in front of him. "They're just going to be inert appendages."

Brenicia said with a chuckle, "It's too bad you two aren't going with me. You'd be good company."

Zeleece abandoned her sparing with Talaan and swiveled toward Brenicia, fairly glowing. "Can we? I bet we could help. I'd love it."

"I don't know if my sponsors would allow it. But if you're serious, I'll ask." She raised an eyebrow at Talaan. "I could use an engineer and a xenobiological assistant."

He nodded his head slowly. "You know, I'd like to do that. My work won't take more than a day or so, and I have a lot of leave accumulated. Yeah, I'd like to have the chance to do something to help xenosociety rather than suppress it."

Zeleece hit him hard in the shoulder. "You piece of orbital junk! You *do* think you're an executioner. You just didn't want me to know how you felt because you were afraid I'd write some little psychoprogram and piggyback it on yours to counteract the genocidal one you brought along." She hit him again. "I knew it!"

Talaan looked at Brenicia in a silent plea for help. She just raised an eyebrow enigmatically.

Zeleece followed his gaze, and her mouth slowly opened. After a moment, she said, "You knew all along how he felt about his assignment, didn't you? That's why you said you would like to have us come along."

Brenicia tipped her head in silent acknowledgement.

Zeleece turned back to Talaan. "Now I'm going to do it. I can get that program written before we land. Your corporate programmers are so stupid, they make huge projects out of the simplest little things. I could've done in about fifty lines of code what took an army of programmers months to do because I'd use the robot's existing psychocircuits to carry out most of it for me, instead of writing all new stuff like they did. And it won't be any harder to undo your xenocidal..."

The thumping and rumble ceased abruptly.

"Thank God the quantumag boost phase is over," Zeleece said as she scooted down in her seat.

"What a relief," the woman with the ruby hair agreed.

The sudden lack of noise was overwhelming. As if some piece of existence was missing.

Perturb.

Perturb? Terry tried to tie it to a source when a wide-eyed Maryann grabbed his arm. Fear strained her voice as she said, "Terry! Why did it get so quiet? Did the engines stop?"

Terry's stomach felt as if it were floating just under his lungs. He felt disoriented, as if he'd been daydreaming. But still adrenaline surged at the sudden shift in sound, but he pretended to be calm as he said, "These new jets are different from propeller planes. I was told they're really quiet. I think we just stopped climbing."

At that moment the Captain's voice came over the loudspeakers, "Ladies and gentlemen, we have reached cruising altitude and you may now move about the cabin. A stewardess will be by shortly to take your meal order. Also, the no smoking sign is off. I hope you enjoy your flight to Hawaii on Trans World Airlines new Boeing Seven-Oh-Seven aircraft."

Maryann relaxed her grip on his arm and said, "You were right. We're just through climbing."

Perturb.

"We're through. Mr. Drake. We're through!" The technician pulled off Jim's ear muffs. She put her face directly in front of his. "We're through! Get up!" she said loudly.

Son of a bitch! He'd done it again. He *was* crazy.

"Get up. Now."

Fuck you—but the words did not come. He stared at the ceiling from his prone position, knowing the stars were out there. He felt himself seeking them, reaching, questing for what lay beyond, for some word or sign of Zeleece. He could feel the pull of interstellar space, an attraction he could not describe. As if that was where he belonged. As if that offered some fulfillment he didn't know had been missing.

"Mr. Drake, get up and get your shirt on. Go collect your things." The woman tugged on his arm and pointed across the room. He shook loose from her. Groggy, disoriented, he sat up, slid off the table, and stumbled to a chair. Put his face in his hands, elbows on his knees.

He was afraid to look around. Afraid of who he might be.

Her harsh voice intruded. "Mr. Drake, I want you to go get your belongings."

Space. The future. The past. He didn't belong in any of those places. Why had he thought he did?

"Stop acting so stupid. The machine is harmless. It did not do a thing to you."

Just as he opened his mouth to tell her to go to hell, a man he had not noticed said, "Marie, let him return to normal. When was the last time this machine was calibrated?" The man had his back to them, and was looking at a monitor screen.

Jim did not recognize him, at least not from the back, but he was probably the psychiatrist Dr. Weagins had mentioned. He had longish hair that curled around his neck, and a good sized bald spot. Maybe this son of a bitch could tell him what was wrong. Maybe even help him. He sure as hell needed it. God, he *really was* crazy. He wished he was a little boy, young enough to curl up in Mama's lap and have her comfort him. He thought of his mother, and her comforting arms. No longer. There was no longer any safe place. He couldn't even depend on the world being here.

"Yesterday," the unpleasant woman responded. "It was calibrated yesterday. It's right there on the log next to you, Doctor." She pointed.

The man still did not turn around, but said, "Something's screwy. Who did it? Was it the same technician that always comes, or someone new?"

"Same idiot as always. He knows what he's doing, he's just a tweeky little sparrow."

"Something's crazy."

"Yeah, I know. But it's not the machine." She looked at Jim out of the corner of her eyes.

The man turned to the technician. "Marie, I don't need your sarcasm. Link these files to the net at once. I want to download them as soon as Mister Drake and I get back to my office."

The technician scowled, and said with more than a hint of belligerent agitation, "Your Mister Drake is already halfway into the next time slot." She turned her scowl on Jim.

"I want it now," the doctor said. "I'll clear it with your supervisor." He glanced at Jim as he walked across the room. "Mister Drake, I'm Doctor Marquand. What kind of drugs have you been using?"

"None."

"No? Well, we're going to draw some blood anyway. They always say no." He wrinkled his brow, then continued to himself, "Could be some odd combination of hallucinogens and psychotropics. I need to check some other things, too."

"I haven't had a fucking thing."

"Then this is really fucking weird." He cocked his head as he looked at Jim, his face alive, seeming pleased at having repeated the profanity. "Fucking weird."

"I know," Jim said. "Believe me, I know."

"I imagine you do. Your brain activity was astonishing. We'll discuss it in my office."

"I hope you can tell me what happened. Cause I just left the damn planet."

"You both have," interjected Marie.

Doctor Marquand ignored her as he raised his eyebrows at Jim and shook his head. "I cannot tell you what happened, Mister Drake. I can tell you what happened, but I cannot tell you what happened. I have brain scans that tell me where and to what extent brain activity occurred, yet they don't tell me anything about what you experienced. I have no idea." He turned away still shaking his head as he mumbled to himself, "Puzzling. Very puzzling. Astonishing pictures. Exciting!" He paused, looked aside, then said to no one, "Just fucking weird." He nodded in satisfied agreement with himself, then picked up his phone and punched some keys. He turned his back and spoke quietly.

Around these people in this drab radiology lab the pull from space was fading, and Jim was almost sorry. With that gone he was left alone to fight a disembodied enemy. Waiting for the next blast of insanity. And no telling where he would go. Or to when. Would the doctor be able to figure out what was wrong, and maybe come up with a cure? Jim looked at him, concentrated on him. Dr. Marquand had a perfectly round head that was more bald than Jim had realized, with just a curly brown fringe above the ears and around the back, the curls extending down the neck, and some frizzy wisps on top. He was wearing a long-sleeve blue shirt with a God-awful yellow-and-blue tie. The blues didn't match. His pants were wrinkled, too big in the waist and too long. His shoes were not shined. Jim figured that's what psychiatrists ought to look like if they were competent, and he felt a slight relief. At least he was in good hands.

"Mister Drake, your things," the technician Marie said gruffly. "Get your shirt on and collect your belongings." She jabbed her arm toward the plastic box where he had put his stuff. "Stop pretending like something happened to you."

"Let him be," Doctor Marquand said. "A great deal happened to him, if these data are correct."

She turned to Jim. "Be that as it may. Mister Drake, this isn't a recovery room." She again thrust her beefy arm in the direction of his personal items. "Or a lounge."

Jim got up without saying anything and began putting on his shirt and retrieving all the objects he had been required to shed. He concentrated on each item in turn, making them real. Understanding the essence of each, the feeling and the heft. His watch, rings, gold bracelet and necklace, keys, change. And his wallet with the credit cards the machine would have erased. It occurred to him that this stuff was all meaningless. None of it would matter after they locked him up. Not one item. Thousands of dollars worth of jewelry, and it was absolutely meaningless.

Marie was staring at him, arms folded, stewing in silent aggravation. Screw her. In a way Jim wanted to aggravate her still more even while wanting to help her, her day was so dissatisfying. Were these episodes going to keep coming? This was the second in two days. If they did, it wouldn't be long until he couldn't function. He'd spend his days slipping from one existence to another, unable to tell if any of them were real. Or would he come to reside permanently as Talaan, or someone else? Maybe that guy Terry going somewhere with Maryann. To Hawaii, they were on their way to Hawaii, and they weren't even married. They were on that ancient jet, and her mother was pissed. That must be what, the early sixties?

Doctor Marquand hung up the phone and turned to the upset woman. "You are to upload the data now. Your patients will be told there will be a slight delay. It shouldn't take you more than ten minutes."

She shrugged in exaggerated indifference, then grumbled to Jim, "I do what I'm told. Doesn't matter what my schedule is, how late I have to stay."

"I want to see the data from yesterday's calibration of the MRI machine, and also the calibration before that one."

She marched across the room to a file cabinet without a word, shoes thunking on the vinyl flooring. She opened a drawer and took out a folder. Tossed it on her desk, where it landed with a whap.

Doctor Marquand picked it up. "Thank you, Marie. I'll return it this afternoon."

"It can't leave this room."

Doctor Marquand rolled his eyes at Jim, opened the folder with a sigh, and began studying the contents. He ran his finger across pages while mumbling to himself. After a couple of minutes he said, "The machine seems to be perfect. However, I want another calibration run today."

"The administrator will have to approve it. It's not in the budget."

"Then call him. Get approval."

"Doesn't work that way. The request will have to come from the plant maintenance supervisor."

"Give me his name and extension."

Marie wrote on a note pad, ripped off the page, and thrust it to the doctor.

The doctor motioned to Jim. "Come with me, Mister Drake."

He walked to the door and put his hand on Jim's back, ushering him through. To Jim's surprise, the doctor's fatherly touch was welcome, grounding him on earth under the doctor's protection. This moved him further away from the now faint tug of space and the stars. And that ancient jet. The future and the past. He was sorry when the doctor removed his hand, and then became ashamed that he had depended on another man for confidence and safety. As he glanced at him, though, he saw the doctor turn and smile at the MRI technician.

Doctor Marquand said, "Have a nice day, Marie."

Jim glanced over his shoulder. Marie had her mouth open, stumped for a response.

Chapter 4

Another kind of day

Dr. Marquand's office, Jim decided, had been furnished either by his wife or an interior designer. It was a showcase of glass and steel and abstract art, of sweeping curves and clean surfaces and back lighting—except for the stacks of papers and folders cluttering the engraved glass top of the desk and credenza, each of which had elaborately carved woodwork supporting the glass, whereas the man himself demonstrated a total unawareness of fashion and appearance, or at least disregard of it. He just didn't fit in here.

The doctor indicated a chair for Jim as he settled himself into the one behind the desk. He made a call and ordered a recalibration of the MRI machine. Then he brought up an image on his monitor, and began flipping from one view to another to another, shaking his head each time. Jim was looking at it almost edge-on, but could see they were brain scans. Every now and then the doctor would pucker up his cheek and make a clicking sound, or lean one elbow on the arm of the chair and twirl his finger through the curly hair above his ear.

He picked up the phone and called Dr. Weagins and asked detailed questions about Jim's blood test. Then he wrote on a form, which he handed to Jim.

"When you leave here, go by the lab again. I want more blood."

Without waiting for a response, the doctor went back to the images on the computer with more head shaking and hair-twirling. Eventually, he turned to Jim. "Tell me what was going on while you were in the MRI machine. I'm recording this." He recited the date and time. Then he nodded at Jim.

"I revisited a far future as a person I'd been before. I was in a spaceship with my girlfriend. But I suddenly left there, and for a brief time I was in the past at a time when jet airplanes were just entering commercial service. I'd never been that person before. Terry Walker."

The doctor held up his hand. "No no no. Back up. Details, Jim. Sights, sounds, thoughts, feelings, voices, smells, people, places. And your emotions. Give me every detail, just as you remember it. Start from the moment you lay down on that table in the MRI lab. Go slowly. Take your time. Give me every detail."

Jim took a deep breath, collected his thoughts, and began.

"Slow down," Dr. Marquand said at one point as he continued writing, "As you can see I'm also taking notes as you talk," he said as he continued writing on his note pad. Jim didn't ask why he didn't use a computer.

He had always admired someone who could talk and write at the same time. Jim had never been able to do that. He continued at a slow pace. As he spoke, the doctor flipped through a series of scans on his monitor, occasionally held out a hand for Jim to pause and asked questions or scribbled notes on his yellow legal pad. Page after page of notes. Picture after picture on the screen. Question after question.

When Jim finished, the doctor sat silently for a long while, nodding his head slightly every now and then, shaking it at others, twirling his hair in between times or tapping a pencil on his knee. Finally he spoke. "I've never seen brain activity like this in my life. What you're going through is utterly unique, Jim. Your experience displayed locational patterns of brain activity much different than any known disorder such as schizophrenia. It was also not much like a dream. I'm quite excited." He nodded vigorously in agreement with himself. "Yes. Quite excited."

"It wasn't a dream. It was real. It was as real as you and me right here, right now." He rapped his knuckles on the desk and looked him straight in the eye. "As real as this desk. It was no dream, doctor."

The doctor said, "You know, many times the dreamer can control his dreams. He can change outcomes. He can back up and go through a sequence again to make it more to his liking. Did any of that sort of thing happen at any point?"

"What the hell is wrong with you? We've both just said it wasn't a dream. How could I change things that were actually going on? That have already happened? Can you go back and change your day? What's done was done. I can't change my life, and that was actual life. I was living it, there and then, at that place and that time. Time passed. I remembered my personal history from moments ago and years ago. I knew when and how I met everyone I was with, where we were, who else was involved in our past and what had happened before that. I thought we'd agreed that it wasn't a dream."

Dr. Marquand showed no reaction. "Tell me about your previous episode. Give me every detail in chronological order, just as it happened. I also want to know what you were doing, what you were experiencing, what you were thinking and feeling and what was going on just before and just after. Take as much time as you need."

Jim took a deep breath. Calmed his anxiety about missing so much time at the office. Refrained from looking at his watch. And began. When he was through, the doctor had filled more pages with notes, had stopped Jim and changed the memory stick once – why wasn't he using the cloud - and had dozens of questions. He scribbled comments during each answer, filling up more pages.

"Why don't you use an iPad or notebook?"

"I'm more comfortable the old fashioned way."

Finally Jim had to ask what he needed to know. "So what the hell's going on, Doctor? Do I have multiple personality disorder or something?"

Dr. Marquand slowly shook his head. "What you are experiencing is something entirely different. I cannot tell you what it is, but I can tell you what it is not. It's not anything I've ever heard of. I can rule out every disorder, every syndrome that I've ever seen or read about."

"Well that's encouraging. So I'm just plain crazy."

"We no longer use that term. But no, I don't think you're suffering from any form of psychosis. Not any known form. That's not to say you don't have some functional aberration in your brain. As a matter of fact you had a very major one during your so-called trip to the future, as well as during the one to the past. I've never seen an MRI like that. Your medial prefrontal cortex, as well as the precuneus and several other areas of your brain lit up the screen like signal flares in very unique patterns."

"At least there is something you can see. I'm mentally abnormal, and not just imagining it."

"That's not a bad way to put it, although unique might be a better term than abnormal. I don't know enough to say how or why it's happening, or what might be initiating it, or what might control it. Or, and I hesitate to say this out loud, and if you mention it outside this room I'll deny it, whether you really are experiencing the future and the past. That would be like something out of a far-fetched movie plot. I wouldn't even mention it to you if it weren't for these damn pictures." He jabbed a hand toward his monitor, then poked the monitor screen with his finger. "Damn pictures." He jabbed the screen again. "There's something going on in there, and whatever it is, it's not your imagination." He jabbed again.

"My imagination's not that good. I literally stepped into another existence, Doc. It was a complete other reality. I remembered making love to my girlfriend the night before. I knew our friends, what we did yesterday and last month and last year. Where I grew up. My parents, my family, my schooling. My childhood friends. I don't remember actually thinking of them or of my family or schooling, but I know I could have if something had caused me to, like Zeleece asking me a question. It was all available to me, all part of the person I was. Talaan." He frowned. "And Terry. I was him too. And neither knew of Jim Drake as far as I know."

The doctor leaned his head sideways and twirled his finger in his hair as he said, "The universe we experience is not necessarily objective reality, Jim."

"Not if you're nuts." This was a fucking waste of time. The doctor had no more idea what was wrong with him than he did. But at least he did confirm that something physical was going on and apparently it wasn't schizophrenia, which was too bad. They could treat that.

The doctor clucked his tongue, then said, "Nuts is a perfectly good term that pompousness prevents us doctors from using."

"So I am nuts."

"Even if a person is normal, whatever normal is, what he or she experiences is merely the view of the world from their own individual mind. It's a subjective universe each of us sees, always slightly different from the universe of realities that are perceived by other individuals. In other words, your universe is not necessarily an objectively universal one. Mine isn't either, and it is different than yours. So-and-so's an asshole to me, but not to you. Blue is appealing to me, but you prefer red. The world is great when things are going my way, but to you the same world stinks because nothing is going right. Normally, in the overall scheme of things, these differences are unimportant. They are subjective, and we all realize they are confined to our own circumstances as we interpret events at the moment."

"I had more than a slightly different viewpoint." He swept his arm to indicate the room. "It was another world, Doctor. Another place. Another time. Other people. Other histories. Or as you put it, another universe." He thought a moment, and nodded. "That's exactly what it was. Another universe. Another existence in another place at another time."

Dr. Marquand looked off into space. "Maybe there *is* something to that parallel universe stuff some physicists have been babbling about." He shook his finger at the monitor. "I don't know if I believe any of that, but on the other hand, perhaps you *could* be experiencing a perceptually unique universe, or a different layer in the multiverse. What I mean is, it could be reality, but reality from your perspective only." He shook his head. "No. There's something more than that going on. I can see it." The doctor got a sparkle in his eyes as he nodded vigorously to himself. "Yes. Yes indeed. A great deal more, and I need to find out what, and why, and how. This is going to be a challenge, Jim. This is a real doozy!"

"I'm glad you're pleased."

The doctor wagged his finger at Jim. "Not pleased. Intrigued. Now, I need to consult with some of my colleagues. Then I want to conduct more tests. Please make yourself comfortable. There are drinks over there in the fridge." He pointed to his left.

"I thought I'd had about every test there was."

"Not even close. We've got PET scans, MEG, various interactive types of functional MRI, quantitative EEG, and others. We may end up using them all. I don't know yet. But before any of those, I'm going to have you undergo a battery of tests right here in my own lab. They will be written, visual, perceptual, and auditory. Fortunately, your company paid for very good insurance so it will cover at least some of that."

"Yeah. I'm the one who pays the premiums."

"Excuse me while I call a colleague at UCLA."

Dr. Marquand dialed a number. "Hello, Doctor Fillmore? This is Aubert Marquand. Yes, good to hear you, too, Peter. I'm glad I caught you at your desk. I've got someone here with something going on that defies everything we thought we knew. You're up on the psychnet, I hope?" After a pause, he said, "Good. U-c-l-a-psy-peter-fillmore?" He fiddled with his computer as he talked. "Take a look at this, Peter."

As the conversation turned to psychobabble Jim tuned him out and looked around the office. He got up to study one picture in particular, an abstract oil, actually a copy of one, that at first glance had looked like a brightly colored Rorschach ink blot. Paint was splotched and splattered in an abstract pattern. But as he shifted his gaze toward the top of the painting he realized it was not random, but a woman in a gown, and the gown was part of the abstraction. He could clearly see her head and an arm. Her filmy gown was a maze of colors that blended into out-of-focus patterns. He looked at a small plaque beneath the artwork to find the artist's name. Mstislav Pavlov, and the piece was entitled *Passion.* He recognized the name, a Russian artist Trina was fond of. He stepped back to better take in the overall impression. It seemed as if the girl was part of a fairy tale. A fairy princess glowing with serenity, yet diaphanous and ethereal, occupying an abstract universe of her own. But at peace with that. Perhaps she had attained that peace by surrendering her tangible nature, her emotions, even her solidity. Maybe, like him, she had slipped into another existence, a different layer of reality. But the one she had found was where anguish and insanity did not exist. Maybe she had risen above all that. But in his case his alternate reality had been far too human, too tangible for any of that. She was angelic while he was beset with faults and problems, with guilt and desire and lust and fear. Could he go there, where she seemed to be? Could he make the transition mentally or spiritually? Was it possible to attain a state of everlasting serenity? Did he want to?

Jim thought about that and realized he could never be content with an existence like that. He had wants and desires and he enjoyed having a lot of them, and wanted to keep them. The blemishes and imperfections—his wants, his successes and failures and the striving after goals. The love and the tears. Anger and laughter and even fear at times. All the uncertainties that the challenges of life brought with them, the ups and downs, the uncertainty and the forgiveness that made up life while increasing wisdom. That is what makes a human being human, he realized

But insanity didn't belong. He didn't want his insanity that took reality and rumpled it up like a piece of paper and tossed it aside, a piece of useless trash that might blow away and be gone forever. In the background of the emotional sea that the painting created he overheard the doctor establish conference links with the University of Pittsburgh Medical Center, and shortly later with New York University Medical

Center. That worried him even more with three major universities involved. He tried not to pay attention. He moved to another painting, but could not concentrate on it. What in the hell was going on, that doctors from all over the country would stop whatever they were doing to discuss his case? He must be a real specimen.

He went back to the first painting, but the serenity was gone. The patterns in the lower part had been transformed into something resembling a nebula out in the cosmos. Dark clouds of intergalactic dust. Stars and galaxies radiating in many colors, whispering their ominous secrets, hinting at unimaginable power. The face now seemed more like one of the Sirens calling the ancient mariners to dive into the water to join them. Beckoning with promises: come into the arms of my radiation field, enter my gravity well.

He looked at Doctor Marquand, who was twirling a finger in his hair. The doctor caught his eye and motioned toward a bar built into the wall. He moved the phone aside. "Help yourself, Jim. Soft drinks, water..." He went back to his monitor and video conference, flipped through his notes, called up a different image on the screen of another monitor. They must be on Zoom or one of the other video conferencing apps. "That particular burst of activity occurred just about when Mr. Drake was…"

Jim tuned him out, walked to the bar and opened the refrigerator. It was packed. Bottled juices. Bottled water. Diet Coke, Sierra Mist, Dr. Pepper. He took one of the designer juices, an orange one and read the label. Carrot juice, strawberry juice, raspberry juice, kale. He put it back and took a Dr. Pepper. Then thought about the caffeine and sugar, and wondered if that could have anything to do with his episodes, and put it back. He took the bizarre juice mixture. Tasted it. Surprisingly, it was not bad. He went back and sat down. Had another sip. He studied the graceful cherrywood curves that formed the base of the glass coffee table.

His gaze wandered to a bone white vase holding white calla lilies on a long, low table under the window. The lilies seemed alive, aware. Aware of him, aware of his psychic deformity. Some were staring at him, some were looking away haughtily. All had their yellow tongues out as if they were tasting the air, tasting for sanity. And disapproving of what they found. Their immaculate pale faces seemed like so many elegant, white-painted geisha, expressionless yet scowling at his condition. He agreed with their assessment.

Finally the long conference call was over. Dr. Marquand sat sideways to Jim staring at the wall, legs crossed, pen tapping on his knee, twirling his finger in his hair. Occasionally he mumbled to himself or shook his head. Then he did both. "Jim," he finally said without looking at him, "we're going to get to the bottom of this."

Jim didn't say anything. That statement seemed to confirm that the doctors had no idea what was going on.

Dr. Marquand turned to face him. "I was discussing your case with two of the most highly regarded experimental psychiatrists in the world, Dr. Peter Fillmore at UCLA Medical Center, and Dr. Maurice Ebenstein at the University of Pittsburgh Medical Center. They both have PhD's as well as M.D.'s. I also spoke to one of the staff at New York University Medical Center."

"So you have no idea what's wrong."

"That's correct, Jim. You are unique." The doctor's gaze did not waver. In fact, the corners of his mouth curled up slightly.

At least the son of a bitch was honest. "I'm pretty sure my insurance will not cover whatever you've got planned."

"Don't worry about it. The initial tests we've decoded to run are coming out of our research budgets."

Anxiety surged within him. "We? Research budgets? Jesus Christ! I came here looking for a solution, not volunteering to have my brain dissected by a bunch of shrinks in white lab coats so they can write research papers and brag to their buddies."

"No, no, no." Dr. Marquand shook his head emphatically. "No, no. This is at my request, and they're willing to help me, but my number one objective is to help you."

"What's in it for them?"

The doctor tilted his head to the side for a moment, then said, "Several things." He tapped a raised finger. "First, because of our relationships. We've collaborated on various projects over the years, and have strong mutual respect. Second," he tapped the next finger, "because this is something that has never before been observed, so it's extremely interesting." He moved to the next finger. "Third, investigating it may open up a new field, or at least extend existing areas of knowledge so we can help others. And finally," he patted a fourth finger repeatedly, "it's a challenge." He nodded to himself. "A real challenge."

Jim said aloud, half to himself, "The operation was amazing, and we learned so much we almost shit our pants. It's unfortunate the patient went bonkers before we finished up."

The doctor chuckled. "Let's hope not. Anyway, Dr. Fillmore has commitments that will keep him occupied for the next couple of weeks, but he'll follow our progress on our network."

"He's at UCLA?"

"Yes. So first, I'm sending you to the University of Pittsburgh for functional MRI testing."

'I can't take the time. I have a business to run."

"Can you run it from your starship?"

"Not funny."

"No it's not. But think about it. What if you have another episode during a business meeting or on a job site?"

"But you just gave me an MRI. Why another one?"

"This is different. It's called fMRI. Basically it's the same machine, but we'll be using stimuli such as light patterns and sound or mental tasks for you to perform while you are in the machine."

"Why Pittsburgh? Why can't you do it here?"

"Dr. Ebenstein and his staff have their MRI scanner connected by a wideband fiber network to a Cray supercomputer at the Pittsburgh Supercomputing Center at Carnegie Mellon. They can create three-dimensional images of your brain activity and send them back to the lab in real time. Very few places in the world can do that. And I can view them right here," he pointed at his computer screen, "almost in real time."

"You mean they can't do that around here?"

"They probably could, but UCLA's system is committed and not under Doctor Fillmore's control, and I don't have a good personal contact at USC or UCI, or up north at Stanford or Berkeley. Besides, and even more importantly, Fillmore and Ebenstein are the best in the field. I've worked with them before, and I want to work with them now."

"So you want me to go to Pittsburgh. When?"

"I don't know." He banged his desk with his fist. "Damn Ebenstein." He banged again.

"You don't know?"

"The man is always fiddling. His machine is torn down for some modifications. It's going to be a couple of days."

"So what do I do in the meantime? Damn it, Doctor, I never had anything like this happen in my life, and now I've had two attacks in two days. What if I have another one? Is there anything we can do while we're waiting, like put me in a padded cell? I hate to say it, but I think maybe you better."

"No padded cell, Jim. I'm going to prescribe some psychotropic medicine which may suppress it. I know a little bit about this syndrome of yours already, namely where in your brain the activity occurs, so I have some idea of what might suppress the onset." He wrote on a prescription pad, saying as he wrote, "Have this filled at once. I want you to take one tablet three times a day." He tore it off and handed it to Jim, then got up and opened a locked cabinet, which he rummaged through. He came up with a pill container, closed and locked the cabinet, and returned to his chair. "Here's a sample. Take one now." He indicated Jim's juice drink.

Jim tore off the seal and removed a small yellow pill. He put it in his mouth and swallowed it with the remains of his drink.

"Second," Doctor Marquand went on, "I want you to refrain from all drugs and alcohol. Not even poppy seeds on your bagels."

"No problem."

"Also, I don't want you to drive."

"That's not realistic."

"Have your wife drive you. Use Uber. Or have one of your employees act as a chauffer."

"I'll think about that."

"You need to do more than think. If you have another episode you sure don't want to be behind the wheel. Also, I'm giving you my cell number." The doctor took a business card out of the holder on his desk and began writing on the back of it while he continued to speak. "If you have another episode, I want to know at once. Call anytime, day or night." He handed the card to Jim.

"Doc?"

"Yes?"

"Doc, I'm... this scares the hell out of me. Like I've never been scared in my life."

"You have every right to be. And it's good to acknowledge it."

"I mean, I'm really... when this happens I lose touch with reality. I'm not here." He tapped the desk with his finger. "And I don't even know I'm not here. Because where I am, that's where I am. Everything's normal. Wherever I am is where I am."

"Yes. Hmmm." Dr. Marquand rocked his head back and forth for a few moments, then said, "It's very odd that everything here, in this reality, disappears. All the people, places, even the century. It's unheard of to be completely in another place and with other people to the extent that absolutely nothing here exists for you, even in distorted form. In fact, it would be unbelievable if it weren't for those damn MRI data. Hmmm. I wonder if it's possible you're bringing to life events you've read about but don't remember. I suppose psychotic fantasy is a possibility, but this is so extreme. The most bizarre explanation is that your mind really is undergoing some sort of time travel. Taking what you've told me at face value, that would be the logical answer except for the fact that it's not logical. It's not only illogical but impossible. So there must be something else, but what, I have no idea. The good news is, there's got to be a reason. There *is* a reason. We see something extraordinary occurring in your brain. We just don't know what's going on or how it's doing what it's doing, or how to suppress it. That's what we intend to find out."

"In the meantime?"

"We're getting you into the Pittsburgh lab as soon as possible. And if you have another episode in spite of this drug, I have other options. Also, I'm scheduling you for a battery of psychological tests. We'll do it here, tomorrow afternoon. One-thirty."

Jim started to get up, then settled back down in his chair. He was afraid to be alone, especially in public. What if his mind just took off again? Sure as hell it was going to happen again. He needed a plan, some sort of a safety net, but as far as he knew none was available. "Dr. Marquand," he said, not knowing what to say, "I want to thank you for everything you're doing, and I don't want to seem ungrateful, but..." He searched for words that did not come.

The doctor got up, came around the desk, and put his hand on Jim's shoulder. "I think I understand, Jim. All of a sudden you're not in control, are you? Your life is being run by something beyond your power to manage, even beyond anyone's understanding. And now you've got to rely on me, and I don't know what I'm doing."

Jim nodded. "That's pretty much it. Well, you know what you're doing, you just don't know what I'm doing. I feel like an out-of-control robot. Or a laboratory animal. Like you're going to have me scurrying around in a cage, seeing if this works or that works and what happens if you poke here or zap there."

The doctor patted his shoulder. "We're intending to study you, Jim, but we're not going to dissect you to take a look. Not physically. Only electromagnetically." The doctor made a sound that was probably a chuckle. "We're going to dissect the crap out of you electromagnetically, Mr. Drake. Poke and prod and twist."

Jim actually had to smile. "Thanks for small favors." He stood up, and the doctor put his arm on his shoulder.

"Hang in there, Jim. We're in this together."

"You can say that, but I'm the one whose sanity is skittering sideways. My grip on reality—when that happens, Doctor, I may as well have left the top of a ski jump spinning and blindfolded. I have no control, no idea which way's which, no idea where I'll land. I step into another universe. But when I'm there, everything is normal. I'm not crazy there."

The doctor nodded. "Yes. Another universe. Hmmm," he mused as his hand dropped from Jim's shoulder. "Very, very odd," he said with a vacant gaze.

"I hate it, Doc. *I hate it!* I've never felt so inadequate in my life, not even as a little kid. I hate the crap out of it."

The doctor put one hand on each of Jim's shoulders. "To be honest, Jim, I don't know if we'll ever fully understand and control these episodes of yours. But I'll tell you one thing. You could not find a better team with better resources anywhere in the world. Your case is so spectacularly unique that three of the top researchers in the world, myself and Doctors Peter Fillmore and Maurice Ebenstein, are dedicating ourselves, our research grants, and our resources to help understand your condition."

"Spectacularly unique, huh? I'd call it spectacularly fucked up, but I guess you guys couldn't put that in your research papers."

Doctor Marquand continued to look into Jim's eyes intently. "We're not in this for the opportunity to publish breakthrough papers in scientific journals, although the possibility is certainly there. Even the likelihood. We three are scientists, and our passion is discovering how the human mind works. Your case is a challenge, perhaps the challenge of a lifetime, and we shall be consumed with getting to the bottom of it. And when we do, who knows, it may be of benefit to humanity."

"I know I should be grateful, and I appreciate your honesty, but damn it, I don't want to be a chapter in a medical book. I want a normal life."

"That's our goal for you too. That would be the perfect outcome."

"Yeah. Perfect."

Jim turned toward the door, head down, feeling the need to summon energy just to walk to his car. Just to continue. And wondered what a normal life was. Would it be boring? What would he do? Would he appreciate it? What *was* normal? Not this. Maybe no one was normal. The doctor had told him that normal was a statistical curve. But on that curve, he was off the chart. By light years.

"Jim."

He stopped with his hand on the door handle, and half turned around. "What?"

"Call your wife or an employee. I don't want you driving."

"Oh yeah. Okay." He started out the door.

"You're not medically fit to be driving an automobile. If you have one of these episodes while you are, the consequences could be disastrous." He pointed back toward his office. "Make the call from here."

Jim thought about telling him to go to hell, but damn! Now he was officially mentally handicapped. The doctor did have the authority to call the DMV and have his license revoked. Besides, he was right. He turned back into the office and fished his phone out of his pocket.

After stopping by the pharmacy for his prescription and the lab to have blood drawn, Jim walked out and sat down on a concrete bench to wait for Trina. He occupied his mind by appreciating the flowers and trees, by trying to be one with nature. But his thoughts kept boomeranging back to his Talaan-self and the starshuttle. To Terry on the airplane with Maryann. To the MRI machine. To Truk Island. To insanity. He looked down at the asphalt.

A jolt of tension stabbed him. Who were these people he became? Then he thought of the old movie *A Beautiful* Mind and terror almost consumed him. That Russell Crowe character, John Nash, was him. Imaginary people becoming real. Jesus! *That was him!* He squirmed, afraid it was going to happen at any moment and looked around, but no one was paying any attention. They were ordinary people coming and going. And so was he, they thought.

He calmed down and thought about the main character in the movie depicting the real-life John Nash. Jim wasn't sure he would have the strength to cope with his own delusions the way John Nash did—by acknowledging that they were delusions, and deciding to ignore them. That would not be possible with Zeleece and Maryann when he was with them. There was no way he could pretend they weren't real. Because they *were* real and Jim Drake did not exist. John Nash's episodes were different. He had remained John Nash, and his wife had remained his wife, and his surroundings remained the same. But with him, Jim Drake ceased to exist. He was literally a totally different person in a different time. The entire present time and place disappeared. Would it be like this for the rest of his life? Would it get worse? It already had. How soon would the next one happen?

He saw Trina pull into the parking lot and stood up. He headed toward the car. She got out and began walking toward him. "Hi, honey," he said as they met. "Thanks for coming."

She hardly broke stride. "I want to talk to the doctor." She passed right by him and headed for the building.

He turned around and followed. "I don't think you'll be able to. I doubt if he has the time."

"He'll make time."

Jim caught up with her. "I doubt it. He's a world-class psychiatrist. He gives lectures all over the world."

"Good. Then maybe he'll be able to tell me what's going on. I sure won't find out from you."

"I'll tell you. He won't be able to see you, Trina."

"Oh, yes he will."

When had she gotten so assertive? She was always meek and compliant except when she was mad. He thought about taking her arm and pulling on it to stop her, but immediately knew he better not. That wouldn't stop her anyway. "I'll tell you everything," he said lamely as they continued walking. "But it wasn't much."

"See what I mean? You're so bad off he won't let you drive, and you say it wasn't much. Jim, I intend to hear that from the doctor first hand."

No need to waste his breath. He walked alongside her as she marched into the building and up to the elevators.

"Which floor?"

"Second. Suite two-sixteen. But you're wasting your time." When they entered the suite the receptionist looked up at Jim and smiled. "Mr. Drake. Did you forget something?"

"No, my..."

"I'm Mr. Drake's wife," Trina interrupted. "I want to talk to the doctor."

"Nice to meet you, Mrs. Drake. Let me see if doctor's available." She picked up the phone and said, "Mrs. Drake is here and wants to talk to you... You have?... Certainly." She hung up the phone and said, "He was expecting you. Come this way, please."

Trina cast a raised eyebrow at Jim that said very emphatically, 'see, you jerk' as she strode through the doorway the receptionist held open. Jim followed silently, knowing he was completely out of credibility.

Chapter 5

The facts

"I'm Dr. Marquand." The doctor indicated the chairs in front of his desk—there were two now, to Jim's amazement. "Please be seated."

Trina sat down and gave Jim another one of those looks as he settled into the other one. He just shrugged.

The doctor said to Jim, "The machine was retested, and it was working perfectly." He faced Trina. "Your husband has some very, let me say, he has some startling activity going on in his brain during these episodes."

"How could you know unless..." her head swiveled to Jim with a look of total disapproval. "Good Lord! Did he have another episode?"

The doctor gave Jim a crooked little half-smile. "I didn't think you'd tell her."

Jim glanced from the doctor to Trina, then back. "I didn't have a chance." The doctor had betrayed him. He felt ganged-up on.

Trina's eyes locked on his, then released him as she turned back to the doctor. "What's going on? What's wrong with him? What caused it?"

"Mrs. Drake, Trina, I don't know. Not yet. Although it may be distressing to you, from my point of view it was most fortunate that your husband had another episode while he was in the MRI machine. Had he not, I would have found everything to be normal and sent him to a practicing psychiatrist or even a psychologist for treatment. But because he did have an episode, I know that conventional treatment would be useless or worse. There's something very physical, something psychochemical and measurable taking place in Jim's brain. Something synaptical and spatially well delimited rather than a more nebulous and widespread phenomenon such as an hallucination."

"Will it get worse? Can you treat it? Is it curable?" She hesitated, then said, "You say you don't know? How can that be? Someone must have studied this."

The doctor laid his hands flat on his desk. "I wish I could answer even one of your questions, but I have no diagnosis. This is something new, Mrs. Drake. It has never before been observed."

"How could that be? Surely someone knows something about it."

Dr. Marquand shook his head. "No. We have never observed such brain activity. No one has, as far as we know. I would never have imagined such patterns were possible. Jim's brain lit up the screen in places and patterns we have never seen."

She looked at Jim with a twisted expression, something between horror and sympathy. "Oh, God." She scanned his face, seeking something from him while radiating a combination of pity and fear. After long moments, she turned back to the doctor. "You keep saying we. Who is we? Is someone else involved?"

"Yes. We're very fortunate to have Dr. Peter Fillmore at UCLA Medical Center and Dr. Maurice Ebenstein at the University of Pittsburgh Medical Center collaborating with me on this."

"Good Lord! Three of you? From around the country? Why? What's going on? What are you not telling me?"

"I involved the other two because what Jim is experiencing is so fundamentally different than anything that has ever been observed—as I said, this is a new phenomenon, Mrs. Drake. It could open up a whole new field. And these two doctors along with myself are at the forefront of experimental psychiatry, conducting experiments on patients and volunteers with some of the most advanced instrumentation in the world. We are the guys who are showing the rest of the world what we have learned and how to do what we are doing, and how to interpret the results."

"You're telling me that three of the top psychiatric scientists in the world are willing to drop whatever they're doing to study Jim Drake? That scares the daylights out of me, doctor." She unconsciously reached over to Jim's hand.

Dr. Marquand leaned forward. "Trina, it's a good thing, not a bad one. Money could not buy this kind of expertise. It doesn't mean Jim's case is fatal. Nothing of the sort. But if we can figure out what's going on, the techniques and the solutions we develop, and the knowledge, may have applications we can't even imagine. It could be of tremendous benefit to humanity."

She looked at Jim. "He seems to think he's actually visiting or existing in the past and the future, living different lives. How could that possibly have any application to *anyone's* psychiatric problems?"

"Hmmm. That's sort of like an accountant at the old Bell Labs asking William Shockley what possible application there could be for his research into semiconductors before he demonstrated the first transistor, long before any applications evolved. Such a question cannot be answered beforehand. The applications of fundamental research can never be predicted, yet every major development has its foundations in so-called meaningless research."

"But Jim needs help, not research."

"If we're going to help him, we first have to understand his affliction." The doctor began twiddling his finger in his hair, then nodded to himself. "Our minds are constrained by the laws of physics, Mrs. Drake, just as every physical system in the universe is. However, we do not know all those laws, and that is more evident when we try to understand what we call mind. These days, we know quite a bit about the brain, but very little about mind. In fact, we know almost nothing deterministic about it, mostly just functional physiometry and some behavioral or experiential tendencies. Through Jim, we may be able to change that situation. I have a strong hunch that what he's experiencing is intertwined with mind."

"What do you mean?"

"It seems that his mind is leaving the present and somehow experiencing a totally different reality."

"Surely you're not talking about time travel."

"No, of course not, not in the classical sense." Dr. Marquand paused as he tapped his pen on his knee. He looked away and frowned, jabbed at his blank computer screen. "Damn data!" He shook his head vigorously and turned to Trina, "No, it can't be time travel." He shook his head no. "Probably not."

"*Probably* not?"

Doctor Marquand seemed not to have heard her. "On the other hand, we do know that in the physical universe, quantum theory allows superpositions of what we normally regard as mutually exclusive alternatives." He focused on Trina and shrugged. "For example, a single particle can pass through two separate slits in a barrier at the same time, which means it exists in two places at once. For another thing, two particles of a system can communicate their quantum state to one another, seeming to violate common sense and physical laws. In other words, Mrs. Drake, a multiplicity of reality is permitted, or at least not disallowed in the realm of quantum physics. So I cannot say no, absolutely not, to anything."

Jim was getting more interested. Maybe he wasn't nuts. He said, "So, if various realities are permitted, does that mean..."

"I'm confused." Trina had a frown, a real frown. One with creases, the sort she never got. "Did you just imply that he, or at least his mind, could actually exist in two places or two times at once?"

"Minds are not free of the laws of physics—nor, I suspect, is the gaze of our consciousness."

"That doesn't answer my question."

Jim felt his eyebrows go up. She sure had gotten assertive.

"I can't answer your question. What I'm trying to convey to you is that his mind is behaving in such a way that, from his perspective, he is experiencing time travel. He is living a multivalued physical reality, qualitatively akin to those quantum behaviors. Within his mind there may be a quantum entanglement between this and some other objective universe."

Trina said, "How is it that you, a psychiatrist, know so much about physics?"

"I completed the course work for a doctorate in physics before switching to psychiatry. I still follow the work in the field."

"Wow!" Trina seemed impressed, and Jim knew he was. "Why did you switch after all that work? Why didn't you complete your dissertation and get the degree before pursuing psychiatry?"

Dr. Marquand studied his fingernails several seconds before saying, "Well, I suppose you need to know. I wanted to find out why I was so different. It worried me and began to consume me, wondering if I was crazy. I had to find out without letting anyone know. So I switched to psychiatry." He looked at Jim. "And I found out I'm not crazy, any more than you are. I'm just me, a little farther out on some meaningless statistical curve than most people. But everyone on this planet is unique. Some of us are just a little more unique than others."

"But how could Jim's fantasies, do you have a name for them?"

"Excursions to insanity," Jim said.

The doctor wagged his finger at Jim. "Don't say insanity." He turned his attention to Trina. "Let's look at it this way. You and I see that Jim is still here during these episodes. He did not leave the MRI tunnel. He did not leave the ball game. Yet at the same time," he pointed at Jim, "you were elsewhere and elsewhen. No question in your mind. You were another person in another place at another time with another complete personal history. In other words, we each had our own perspective. A panoptic outside observer would say that Jim was experiencing a multivalued physical reality. Is it all in his mind? Almost certainly. Is that time travel? Your answer is as good as mine, because I can't answer that question. I don't even know what time travel would be in this context. If you mean does he undergo a physical temporal excursion, then no. If you mean his mind does, then perhaps."

"Why did he suddenly start having these experiences? What went wrong? What changed?"

"I don't know. No idea. Not yet." He tilted his head to the side. "Did you know that space, and even time, are probably quantized? The idea is that space, and time itself, may not be continuous but composed of discrete elements. It may be that the string theory or loop quantum gravity is leading us in that direction."

"Doctor, I don't care about that. I want..."

"Mrs. Drake, we are extremely ignorant here, even more so than the physicists trying to reconcile the theory of relativity with quantum mechanics, which is what string theory is about and what I was getting at. If the radiation from black holes, where the theory of relativity applies, can be explained quantum mechanically, as Stephen Hawking tried to do by looking at Plank unit areas on the event horizon of black holes, then why should the brain and the mind be uniquely excluded? And by the way, I want to reiterate that we're dealing not just with Jim's brain, but also his mind. His personal experience of his reality at the moment."

"Yes, I can see that."

"When we try to define the link between the physical brain and the subjective or creative or spiritual mind—between chemical reactions and abstract, intuitive thought—between neuronal activity and the essence of what each of us consider to be our unique selves at the deepest level—what some would call our spiritual self—we know nothing."

"But..." She turned to Jim with a silent plea for help. "Quantum effects?" She looked at Jim.

He shrugged.

Dr. Marquand said, "It's certainly not a foregone conclusion that they are important at this interface where brain activities transition to mind, to imagination, to abstraction—at the level where electrochemistry metamorphoses into, or gives way to what we consider being or essence. Perhaps that part of Jim is time tunneling to different universes or realities."

"I don't know what to say."

"Nor do I. And I most definitely could be completely off track. Miles off. We have entered uncharted territory, Mrs. Drake, and what I'm speculating is that in Jim we may be witnessing some manifestation of the interactions at this boundary between the physical brain and the essence of what a human being is. And that's what is so intriguing to me and my colleagues."

"If it wasn't for those high-powered colleagues I'd be wondering about you, and questioning what you said even more than I am."

"You may anyway, if you wish. That's perfectly acceptable. I sometimes do myself. In fact I am now. But I'm not collaborating with these men to lend legitimacy to a wild theory, because they would not agree with a thing I just said. They each have their own ideas. And by the way, neither of them is what you might consider eccentric. They are perfectly normal, and entered psychiatry because they are intrigued by the mind and by how much we don't know about it."

"I have to take your word for that. What's the next step?"

"Well, I'm conducting a whole series of psychological tests on Jim here tomorrow afternoon. Then I'm sending him to Pittsburgh for functional MRI testing."

Jim felt impersonalized, as if they were discussing someone who wasn't here. He decided to complain, but before he could Trina said, "That's where they apply sounds or images while he's in the MRI machine to see how his brain responds?"

The center of Dr. Marquand's lower lip pushed upward in approval. "Exactly."

"Then what? What will that tell you?"

"I don't know. I truly don't know. We'll have to learn as we go along. The results of one series of tests will, hopefully, lead us to the next logical step in the process of unraveling the mystery. I expect we'll have him undergo additional testing, which may or may not include PET scans or MEG testing at UCLA to fill out the picture. Also, UCLA has a fairly new system from GE that combines three-dimensional x-ray and magnetic resonance images. That may prove useful, if we can get access to it."

Jim said, "Why don't you save time and send brain samples everywhere?" He mentally kicked himself. That was stupid.

Trina scowled at him; the doctor smiled.

She said, "You saw something going on at certain locations in his brain when he was in the MRI machine here. Can you give him medication to suppress activity in those regions without numbing him with narcotics?"

"I already have. I gave him a prescription that has had beneficial effects on some patients suffering from completely different disorders, but which manifest activity in some of the same parts of the brain." He looked at Jim. "However, as I said, it's nothing more than an educated guess. If it doesn't work, we'll try something else."

"When is his appointment in Pittsburgh?"

"I don't know exactly, but as soon as Dr. Ebenstein's functional MRI system is back on line."

"But facilities all over the country can do functional MRI. Why Pittsburgh?"

"Most require hours if not days to correlate the response to the stimuli and come up with a useful brain map. At Pittsburgh they do it in real time. Even more importantly, that's where Dr. Ebenstein is. He and Dr. Fillmore are the ones I want to collaborate with."

"A lab animal."

Trina looked at Jim with what seemed like pity, and sagged in her chair. "He's right. He almost is."

Doctor Marquand looked at his fingernails again, seemingly mulling over what she said, gave two brief nods of agreement to himself, then said, "Mrs. Drake, I am going to need your help."

She brightened visibly. Scooted to an upright posture.

The doctor continued, "I've given Jim my cell phone number, and I'm going to give it to you too. If he has another episode I want to be notified immediately. I also told him no alcohol or drugs of any kind. Not even caffeine."

"He used some psychedelic drugs twenty or so years ago." Trina looked at Jim in disapproval. "Could this have anything to do with that? A flashback or something?"

"No. This is totally different."

"What do you want me to do besides watch his diet?"

"If he has another episode write down, to the best of your knowledge, everything he ate, drank, and said prior to the attack. What he was doing. What he was hearing and seeing. How he looked and acted. Anything you can think of that might be pertinent."

"If he does have one, what should I do? Just let him be, or shake him, or what?"

"Shaking might be good. If that doesn't bring him out of it, try hitting him hard in the shoulder. Or slapping him."

"Tell her to shoot me, Doc." Stupid remarks always popped out at inappropriate times, even when he didn't feel like joking.

Trina scowled. "It is tempting."

The doctor said, "Humor can be good medicine."

He felt desperately alone. And hopeless. He needed to be involved. "I need to do something, damnit. I'm not helpless."

"You're absolutely right. I was about to get to that. I want you to keep busy mentally, Jim. Very busy." The doctor tapped his pen on his knee. "Tell me, what do you like to do for fun?"

"Have sex."

Doctor Marquand erupted in a chuckle and Trina glowered. The doctor said, "Good answer. But that's not what I meant. What hobbies do you have, what avocations, what diversions that really interest you?"

"I just work."

"Bad." Doctor Marquand shook his head and looked at Trina. "That's not good."

She said, "He's a darn good architect. Before he started his business he used to spend evenings designing our dream home."

"Ah! Good. Good. Anything else?"

Trina had a far-away look, then held up a finger and said, "Yes. He also used to play chess."

The doctor turned to Jim. "There's your answer. Do that."

"Play chess?"

"Yes. And design your home. Engage in activities that completely absorb you. Leave no opportunity for your mind to wander."

"I don't have a chess partner anymore."

"There are numerous sites where you can play online, either against a computer or against other players. I recommend you play against the computer so you don't have down time waiting for your opponent to make a move. Keep trying to improve your play, make it a challenge to move up in the rankings. When you're tired of chess, devise whole new floor plans for your dream home. New exteriors, new surfaces. New and different everything. Make it difficult to build, and then figure out ways to do it."

"And let my business go to hell."

"Yes. If that's what it takes, yes. Absolutely."

Jim looked at Trina for support, but she said, "He can do that. Abby can handle the business for a while. I can help her."

Jim rolled his eyes upward. "God help the construction trade."

The doctor rose from his chair. "And keep wisecracking, Jim. That's good. Yes indeed." He looked aside and, nodding with vigor, said to himself, "F-ing good." His head snapped back to Trina. "Ooh! Sorry. Jim and I... never mind. Sorry."

She looked at Jim quizzically.

"Just a phrase we shared," he said.

"Lord, Jim, you're even a bad influence on your doctor." But she almost had a grin.

"Don't forget to get your prescription filled. And be here tomorrow by one-fifteen."

"I already dropped it off downstairs." He turned to Trina. "It's probably ready."

Chapter 6

Chess Master

He was amazed at how much chess he'd forgotten. He'd even had to stop and think about how some of the pieces were allowed to move. Most of the opening gambits and basic strategy eluded him. In the first game the computer blew him away in five moves. Now, after dropping down in class three times he had stretched a game out for twenty moves before being declared a loser, and was pretty sure he could win at this level next time. Maybe.

Loser! He hated that word and all it implied—someone who wasn't capable, or kids who messed with drugs so much, thinking they were cool, that they eventually dropped out of school and then out of society and would never have a nice job, a nice home, make a decent living or have a satisfying life. He'd never been like that. Until now. In sports, in dating, in school, in business, he always worked to become a winner. But now. Jesus Christ. He was a certified lunatic reduced to playing games on a computer because he couldn't be trusted in public. Next? Soaps and game shows. Maybe he should start making fringed leather vests or molding crooked little vases and coffee cups out of clay.

"Are you hungry?"

The voice startled him, then he felt foolish for having been startled. He turned to her. "I hadn't thought about it."

"You've been sitting at that computer for four hours."

"Four hours? How time flies when you're having fun." Stupid ass. He hated who he'd become. He sought within for the old Jim and found remnants lurking here and there alongside anger and yes, fear. Fear of not being in control. Fear of not being normal. Fear, fear, fear. Like a little kid or a hypochondriac. Screw this. He breathed a deep and determined breath and took control, shoving that pitiful self away. "Now that you mention it, I could eat. After all, I've been playing chess all afternoon, and that's after going to an alien planet and back this morning. That'll work up an appetite like nothing I know."

"You *are* sick. But thanks for staying home the rest of the day. I feel better knowing you're here in the house."

Yeah. He needed to be watched. He might end up wandering the streets babbling to aliens, or climbing up the neighbor's chimney. "I'm going to work tomorrow morning."

"I'm driving you."

"I know, I know. But after that, I think I'll have one of the men pick me up."

"That's fine. Now, let's go eat. I haven't had anything all day and I'm starving."

Without even asking what he wanted, she drove to Dos Amigos. It was late afternoon but well ahead of the evening rush. They were seated immediately. The busboy brought water, chips and salsa. Jim loved chips and salsa, and dipped right in. After crunching the first chip in his mouth, he said, "How come we always end up here? There are lots of other good Mexican restaurants around."

"You ask me the same thing every time. I love their burritos, and can get them without beans. Less fattening."

"I'm going to have a burrito this time too. The chili verde one. With refried beans on the side." He put down the menu and picked up a chip from the basket. Dipped it into the salsa. "The salsa is good."

"It's too hot for me."

Jim had another chip, loaded with salsa. "Perfect."

A cute little waitress came up and asked what they wanted to drink. Trina said, "Just water. And I want the chicken burrito, no beans, à la carte."

Jim said, "I'll have a Corona and a chili verde burrito with refried beans on the side." Then he remembered, slumped in his chair, and said, "Scratch the beer. Just water."

"Whatever you want, honey," the waitress said before she sashayed away.

Jim noticed Trina looking at him intently, and he said, "It sounded good. A margarita with a double shot would be even better." He took another chip. Dunked it in the salsa.

"How about a double shot to the head."

"What's that about, Trina?"

"Are you trying to hit on that waitress?"

"Of course not. What gives you that idea?"

"I don't know. That's silly. I'm just upset. This problem of yours. I'm really worried, Jim." She daintily picked up a chip, nibbled at it. "Our world seems as if it's turned upside down. This is something that just shouldn't happen."

"I know. I'm afraid to make a move or look at anything or listen to anything for fear it'll trigger another episode. But at the same time I have to make a constant effort to keep my mind off it. And this drug he had me take, I don't like it. It feels like I'm an onlooker, not involved with life." He took another chip, loaded it with salsa. He looked at the mural painted on the wall. It was a tropical setting, palm trees on a beach. It was not well done. The painter had no concept of perspective, but the location did look inviting.

Trina saw where he was looking, and said, "I can't wait until we go back to Hawaii. Remember that hotel where we stayed? Remember the open dining area where we would have breakfast, and the birds would fly right in?"

"There's one of them now. Do you know what kind they are?" He pointed down the beach where the water was rolling back to sea, exposing fresh wet sand, and birds were pecking to see what they could find.

Maryann said, "Terry Walker, you know I don't know one bird from another. I just call them, not ragamuffins, what's that new slang term we heard those kids with the surf boards call themselves?"

"Beach bums."

"Yes. Beach bums. That's exactly what these birds are. Loafing on the beach, waiting for food to be delivered to 'em. They're unbelievably tame though, aren't they, the way they came right up to our table this morning looking for handouts? Cute little devils."

Terry laughed in admiration of her infectious enthusiasm, then noticed a 1961 Thunderbird driving up the street. He pointed. "How could Ford have screwed up such a terrific car? They were great when they first came out. Now look. Why would anyone even buy one? I'm getting a Corvette this fall when the new ones come out, even if they are made by General Motors."

"They're terribly expensive. Gosh, over four thousand dollars. And we're going to need a house."

"But the wedding isn't for another year." He saw her look. She was always practical and conservative, always disapproving of his recklessness. "Well, maybe I'll get a used T-Bird. That would be okay. A '55, 6, or 7." He put his arm around her waist, feeling the smooth texture of her blue one-piece bathing suit. "Too bad we have to go home tomorrow."

"I know. So let's go swimming now." She took his hand and pulled him toward the ocean. "Let's get our money's worth."

"Money's worth? I wasted a lot of money getting two rooms. You haven't even slept in yours."

Maryann blushed. "Terry, not so loud." She looked around to make sure no one had heard, then added softly, "But if you want, I'll sleep in it tonight."

"I'll join you," he said in her ear.

She shrugged away from him. "I'll have to think about that," then she laughed as she tugged his hand. They ran into the ocean hand-in-hand, water splashing.

A short time later they collapsed on their beach towels. Terry squirmed to smooth out the lumps in the sand under his, and felt the salt water prickling his back as the tropical sun dried him out. The sound of the ocean was lulling, the breeze soft and warm, the world far off. He had just about dozed off when Maryann said, "I need to get back to that little store before we leave. I want to buy that coral necklace for my mother."

"You better do something. She sure wasn't happy about us coming over here unchaperoned before the wedding. Why don't we shower and do that now? We can have lunch while we're there."

"Okay."

They got up, picked up their towels, and headed toward the hotel.

He looked at her and smiled. A wind-blown wisp of brunette hair obscured her eyes. Then he looked at the palm trees at the edge of the sand.

Perturb.

"I love Hawaii."

"I do too, Trina." He glanced at her, then looked away quick so she wouldn't see the panic he felt. He realized he had crumbled the chip in his hand, and he let the crumbs trickle onto the table.

"Jim!" Panic surged in her voice. "What's wrong?"

He played with the crumbs, pushing them into a pile with his finger, avoiding eye contact. "What do you think? I'm going nuts, that's what." He wanted to crush the whole bowl. Dig both hands in and crush them all. Throw the bowl. Run and cuss and do something to stop this. "I don't want to talk about it."

"Jim, have you..."

The waitress magically appeared, saving him. "Here are your burritos, folks." He couldn't even think. What the hell happened? How may lives was he living? What brought this on? Who the hell was Terry Walker? This was the second time he was Terry. And Maryann? How could he act normal so Trina wouldn't know? God, she'd go ballistic, and drive him back at the doctor's office. Or try to make him stay home in bed. He had to do something. Something normal. What was normal? The waitress. He needed to order something. "Brooke," he said, "would you bring me a lemon wedge for my water?"

"Of course," Brooke said sweetly and touched his shoulder, then turned away.

Trina's voice was harsh. "How do you know her name?"

Son of a bitch! Jim closed his eyes. He took a deep breath, fixed his attention on his plate to make sure he stayed here. "From her name tag."

"She acted like she knew you."

"Trina, for Christ sake. She's just a girl."

"So was Lolita."

"So put her in your goddamn book."

They ate the meal in awkward silence after that, for which Jim was supremely grateful. One quick glance revealed that Trina was wearing her frown-without-a-wrinkle face. Hell with her. He had his hands full pretending to be sane. He was on the verge of a panic attack. His heart was going like crazy. His hands were shaking, so he held the burrito with both hands. He made sure not to look at the mural. Terry Walker? Maryann? Nineteen sixty-two? Good God! Terry Walker could still be alive! What the hell *was* going on? What if they met? Damn, he had to stop thinking. Damn, he wished he could get drunk.

God, please help me!

He forced down a second bite of burrito, and that was it. Drank his water so he could swallow. Tried to keep focused on his plate and the squished remains of the burrito. The pile of crumbled tortilla chip next to it.

"I thought you were hungry."

"I'm full."

The silence resumed. He kept his eyes on his plate. And the knife. And the fork. And his water glass with the lemon wedge in it. His plate again. Calmed his breathing. Realized his teeth were clamped together, and relaxed his jaw. Finally she was through. He stood up and said, "You pay. I'm going outside. I need some air." He went outside and stood staring at the hood of her car, at the three-pointed star of the hood ornament, afraid to do anything else.

Trina drove home in silence. As soon as they got in the house she went into her office, but left the door open. She was probably going to work on her book. Jim was irritated that she was more concerned about Brooke than him, that she had not guessed that he'd had another trip. He wasn't about to tell her. Instead, he said loud enough for her to hear, "Going to add Brooke to your cast of characters?"

"Should I?" The tone of her voice said yes. Brooke belonged.

"Why not? Since it's becoming a soap opera."

"So is our life. It's just that no one's been murdered yet." The office door slammed.

Jim went into his own office. Found Dr. Marquand's card. Added his number to his contacts and called.

"I was afraid of that. I have another drug standing by. We'll try it."

"Doctor, what if that guy is alive and we meet? Terry Walker."

"I doubt if that's possible. I think it would be against the laws of physics."

"Which laws, doc? Relativity? Quantum mechanics? Your loop gravity one?"

"That's a darn good question, Jim. Ones we don't know, I guess. But I just don't think nature would allow something like that."

"I sure as hell hope not."

"Give me directions to your house. I'm bringing this medication over."

"If you make a house call aren't they liable to yank your license to practice?"

Dr. Marquand laughed. "Just don't tell them. But I'm glad you can still crack a joke. That's good."

"I'm on autopilot. No brain activity. Words just dribble out."

Now Trina was going to find out he'd had another episode. May as well get it over with. He took a deep breath, and walked to her office. Knocked.

Chapter 7

Unexpected help.

Jim expected his desk to be mounded with paperwork, but it was more orderly than he'd seen it for – maybe forever. He would have every square inch covered with blueprints and quotation worksheets. Plus invoices and work orders covering the credenza. Instead, vast expanses of well-oiled walnut were showing.

He began looking through the few small, neat stacks. There was nothing urgent, just items for his information, a few checks he needed to sign, and even two quotations. Abby, his assistant for over four years now, had actually completed two small job quotes and had them waiting for his review. He knew she was sharp, but this was unexpected. It looked as if he should be giving her more responsibility. And a raise.

He heard the front door open and looked out through his open office door to the reception area. It was Abby. Ten minutes late, as usual.

"Hi, Abby. Have a good sleep?"

Her smile was genuine. "Welcome back, boss. Feeling better?"

She looked sexy in her short skirt and a blue blouse that seemed to accentuate her big brown eyes. "I guess," he said, then wished he'd been more positive. "Yeah. Great."

Her smile did not waver as she walked into his office, sparkling with sexual allure and knowing it. He couldn't help but compare her with Trina. Trina was sexy, but in a much more understated way. Elegant, slender, classy, intellectual. Abby was the opposite in many ways: her sexuality was front and center without her seeming to make any effort to appear that way. She was care-free and at ease with herself. Trina struggled to be secure. She was not a people-pleaser, but nonetheless was always concerned about what others might think. Abby, on the other hand—if you did not approve of Abby, too bad. Your problem.

"What do you mean, you guess?" she said as she sat down in the chair at the end of his desk. "You look healthy as a horse."

She had obviously been to the beach or out by a pool; her body glowed with burn turning to tan. "Maybe so," he said, "but my brain's more like a jellyfish."

"Poor baby." She obviously thought he was joking. She patted his hand. "You better get it together. We've got a government quality assurance inspector coming this morning. In about half an hour."

"Oh, crap. We may have a problem. Where are the mill certs for that government job?"

"We're okay, Jim. I caught your mistake on the material thickness and changed the order. I think we're in good shape."

"You changed it? There goes our profit."

"Oh, don't be silly. It only added two thousand dollars to the total cost. You're still going to make at least seventy thousand on the job, unless you have a lot of overtime. And I don't think you will. The foreman was in yesterday and looked over your estimated labor, and said it should be no problem."

"There goes my Ferrari."

"What, you clear seventy-two thousand and you can get one, seventy and you can't? Seventy thousand net for a three month job isn't chicken feed. I'd like to have just ten percent of that."

"That's about what you gave away."

"You mean you lightened up the material on purpose?"

"They over-engineered it. I've done lots of jobs similar to this, and they all used lighter material. And they're still in good shape years later."

"You might have had a little problem convincing the inspector."

"I wasn't going to show it to him if he asked. But no one ever asks. I've never had a single customer ask for material certifications."

"I didn't know that. I thought you made a mistake." Abby had a little frown, obviously worried that she had screwed up her first time being in charge. Or maybe she was uncomfortable with Jim fudging on the job. She squirmed in her chair.

Jim had intended to alter the order himself just because it was for the government, but with the events of the last days had forgotten. He put on his most reassuring smile for her. "Actually, Abby, this is the first job I've done for the government, and they just might ask. So I think it's best that you did change it. I was going to do it myself, but it totally slipped my mind. You did a good job. Perfect."

Abby visibly relaxed. She crossed her legs, great legs, fantastic legs, and when she caught him looking she uncrossed them.

"Getting engaged to this Jeff guy kind of changed you, huh?"

"I want to get an idea of whether I'm cut out for marriage. And I think that ought to involve fidelity. Not just physical, but emotional and even my thinking."

"Actually, I think you'll do just fine."

"I think I'll like being monogamous. That makes it feel like a real commitment."

He smiled, "Then don't cross your legs like that in front of the wrong person."

She laughed, lifted her leg to give him a flash of pantie, then slapped at his shoulder playfully. "That's all you get."

"Probably all I can handle. And more than I need."

"You know," she said, "when I came in here looking for a job, I was just out of high school. I thought that if I wanted to get anywhere I should have sex with you. Now I know better. You're a way better man than you want people to think."

"You're fired."

"Screw you. I'm the one who runs this place, not you."

They both laughed. "You're right," he said. "Even Trina says I'd be lost without you. At least when she's not wondering what we're up to."

"Jim, Trina needs assurance. She wants to know that you love her."

"Abby, I do love her."

"I know that, but I'm not sure she does. She needs you to show it more."

"I don't need you to nag me too. That's her job." Abby's expression jolted him as her face transmitted emotions somewhere between hurt and mad and surprise, and Jim realized he had violated the unspoken bond of their relationship. "No, that's not true. You're right, she needs it, and I've been trying to let her know. To make her believe. I'm trying."

Abby's face relaxed and the rift was healed as quickly as it had formed. "Good. Because you know she suspects there's something going on between us."

"I think she's plotting my death in her book."

Abby grinned. "You're so full of it."

"She's working out how do it, how to get away with it."

"Go home tonight and make love to her. Be caring. Think of her feelings, her needs. Do little things for her."

"Like what? I just bought her a Mercedes."

"That's exactly *not* what I mean. That's trying to buy her, or at least it feels like it to her. That's not what she needs. It's the little things that matter, Jim. The thoughtful things, not the big expensive ones. Send her flowers for no reason at all. Call her in the middle of the day and say you were thinking of her. Cook her dinner, do the dishes, bring her breakfast in bed. Stuff like that."

"Abby, I'm not that kind of guy."

"I think you are. You just try to hide it. Let it go. You'll be even more attractive."

"Yeah. Whatever you say." He looked at her and smiled. "Even more attractive, huh?"

Abby just smiled coquettishly, the look that said 'come hither' to him but that he knew wasn't really her intention, then abruptly the smile faded and she changed the subject. "Now tell me what's wrong with you. You've been out all week."

"I'm going crazy, Abby."

She started to laugh, but when he just looked at her she put her hand over her mouth. "What do you mean?" she mumbled, eyes wide above her hand.

He gave her some of the details. Abby remained wide-eyed as he spoke, but eventually dropped her hand from her mouth. When he was through, all she could manage was, "God, Jim, that's scary."

"You don't have to tell me. I'm scared like a little kid."

"Oh, God, Jim." She got up and stood behind his chair, bent over and put her arms around his chest. Pressed her cheek against his. He felt a tear on her cheek. Or was it his? She moved her head away and wiped the wetness with her hand. "I wish there was something I could do."

He stood up and put his arms around her and hugged her, and to his surprise all he wanted was to be comforted. And he was. They stood there silently for long moments.

"I'm so sorry, Jim." She backed up, brushed his forehead. "You know, I can run this office. The only thing I can't do is some of the non-routine stuff like bid on custom jobs. But I bet I could even do that, if I had to. With Salvador's help. He's the best foreman you ever had. So don't worry about the business."

"Thanks, Abby. I'm really glad you're here."

"Thanks," she whispered. "You're not the asshole you want the world to think you are, are you?"

"Yeah, I am."

She whirled around and headed for her office, but he saw her wipe away a tear. He said, "I'm giving you a ten dollar an hour raise. Even without sex."

She turned and smiled. "Thanks."

"It was going to be twenty, but you told me how the big expensive things aren't what women want."

She said, with her back to him, "Asshole." He could tell she had a big smile. She wiped at her face again.

A half hour later Abby rapped on his already open office door, then ushered in a slight man of about fifty. He had a full head combed back of hair that was well on its way from brown to gray. He looked very serious or perpetually worried, with deep wrinkles in his forehead and no hint of a smile.

"Mr. Drake," Abby said, "this is Mr. Adams. He is with the United States Government Procurement Office."

Jim stood up and came around his desk with a smile, his hand extended. "Jim Drake. A pleasure to meet you, Mr. Adams."

The man's handshake was limp. "Likewise." He did not smile, nor did he sound pleased to meet him. "Let's get right down to business, Mr. Drake. The first thing I want to see are the mill certifications on the material you purchased for this job."

Jim felt a rush of adrenaline, but he said calmly, "Of course. Please be seated." He indicated the visitor's chair in front of his desk. He looked over to Abby. "Abby, will you pull that file please?"

She flashed a smile that said volumes, obviously more than a little pleased. "Right away. Would you like some coffee or a soft drink, Mr. Adams?"

"No thank you."

Abby hesitated at the door with a raised-eyebrow, I-told-you-so look that she made sure Jim saw before she turned to get the file. Jim had to smile inwardly. He knew everything having to do with this job was perfect.

"Everything is perfect, Mr. Drake. It's rare that I can say that to a contractor."

"I expected it would be." He looked at Abby, who had helped him with the review. "We have Abby to thank for that," he added with only a tiny pang of guilt.

She almost blushed, something he had never seen her do. "Thank you," she mumbled.

The inspector looked at his watch. "Ten-thirty. I get to have a long lunch today. Maybe I'll shop for my wife's birthday present." He actually smiled as he stood up and shook Jim's hand, and then Abby's. "Thanks to you, apparently," he said to her.

After he left, Jim said, "Abby, you earned your raise today, and I have a feeling I'm going to be depending on you a lot until I get this thing resolved." He tapped his head.

"I'll be here."

Jim looked out the window without seeing anything. How had this happened? Suddenly he wasn't even capable of running his business, the one he had built from scratch. What if his crew found out? He couldn't let them know. He turned to Abby who was standing there awkwardly. "Don't tell anyone, Abby. Not Salvador, not anyone. If they ask, tell them my mother's sick. Or something. Tell them anything. But don't tell 'em I'm crazy." He didn't say, don't tell them I'm visiting aliens. "Don't tell them I'm off time traveling."

"I won't." She stepped forward and put her hand on his cheek, and seemed about to say more, or to kiss him, but instead dropped her hand. "I won't."

Jim said, "I'm going to take off now."

Abby frowned. "I thought Trina was supposed to be your chauffeur."

"Yeah, well, she had a manicure appointment at eleven o'clock. I'm going home to get some rest before those tests this afternoon. It's only five miles. I'll call her and let her know when I get home."

"Why don't I drive you?"

"No, I'll be all right. Besides, if Trina found out, she'd imagine all sorts of things."

"How about I call Uber?"

"I'll be fine, Abby. I'll just take the Ford half-ton."

Chapter 8

It happens

The traffic was already beginning to get heavy, so Jim relaxed and took his time. Eased into the freeway, then over one lane, then another, to the next-to-fast lane. It was moving as fast as number one, so he stayed here. He checked his speedometer. Forty-three. Not bad. He found himself being drawn into the hypnotic rhythm of the song on the radio and as soon as he realized that, he switched to a news station so he wouldn't get yanked into some other time and place.

He kept his mind occupied on the traffic, on how far he was from the car in front of him. How close the car behind him was. People changing lanes up ahead. The stock market was up, and so was the cost of living. He looked up at a freeway sign. Three miles to his off ramp.

Bored with the news he tried a different station. It was music from the Swing Era. That seemed safe. One of the big bands of the time was playing *A String of Pearls.* He had no idea who the vocalist was, or even what band it was, but he had heard the song before. "Till that happy day in spring, when you buy the wedding ring. Please, a string of pearls."

She held it up to her neck. "Isn't it beautiful?"

"I thought we were buying something for your mother." But he couldn't help grinning. Typical woman. Go for one thing, buy two others. She was right though, it was nice looking and her smooth skin sure did set it off. "It's probably more than I can afford."

Maryann's eyes were dancing. "Oh, I know. But isn't it beautiful?"

"How much is it?" Terry asked the sales person.

"Four dollars and thirty cents."

He mentally counted the money he had left, and thought he could probably buy it if the gift for her mother wasn't too much. But he had to leave money for the taxi. "Maybe we better see how much your mother's is going to cost before..."

Perturb.

Talaan and Zeleece stepped out of the body shop entrance and moved onto the flowwalk. Flowwalks were fairly new. They used an engineered material that moved in the center but was stationary at the edges. The moving central section glided people along smoothly but quickly. When the person got near where they wanted to go, they simply made their way over to the edge and stepped off. At first Talaan felt a little off-balance, but that quickly passed. They weren't moving much faster than a brisk walk.

Zeleece squealed and grabbed his arm as they rounded a corner and the sun hit them. "Zang, Talaan , I love it. I just love it. Look at you! You look like a walking Buddha statue, only thin. Zang!"

At Zeleece's urging, he had just had his skin color changed to gold in the body shop. Glimmering, jewelry-like gold. It felt a little crawly right now, but the technician said that sensation would go away in a couple of hours. Talaan held out his arms and looked as they glided along, rotated them as the sun reflected off them in shimmers. "Well, I'm... I'm kind of spectacular, aren't I? I'm not sure I'm going to like it."

"Oh, I just love it. I can't wait until we get to the party tonight. Glenoya will be all over you. When I told her what you were doing, she already asked me if the three of us could have sex tonight."

"Why doesn't she get her own lover?"

"You know her. Sample this, sample that. Avoid sameness at all cost. Especially, avoid commitment. Remember how upset she was after her last love-pledge fell out? I guess this sort of thing is easier for her right now. So what do you say?"

"I say I'd rather be with just you, but if you want..."

"Oh, oh, oh!" Zeleece tugged on his arm. "Come on. Get off. Hurry." She pulled him off to the side of the flowwalk. "Look what's playing!" She pointed to a sign cube advertising an immersium. *Earthland Gangsters Invade the Seventy-Fourth Century*. She squeezed his arm, wriggled, eyes sparkling. "Let's go in and see it. I just love that shit. Can we? What are gangsters? Are they criminals?"

"Yes. It's an old, old term." Her unselfconscious enthusiasm over life was infectious, one of the things that attracted him to her. He couldn't quite let life run free like that, but being around her helped. Hell, getting this skin job had been a big step, but for her it would have involved no more than five seconds of consideration, if that.

"Can we go in?" Talaan had to laugh at her excitement over such a silly little thing as a cheap, half-serious and no doubt poorly executed immersium.

He put his arm around her waist and gave a squeeze. "Sure," he said. "Why not?"

After an iriscan to debit his account and entering through the polarizing photon portal, they stepped onto a sidewalk in an ancient city. The sidewalk was actually concrete! And cracked! Not only that, but recyclable hydrocarbon-based materials such as—what, pouches or bags of some sort—were scattered along a dam-like ledge where the sidewalk dropped several inches to a wide, lower-elevation area. As they walked along, he searched his memory and came up with the ancient word: street. Streets were used for wheeled vehicles to travel on.

Signs glowed in every store front in multiple colors. One of them said, *Buy Blatz Beer and Get Drunk Today*. Others advertised Dominator Pizza, Colt Submachine Guns, Murphy's Snake Oil, It's Your Life Abortions, Lucky Strike Cigarettes, Standard Gasoline, and Bayer Replacement Organs.

"You studied ancient history, Talaan. Is this the way the cities looked?" Zeleece asked.

"It's pretty accurate."

"Lucky Strike Cigarettes? What are cigarettes?"

"They were a way to ingest a narcotic," he said. "They took the leaf of a certain plant, I think they called it tabico, and dried it out and crumbled it up and rolled it in a paper tube. Then they would set fire to it on one end, and inhale the smoke by sucking on the other end."

"Zang! Why?"

Talaan shrugged. "To get euphoric, I guess. I do know that this tabico was highly addictive."

"And it was legal?"

"It must have been, they advertised it right out in the open like this."

"Didn't the addicts contaminate the shit out of their lungs? I bet they had to have new sets installed pretty often."

"Probably."

"What's gasoline? And what would anyone do with snake oil?"

Talaan was about to try to answer when she tightened her grip on his arm.

"What are those things carrying people?" She pointed to some wheeled box-like things on the street. "Are those what they used for transportation, things that had to stay on the ground?"

"Yes. They were called automobiles, and that area they roll on is called a street. I don't know why they were called automobiles, though, they weren't auto for a long time after they were invented. People actually had to steer them and make them start and stop and decide when to turn. That's why they crashed into one another all the time."

"Really? Did the occupants get hurt?"

He shrugged. "I guess so. Probably." Talaan had studied automobiles for a class project. He pointed to an old Packard and said, "There is a Ford Model A, one of the first automobiles made in any volume. And there's a Mercedes built somewhere around the year 2000, and a two-thousand-twentyish Honda." Or something like that. She wouldn't know the difference.

Every car made a clatter-clatter sound superimposed on a loud rumble as it passed by. They all emitted great clouds of black smoke from a tube under the rear. The smoke was evil smelling and burned their eyes.

"Zang!" She waved her hand in front of her face. "That's terrible." She pointed to the Mercedes. "Even without the smell and the eye burning, can you even imagine riding in one of those things for more than five minutes?"

"Not with a human actually controlling it."

"That's what I meant. Especially after smoking a cigarette or drinking Blatz Beer. But I thought this was a gangster immersium."

Just then a black, boxy car came careening around the corner. A barrage of machine gun fire erupted from it, spitting flame and shattering the window of the restaurant next to them. Shards of glass flew everywhere. Talaan and Zeleece both ducked in spite of knowing it was a simulation.

"Zang!" Zeleece stepped behind him.

Machine gun fire erupted from the restaurant. As the car started moving down the street bullets from the restaurant punched holes in it while the occupants kept firing their guns at the building. The car swerved and bashed into other cars, sending some of them into buildings and others into pedestrians. One automobile caught fire. Bleeding pedestrians littered the sidewalk.

"I just love this shit." Zeleece had an iron grip on his arm.

Another black car came tearing into view, and it too had guns firing from the windows. It skidded up next to them with a great screeching sound. The back door opened, and a man wearing a black hat said, "Get in. Quick!"

Zeleece scrambled in, dragging Talaan along, and even before the door closed the automobile accelerated with much jerking and roaring. A second car pulled along side them, and a black-hatted figure raised a machine gun and began firing at them.

"Zang!" Talaan and Zeleece ducked down.

There was a whump that Talaan felt in his chest.

"Bastard! He's trying to run us off the street," shouted a man in the front seat as he twisted around. He held a huge black handgun in one hand, aimed it at the other car, and began firing. He must have fired twenty shots as fast as he could pull the trigger.

Talaan raised his head and saw the other car swerve into theirs again. Their car jerked sideways and banged into the curb, then the other car, then back into the curb. It tilted way over, up on two wheels, and the driver began cursing. Then the car seemed to be settling back when there was another hard bang and it slowly rolled over on its side. It skidded along the street with the grating sound of rending metal and the crash and crunch of shattering glass. They bounced off a lamp post or building, Talaan couldn't see which, spun around and came to a rest.

Zeleece, asprawl on top of him, screamed, "Zang, I love this shit!"

Perturb.

All was quiet.

Except for the radio. A soothing voice advised buying a policy from New York Life Insurance Company. Jim shook his head, trying to orient himself. He was hanging by his safety belt, right side down, the now-deflating air bag in his face. He worked it aside, then pushed on the center console and passenger seat with one arm and leg to relieve the stress on the belt, and was able to unbuckle it. Then he planted his right foot on the passenger-side door while holding the steering wheel. He pressed the button for the drivers-side window, and to his surprise it worked. The window went all the way down. Jim put his arms through and got his head and shoulders out. He repositioned his arms and hoisted himself the rest of the way out, then sat on the side of his truck, legs over the roof. The underside was against the center divider.

Three other vehicles were wrecked, one next to him sitting sideways on the freeway and two others behind that, one backwards and one sideways.

"You crazy son of a bitch!" one of the drivers yelled at him. "Get down from there, I'm going to kick your ass." The man wasn't all that big, but he sure did look mad as he marched toward Jim.

"Sorry. I guess I passed out."

"Drunk, huh? You son of a bitch."

The guy was almost up to the truck, so rather than give him the chance to pull him down by the leg, off balance and defenseless, Jim dropped to the pavement and faced him. "No, I'm not drunk, so you better back off, you little fucker." At six-two, Jim was a good four or five inches taller than the outraged driver, who lost some of his steam right away when he saw Jim towering over him ready to fight.

"What the hell's the matter with you? You swerved right into the side of my brand new Toyota." The man was red faced and wild-eyed, animal-like, but he obviously retained enough wits to not take a swing at a much bigger and considerably younger man.

"Yeah, like I did it on purpose."

"Look at it! I just bought it yesterday." His rage, his frustration were on the verge of bringing him to tears as he pointed to a new Toyota with the side smashed in.

"It's just a car, for Christ sake. Lets go see if anyone's hurt." Jim started walking back up the freeway toward the other two cars.

"What do you mean, just a car?" The man's tone became more defensive than aggressive as he followed Jim up the freeway. "I've been wanting a new car for years. And I just got it yesterday."

Jim didn't bother to look back at him. "Stop your goddamn whining. I've got insurance."

The fast lane of the freeway plus the carpool lane were blocked, and cars in the other three lanes were slowing nearly to a stop to look. Some of them had pulled to the shoulder. Several people from vehicles behind them were coming up now, probably to see if anyone needed help. The two people who had been in the farthest car were already out, standing together next to it. They seemed stunned. The other car had only one occupant, a woman still sitting behind the wheel.

Jim walked up and motioned for her to roll down the window. She seemed to be in shock. Just sat there.

"Roll down your window," Jim shouted.

She turned her head and stared at him with a blank expression, not seeming to see him.

A woman from one of the other vehicles tapped on the window. "Roll your window down." She twirled her finger in a circular motion. "Roll your window down."

Finally a shade lifted from the woman's eyes, and she focused on the other woman.

"Roll your window down," the woman repeated.

The driver nodded, and opened the door. She started to get out, but bent sharply at the waist as her safety belt refused to yield. The other woman reached in and released the latch, then almost let the dazed woman fall as she lurched from the car with the sudden release of the restraint. Jim saw what was going to happen just before it did and stepped forward to catch her, but was too late. She would have fallen right on her head if the second woman hadn't been there, but she was about to collapse. Jim grabbed one arm of each of them, and managed to stabilize the two.

Jim looked in her eyes, and she seemed alert now. "Are you all right?" he said.

She nodded. "Yes." She rubbed her waist where the seat belt had restrained her. Someone else came up and offered a bottle of water, and she took a sip.

A police car pulled up against the center barrier on the other side of the freeway and moments later a second one did the same. Three officers climbed over the median and came up to them.

"Anyone hurt?" one of them asked.

"No, I don't think so," Jim answered.

The policeman looked at the woman with the water bottle. "Are you all right, ma'am?"

"Yes," she said faintly. "Just shook up."

The man with the new car pushed his way in. "And that son of a bitch caused it!" He pointed at Jim.

The officer glanced at Jim, then turned back to the man. "How much have you been drinking, sir?"

The man took a step back from the officer. "I... why... just a couple of beers. But I didn't do anything. I was just driving along and..."

"Which vehicle is yours?"

"That gray Toyota. Brand new. Now look at it."

"I want you to step over there," said the officer, pointing to a spot next to the center divider. "Joe," he said to an officer in a police car across the divider, who was talking on the radio, "bring the field sobriety kit."

"Officer," Jim said, "I was the one who caused it. I don't know what happened. I blacked out."

"Which is your vehicle?"

"The Ford pickup."

"Have you been drinking, too?"

"No. Nothing."

"Do you have a heart condition, or epilepsy, or anything of that sort?"

"No, but I've been having these spells lately. The doctor didn't want me to drive, but I thought it would be okay. I just had a few miles to go."

"You step over there too." He looked at the officer named Joe, who was in the process of stepping over the barrier. "Joe, call an ambulance."

"I already have."

"I don't think anyone needs one," Jim said.

"You have a spell where you black out, and you expect us to just turn you loose? Whether you think you need an ambulance or not, that's the way you're leaving here.

Jim looked at the officer and nodded his head. "You're right." He turned away and stared down at the weathered, inert pavement. "I'm not capable," he added to himself.

***

Trina peeked inside the curtain separating his hospital bed from the others, then pulled it aside and sidled in. She minced over to his bed, bent over and looked into his eyes. Stroked his forehead, then kissed it. She looked haggard. "Jim, are you all right?"

"Yeah, I told you on the phone. I'm fine." He sat up. "They said I could leave as soon as you got here."

"Who's your doctor? I want to talk to him." She looked around, then walked over to peer out the curtains, looking in both directions. "I'll be back." Trina left without waiting for a response.

Jim got up from the bed, took off the stupid gown that opened in the back, and put his clothes on. When he was dressed, he walked to the nurse's station where Trina was talking to the doctor who had examined him.

The doctor turned to Jim. "Mr. Drake. I don't want you drinking any alcohol. No drugs either unless your doctor has prescribed them and is aware of this condition. Is that clear?"

Jim glanced at Trina, who had her frown-but-not, then said to the doctor. "I haven't taken any drugs, and I haven't been drinking."

"Call your doctor first thing in the morning. Did the police keep your driver's license?"

"Yes."

The doctor nodded, then turned and walked away. "Don't forget. Call your doctor," he said without looking back. He disappeared around a corner.

"Oh, Jim." Trina put her arm around him and leaned her head against his shoulder as they headed toward the exit. "What are we going to do?"

He had no answer.

When they got home, Trina pulled into the driveway but left the engine running. "You go in. I'm going to pick up some food. Chicken raviolis okay?"

"Get some plain cheese ones, too. Not just chicken."

"Okay." She activated the phone to place a to-go order.

Jim opened the door and stepped out. He walked around the front of the car, where the cabbie met him with their bags. "That's two dollars," the driver said.

Terry, trying to impress Maryann, gave him a fifty-cent tip. "Here you go, two-fifty." They entered the terminal area, showed their tickets, and headed toward the airplane. Maryann grabbed his arm.

"Wow!" she said. "Look at that!"

Their plane was a sparkling new 707. "How can something that big fly, and without propellers? That's amazing."

"Yeah, it really is."

A baggage handler took their suitcases and put them on a cart, and they made their way up the stairs and into the plane. A stewardess showed them to their seats and explained how to operate the overhead air vents and reading lights.

Maryann took his hand. "They think of everything, don't they?"

"Just about." Terry opened an air vent and a flood of air wafted over his face.

Perturb

He was vaguely aware of being in a dream-state, but unable to do anything about it. Names, strange names, floated to him: D'zeos. D'zeos? Somehow he knew that name should be familiar. But it wasn't. And someone else was here in this half-life. Vanqa? What nationality was that? He tried to pull in the threads of memory, to get a grasp on reality, but nothing would solidify or come into focus. There was no face to go with the names, no recollections.

Fear stirred and in spite of his will surged in a mighty blast. He looked around wildly seeking anything, any one thing that appeared solid, but there was nothing. Nothing. Blank nothingness. There was no world. He struggled to push his consciousness foreword but could not. Then he tried to leave this place, but could not. Could not. Could not. He focused. Concentrated. Could not.

Perturb

"You're hurting my hand, Terry."

It was a relief to realize he was still in airplane. "Sorry." Holy cow! That was bizarre. He must have blacked out. Terry leaned his head back and tried to reorient himself. He closed his eyes and let the air from the vent caress his face. What in the world had happened? It had seemed... for some reason it had seemed that he had been way, way in the future. Thousands of years. He knew that, but didn't know how he knew. Or if he knew. It made no sense. He shook his head and pushed the memory away, then opened his eyes and watched passengers filing into the airplane. Some were chatting excitedly, some trying to act bored, one seeming preoccupied. Had he dozed off? Was something wrong with his heart? Boy, oh boy! This place had just faded away. It was like part of him had been transported somewhere else.

"Are you okay?" Maryann brushed his hair with her hand.

"Yeah. Sure. I was just, I felt a little disoriented for some reason." He wanted to change the subject. Push the recollection away. "Great vacation, huh?"

She put her hand on his arm. "You know, it should have been our honeymoon."

"It's your mother who insisted on a long engagement. We've got another year."

"I know." Maryann giggled. "I bet she's sorry now, though."

"If she's still talking to you." This helped. Stupid, everyday conversation. He was focused, not dreaming.

"She'll get over it." Maryann had been rummaging around in her purse as they spoke, and now she came up with a little packet of cheese, and another of crackers.

Terry said, "They're going to feed us, you know."

Perturb

"If you eat a little something, maybe you'll feel better." Trina sat containers of food on the table. "I got some garlic bread, too."

Jim looked at Trina, but she was getting glasses out of the cupboard. He looked out the window as panic boiled. He could smell the food. It was here. He reached out, and could feel the warmth. His arm pits were wet. "Whoo," he said under his breath, trying to slow down his racing mind. "Steady, boy."

Trina whirled around. "What!"

"Nothing."

Her eyes bored into his.

"Just admiring your fanny," he said.

Trina shook her head. "You have a nonlinear personality, Jim Drake."

Nonlinear mind, he thought. Nonlinear reality.

He gritted his teeth to try and maintain control. Damn! What was happening to him? What could he do? How could he trust himself? He needed to run. But there was no place to hide. He couldn't sit here. He had to do something.

Trina sat a plate of raviolis in front of him. "Here, eat this."

He dared not look at her. She would know. She'd see the panic. He had to maintain control. Focus on the food. Eat a ravioli. Chew. Swallow.

Trina sat a glass of water down for him. He took a drink. Could feel her looking at him, so he kept his eyes down. He cut a ravioli in half with his fork. She was still looking. "Thanks," he said.

She turned away to get her own plate.

That airplane. Something was wrong there. It felt ominous. He was afraid. Something was really wrong with that situation. It felt full of danger. What airplane, stupid? It wasn't real. And now he'd had an episode of time travel inside an episode of time travel. But this was too much. He was about to explode. He had to... shit!

"Trina, I've got something to tell you."

"What?" She turned around, and her face went ashen. "Oh, my God!" She stumbled over to the table, sat down, and put her hand on his. "We've got to do something, Jim!"

Chapter 9

A crack in the world.

Dr. Marquand sat quietly behind his desk, legs crossed, tapping a pen on his knee as he stared into space. Occasionally he would nod his head in agreement with himself, or shake it no with a frown. Jim looked in the direction he was looking, toward the window with the long, low table beneath it. The vase of calla lilies was still there on the table. Just like before, each lily was tasting the air with its yellow tongue, their pasty white faces arrogantly turned aside, devoid of expression yet conveying utter disapproval of Jim and his condition.

"The results from the battery of tests I gave you confirm that you do not have schizophrenia or any related disorder," the doctor said softly, still staring out the window as he rocked back and forth in his chair. "No serious disorder of any sort that I can identify."

The unexpected speech jolted Jim from his interlude with the calla lilies. "I thought you knew that from the MRI."

Doctor Marquand continued as if Jim had not spoken. "To be honest, the fact that it's not anything familiar, plus the increasing frequency of your episodes, is rather troublesome."

"Well, how do you *do*! You surely did earn your pay with that." Jim instantly regretted saying that. He wasn't in any mood to joke or make smart remarks, it had just popped out. "Sorry."

Dr. Marquand swiveled his chair to face him. "You are free to speak whatever you want in front of me. It's healthy."

"At this point, I'm not sure that matters."

The doctor pulled himself upright in his chair. "I have noticed several tendencies in your episodes, although perhaps it's too early to say they are trends. First, it appears that for whatever reason your episodes are tending to take place in time progression. In other words, time is moving forward in each of your situations. If that proves to be consistently true, what it means is unclear. But there could be some sort of a clue there. Second, you have never gone back to the first personality, Philip Osborne, where you were a soldier. You say you think Philip may have died on Truk Island. So maybe he did. Third, you have revisited Talaan, but apparently at relatively widely spaced time intervals. Weeks, if not months or more passed in that time frame between visits. Fourth, you have become Terry Walker in the nineteen-sixties more than once, but with very short time lapses between sequences there. Just hours. Again, you're involved with a pretty girl, Maryann. This man Terry, of course, could still be alive today, which raises some very troublesome questions as to how you're going to resolve that one."

Jim felt a flush of anger. "How I'm going to resolve it? How *I'm* going to resolve it? What the hell is that supposed to mean? How..."

"Yes, you." The doctor jabbed his finger. "You are, or perhaps your subconscious will. And finally, the last time you were Terry you brushed against some other place and time, but nothing would come into focus for you, and that episode was very disturbing to the Terry personality. It was a trip within a trip. A compound trip."

"That was *really* weird. It felt different, like that time and place had some sort of connection to something important that I should know about. But nothing would solidify. It was just a fog of nothingness. I don't know. I, that is, Jim Drake, wasn't there so it must have been Terry. The thing is, it seemed different."

Doctor Marquand slapped his desk with a whap that startled Jim. "Good," he said. "Very good. Excellent. That must be your subconscious. It's becoming awakened or aware. It must be trying to take control and stop these episodes."

"It sure as hell didn't feel like that. It felt like things were going from bad to worse."

"We'll have to see how that develops. But it certainly is an intriguing development. Very odd, too, that it came through Terry Walker. I would have expected it to have come directly from you."

"Speaking of Terry Walker, that situation feels ominous somehow. To me, Jim Drake. Not to Terry. It's nothing I can put my finger on, I just have more of an uncomfortable feeling than when I'm Talaan. Do you have any idea why that would be? What it means?"

"No. Unless it's your subconscious battling to preserve reality."

"That place where nothing would come into focus, I think it was way in the future. But I don't know why I think that. As a matter of fact, I don't know shit, and I hate that. I'm really frustrated."

"No, you're frightened." The doctor began twirling his finger in his hair. "But that could mean that you are more in control of these episodes than you realize. At least subconsciously."

"I hope so." But he knew he wasn't. There was not anything within himself battling these trips. He was afloat on a raft in an endless gray sea with no paddle, no horizon. No sun or stars visible through the overcast.

The doctor said, "We're going to have to let that play out, at least for the time being. Now, I want to get back to the original episodes, specifically those with Maryann and Zeleece. There could be a clue right there as to what the driving force is. After all, sex with an attractive partner is a powerful stimulus. Maybe you wanted to be with them."

"Do you think I'm fantasizing all this to fulfill some sexual inadequacy of mine? If so, that's a bunch of crap. I have never felt uncomfortable around women, I've got a beautiful wife, and I function very well, thank you." He looked at the doctor and thought, you crazy bastard. How about you? I'm surprised you even found someone to marry you. Probably another kook hiding out in graduate psychology classes trying to find out why she never had a sex partner. No, that wasn't good thinking. Doctor Marquand was a good man, and very intelligent. Jim did like him. He was just frustrated. No, he wasn't frustrated, it was fear like the doctor said. "I don't mean to be so damn confrontational, Doctor Marquand. I know you're doing your job."

The doctor just smiled benignly. "Being tied to just one partner can cause major subconscious conflicts with some people, such as feelings of being repressed, or of imprisonment. Have you come out of any of your episodes to find yourself sexually aroused, or masturbating?"

"No." He felt his face flush. "Doctor, you've been reading too damn much Freud."

"Actually, I haven't. I don't agree with very much of what Freud said. But I have to consider all possibilities."

"So you still have a puzzle."

"Yes we do," the doctor replied without hesitation.

"Yeah," Jim said. "We. Or me. Meantime, complete insanity looms as the most likely outcome."

"I'm going to prescribe..."

"I know. Another drug."

"Yes. Also, I'm going to push Dr. Ebenstein at Pittsburgh to get you under his machine the minute it's back online. In fact, I'm calling him now."

***

Jim watched as the flight attendant picked up her microphone. "Welcome to American flight ninety-four, nonstop to Pittsburgh."

He turned to Trina to see how she was doing. She did not like flying. He saw that her face was tight, her body tense, her shoulders pushed up, so he reached over and patted her hand. She leaned his way, seeming glad he was paying attention to her, and said, "Maybe that new medication is working. You went all yesterday afternoon and all last night and all this morning without an incident."

They had mentioned this before. He knew she was just talking to avoid thinking about flying, but he played along. "I hope so. When those episodes come one after the other, it feels like... it scares me even more."

She captured his hand. He gave a little squeeze. Reassurance for both of them. The plane began rolling and he visualized what it would be like when they were up in the air looking down on vast ranges of mountain and desert, dirt roads and highways and wilderness and forlorn ranches hidden away. Little dust blown towns that no one had ever heard of and couldn't find if they tried, towns that were disjointed from so-called progress, immune to the frantic pace and the drive-by shootings. Peaceful towns. He turned his gaze from the window and studied her fingernails. The geometric curves of her nail tips mirrored the shape of the cuticles. He noticed how much wider his fingers were than hers. He turned her hand over, and it seemed so good a fit in his palm, and so soft. It belonged there.

Trina turned to look out the window, but her grip tightened as the engines revved up and the plane shuddered. He could see the tension tighten her face even more. The engine noise ramped to a subdued roar, then he felt himself pushed back into his seat as they began their takeoff run. She turned her head away from the window to stare down at her lap.

He knew what she was thinking. That if they died, at least they would die together. He put on his most confident smile and stroked her arm. "Trina, relax. It's okay."

She did not acknowledge his reassurance.

He heard, or felt, the wheels leave the ground then the push down into the seat that told him they were gaining altitude. In a moment the plane began a bank, and he pointed out the window. Maryann looked, and gasped at the beauty of Oahu from the air. She relaxed almost at once, and flashed a smile at him before returning her gaze to the scene out the window. The plane finished its turn and the island disappeared from view, then they made another maneuver, perhaps leveling off, and a sense of weightlessness overcame him.

Perturb

"This is so exciting," Zeleece squealed.

Talaan wasn't so sure, as his stomach began searching for down. He knew, he knew it had been a mistake to let her talk him into booking an 'encounter room' for zero-gravity sex for the one year anniversary of their first date. And first sex.

"Let's go," she said. "I just can't... can you imagine the possibilities!? Zang, Talaan! There won't even be a top and a bottom."

They pushed off the hand rails and floated out into the encounter chamber naked, clinging to one another. Talaan hated the lack of control. He tried kicking his feet to change his orientation. It didn't work. In fact he rotated opposite to what he had intended.

"Relax, Talaan. Just hold me for now."

"I think we're drifting into that wall."

"It won't hurt. It's not really a wall."

"Right."

"Nothing is the way it appears."

Perturb

D'zeos frowned and said, "Damnit, Vanqa! You interrupted my sexual encounter." He looked around. "Where am I, anyway?" He didn't seem to be any place. It was alien. Everything about it was alien. "Why am I bouncing around in time? What do you want with me? Why do you want me here? How do I even know you? I don't even know who I am."

"You're a bit jumbled up," Vanqa said in a peculiar sing-song voice. "You're not in a reconciled timeplace."

"Why not? Then where am I?" The walls were featureless. Off-white and slowly undulating like clouds, swirling fog. D'zeos couldn't quite focus on anything. He could not tell the size of the room, or even if it was a room. And it was silent, disconcertingly silent. But not as bad as last time he was with Vanqa. At least he seemed to be in a space, even if a boundary was not definable. "Where am I?" he repeated.

"Actually, you are nowhere certain. You're extremely fractionated. You best leave."

The scene wavered, and he had the impression he was looking through a crinkling piece of plastic wrap.

A distant roar gradually formed out of the immense silence, then quickly diminished as the engines throttled back. The plane was apparently at altitude.

Perturb

Son of a bitch!

He glanced to the side, but Trina was still looking out the window. He eased his hand out of hers. Then wondered why he had. He wanted it back. It was an anchor to reality. A connection to sanity. To now. Now. He wanted to scream it. Now!

He quietly took a deep, slow breath, then another one, and his head cleared a little. He wished he could go back to before this started and make everything the way it used to be. Even way back like when he was a little kid and could depend on the strength of his father and the tender arms of his mother. They would shield him from the dangers, from the monster hiding in the dark closet. He looked down at his lap, at his hands gripping one another. They were a man's hands, but inside he felt like a helpless little boy. He took another deep breath and wanted to give up, really wanted to. But give up to what? What would he do, sob in a corner? He had to fight. But there was nothing to fight against. He just had to be stronger. Pretend that he could fight against the unreal. But when he went to these crazy places, it was real. He could not tell it was not, because at that moment it was. He had to hold on to this this reality. This world. The Jim and Trina Drake world.

He concentrated on the sound of the engines and the captain making meaningless announcements about flight conditions and landmarks along the planned course. He concentrated hard, even though he knew it would not keep him here in this reconciled timeplace, as the mystery man Vanqa had called it. Earth, twenty-first century earth. Jim Drake. Jim Drake was real. Who the hell were Vanqa and D'zeos? No such persons existed.

Had his subconscious invented them as a way to return to reality? Was that his door to sanity? Was the doctor right? Was Vanqa the magic word, like *open sesame* was for Ali Baba? Maybe becoming D'zeos was the door to get home. Yet deep down he feared that was not true. So he formed a mental image of Jim Drake the body and Jim Drake the inner person. Christ he was scared! Jim Drake. Jim Drake, the not-schizophrenic. Jim Drake, nut case. Jim Drake. Jim Drake.

Chapter 10

The mystery deepens

"I'm Doctor Ebenstein." The doctor had a firm handshake. The man was a Ferrari at idle, exuding fitness. He was poised, with the bearing of an athlete. Jim wouldn't be surprised if he could walk down the hall on his hands.

Doctor Ebenstein turned to Trina and shook her hand, and a little twitch raised the corners of his mouth as he did so. It came and went so quickly it almost didn't exist, but apparently it served as a smile. "Come with me," Dr. Ebenstein said as he turned and waved for them to follow. Without further ado he exited his office and headed down a hallway.

Jim and Trina shrugged at one another and followed. The man was not exploding with social grace, only energy. He walked fluidly and rapidly without apparent effort. He seemed too athletic to be a doctor, but Dr. Marquand had said he had an M.D. as well as a Ph.D. Doctor Ebenstein opened a door and gracefully motioned for them to enter ahead of him. Perhaps Jim had misjudged his social attributes. He often misjudged people.

They entered an examination room where two assistants were waiting. The doctor gestured casually toward an upholstered side chair. "Mrs. Drake." Then he said to Jim, pointing to a plastic chair with flat arms on each side, "Sit there so Max can draw your blood."

How many times had they drawn blood the last few days? But what could he say? They were trying to help. They were doing their job. The lady named Max drew four vials with practiced efficiency and no pain, then taped a piece of cotton over the puncture.

"Now take a seat over there." Dr. Ebenstein unfolded his crossed arms and motioned toward a chair with padded arms as Max exited with his blood.

As soon as Jim sat down the second assistant began connecting electrodes to him. "What's this, another EKG?" Jim asked.

"No. A polygraph. I'm going to ask you a series of questions." The doctor turned his back to Jim and pulled a school desk into position, dragging it across the vinyl floor.

Jim looked at Trina, and she just sort of smirked. In fact, he thought she seemed rather pleased. Had she wanted this done all along? He would if he were in her place But he had done his best to tell her everything. Well, almost everything. He was trying to decide whether to be angry or not when the technician said, "He's all hooked up," and began doing something with the machine. After another moment, he said, "Whenever you're ready, Doctor Ebenstein."

The doctor sat in his chair and laid an iPad down on the paddle-like writing surface, then fished a writing stylus out of his pocket, all the while looking at Jim intently. Jim wondered why he didn't just use a keyboard. The doctor continued holding his eye for a long moment, then jabbed a finger toward Trina. "Is this your wife?"

"Yes."

"How long have you been married?"

"Umm, nine years, I think."

Trina frowned. The one without wrinkles.

"How many children?"

"None."

"Did the police take your driver's license?"

"Yes."

"Should they have?"

"Yes."

Doctor Ebenstein was taking notes on his iPad. He now glanced at them, then asked, "Is Zeleece your girl friend?"

Jim felt a pang of anxiety reverberate through his body, and he glanced at Trina, who raised an eyebrow slightly. Then he turned back to the doctor and said, "She is Talaan's girlfriend."

"Are you Talaan?"

"Yes. Sometimes. When I'm there."

"Where?"

"In the future. The year seventy-three sixty-six, I believe."

"Is Zeleece good in bed?"

What kind of bullshit question was that? What kind of an asshole would ask something like that in front of a man's wife? Jim stuffed his retort and said simply, "Yes."

"Better than your wife, Trina?"

"That's a bullshit question and you know it. No one asks a man a question like that, especially when his wife is sitting right here. No matter what the answer is. What the hell are you trying to do?"

"I'm not posing as a marriage counselor. I'm measuring your responses to various sorts of questions."

"Well, you can take that line of questioning and shove it."

The doctor looked at the polygraph technician, and out of the corner of his eye Jim saw her nod in the affirmative. "Very well. Let's move on." He wrote something a couple of lines long, then said, "Terry Walker. Tell me how old Terry Walker is."

"Twenty-three."

"In what year?"

"Nineteen sixty-two."

"Is he alive today?"

The anger dissipated as anxiety coursed through those veins of his. He wondered if fear would show up in his blood, maybe in a panel called the Stupid Factor. But the possibility that Terry Walker was alive and they would meet was ominous. Jim glanced at Trina again, then said, "That's one of the questions that's been nagging me. I don't know, but the possibility is frightening."

"Just answer the questions. I don't want a dialog or your opinion. We'll discuss these issues later, if I think it's appropriate."

"Yes, *sir*!" What an asshole. Or was he doing this deliberately to evoke responses for the polygraph technician? More likely he was an asshole.

The door opened, and a young woman came into the room. "Sorry I'm late."

Doctor Ebenstein glanced up, and said, "This is Sylvia Maynord, a graduate student of mine. Late as usual."

Jim nodded hello and was about to greet her when the doctor said, "Does Terry remember his mother?"

"Of course."

"What's her name?"

"Melinda. Maiden name Jasper. oops. Sorry for giving you too much information."

The doctor looked at him for a moment, an expressionless yet hard and unwavering look, then he went back to taking notes, or whatever it was he was writing. "How do you know that?"

"Know what?"

"Her name."

"What do you mean, how do I know her name? I told you, when I go there, I'm Terry Walker. I have a past. I have friends and relatives, all of whom I know. Of course I know my mother's name."

"How is it you still remember, now that you're Jim Drake?"

"I don't know. But some things I don't remember."

"Like what?"

"Well, let's see. I can't remember the color of my dad's car. Terry's dad. It's a fifty-eight Desoto, and it's two-tone, but I can't remember the colors."

"Jim, have you ever seen a fifty-eight Desoto?"

"Not as far as I know. You don't see many De Sotos these days."

"Are you sure his father had such a car?"

"This isn't déjà vu, doctor. When I'm there, it's life. I know and remember everything. Births and deaths and parties and weddings. All the details. Cousins and friends and disagreements and poker games."

"Is Maryann pretty?"

"Yeah. She's not beautiful, but she's cute. And real sweet."

The doctor looked at his graduate student. "Sylvia, write this down." He turned back to Jim. "What is Maryann's full name, and when and where was she born?"

"Maryann Bethamy Sue Jacobson. Born in nineteen forty-four in Montebello, California."

"What was her mother's name?"

"Bethamy Sue Iverson."

"What is Terry's full name, and where was he born and raised?"

"Terry Martin Walker. Born in Salem, Oregon on October 3, 1943. Raised in Whittier, California. Went to Whittier High School."

"What about Philip?"

Jim chewed his lower lip as he tried to remember back. "Philip Andrew Osborne. He was born on May 21, 1925 in Norwalk, California."

"Does Zeleece love you?"

"Yes."

"You didn't hesitate."

"No."

"How do you know?"

"By the way she acts."

"Did Trina act the same way when you two were engaged?"

Jesus Christ, here he went again! He *was* a asshole. Jim started to tell him so, but swallowed it one more time. He looked at Trina and tried to smile, but it felt fake, and he felt guilty because it wasn't genuine. He was stressed over the question, and what he should say, and how she would react. So he said to the doctor, "More or less."

"What does that mean?"

"It means more or less." He caught himself in time to not say 'asshole.' He went on to explain, as much to Trina as to the doctor, "They are different people, so they respond differently to the same sort of situation. Besides, the cultures in which they live are different. The morals and the social expectations are different. But the emotions are the same. They both love me. That is, Trina loves me, and Zeleece loves Talaan. And I love them."

"Jim, what's your full name?"

"James Cornelius Drake."

"Where did the name Cornelius come from?"

"My grandfather on my mother's side."

"What was his name?"

"Cornelius Christofides."

"Greek?"

"Where else would they come up with a name like that?" Idiot.

Trina chuckled, and the doctor almost smiled. His little twitch. Dr. Ebenstein turned to his graduate student. "Sylvia, go run a search for Terry Martin Walker and Maryann Bethamy Sue Jacobson. Place of birth, any available statistics, death notices if any, and so on. I especially want to know if they're still alive. Also look for a Philip Andrew Osborne." He was talking to Sylvia, but looking intently at Jim. Jim just stared back, right in the eye. The asshole. What did he expect? What was he looking for? Lies, of course. Nervousness. A break of resolve. Screw him!

Sylvia said, "Right now?" It was more a plea than a question. She obviously wanted to stay.

"Right now." He was still staring at Jim.

The girl started to say something, then turned and left.

Dr. Ebenstein said, "Who is Vanqa?"

And so the questions went, for almost two hours, circling from the mundane to the far future, with numerous repetitions using different phrasing.

Finally, Doctor Ebenstein said, "Okay. That's it for today. Tomorrow morning we're going to do some tests in the machine. Be at my office at nine am."

"Did you find out anything?" Jim asked.

Doctor Ebenstein gave him that steady look and said, "You're not lying."

***

There was a polite tap on Maurice Ebenstein's office door. "Yes," he said without looking up from his desk. Sylvia came in, and he said, "What did you find?"

She sat on the edge of the wooden chair at the end of his desk and laid some papers in her lap. "I couldn't find any record of a Terry Martin Walker born in Salem, Oregon. I searched the County Health records and the State and County Archives. Nothing for the period from nineteen-twenty to nineteen-thirty. But then, I'm not sure all births were recorded back then. Salem was pretty rural."

"That could very well be. But I need facts. What were you able to dig up?"

Sylvia seemed to relax a little with his indirect, sort-of acceptance of her statement regarding the absence of data. "There is a record of a Terry Walker graduating from Whittier Union High School in nineteen sixty-one."

"Hmm. Open records, though, available to anyone, including Jim Drake. What else?"

Sylvia looked at him, excited, then glanced back down at her notes. "I got a good one from LA County, but I'm not sure it's them. Not unless they took a trip to Hawaii before they were married, which was not socially acceptable back then."

Maurice felt himself blanch. "Mister Drake told me they did."

"Oh, my God!"

"What's wrong? What have you got?"

"The only Maryann Bethamy Sue Jacobson on record in LA County was killed in the crash of a Boeing 707 on a Honolulu-to-LA flight in nineteen sixty-two. A Terry Walker was also on the passenger manifest, but I couldn't find a death notice or certificate."

"I'll be a son of a—" Doctor Ebenstein tensed up, then leaned back in the chair and chewed his lower lip. "That's most, uh, Sylvia, this could be serious."

"What do you—Oh, my God!" Sylvia covered her mouth and said, "If Jim Drake becomes Terry Walker when Terry dies in the plane crash..."

"Right. I think we've solved the puzzle, Sylvia. Mr. Drake wants to die! Those records were no doubt accessed by him too. I didn't consider that when I was testing him this morning. But I did find out he definitely believes he becomes Terry Walker. The only thing we don't know beyond doubt is, does he know Terry Walker dies in an airplane crash? He almost surely does, and thinks that by becoming Terry, he's going to die in this life."

Sylvia was pale. "Would he? Could he?"

"It's certainly possible."

Sylvia leaned forward. "Doctor Ebenstein, Mr. Drake's suffering from a very serious psychosis."

Maurice nodded. "Yes. Which we could potentially treat."

Sylvia sat back in her chair with the satisfied expression of a job well done, and a solution in hand. Then she got a frown. "But what about this Private Philip Osborne? It seems like maybe he died, but Mr. Drake survived."

The doctor crinkled his forehead. "It could have been a failed test run on Mr. Drake's part. Maybe he wasn't there during the actual death. He came back too soon. Did you find anything on Philip Osborne?"

The look of satisfaction evaporated from her face. "I'm afraid I stopped looking after I found the information on the 707 crash, and I came right over here."

"Well, let's look now." He turned to his computer, then motioned to her with his finger, "Scoot your chair around here so you can see too."

He accessed LA County records and soon found not one, but three Philip Osbornes born between nineteen twenty-three and nineteen twenty-seven. However, there was no record of the death of any of them in the nineteen-forties.

"How about checking the Social Security records?" she said.

He found the government web site without any trouble. "No. Nothing," he said, then another thought occurred to him. "Lets see, how about the California Bureau of Vital Statistics?"

"Those are private records, doctor. We can't gain access."

"Okay then," he said, "let's check the obituary archives for the *LA Times*."

After considerable help from Sylvia, he gained access to the records. And found nothing.

He said, "Find out what other newspapers were in publication at that time." He scooted the keyboard over to her. Being a graduate student she knew where to get information, and soon had the obituary archives for the now-defunct *LA Examiner*. No notice of a Philip Osborne.

"There were two other newspapers," she said.

After about five minutes she had the long-out-of-business *Los Angeles Evening Herald and Express* records. Again, no notice of the death of a Philip Osborne. "I'll try the *Daily News*," she said. "That's the only other LA paper in publication back then." After several minutes, with Doctor Ebenstein looking over her shoulder and making her nervous, she said, "No record of a Philip Osborne."

"Try the Honolulu newspapers." Dr. Ebenstein got up and walked to the window while she clicked away on the keyboard. The more he thought about it, the more obvious it became that Jim had found information on Terry Walker and now planned to die in the airplane crash when Mr. Walker died. It was hands-off, guilt-free suicide. No doubt planned mostly below the level of consciousness.

"Doctor Ebenstein," Sylvia said at last.

He turned around. "Yes?"

"The two major English language newspapers of the era were the *Honolulu Advertise*r and the *Honolulu Star-Bulletin.* There is no notice in either of them regarding a Philip Osborne."

"Do you have any other ideas?"

"Yes. I ran across a mention of the Hawaii War Records Depository. Let me check that."

"I suspect you'll find it there. I bet Mister Drake did, too."

After several minutes, she said, "No. Nothing. No record of him."

"Too bad. I guess that's all we can do. I'll run some fMRI tests on our patient tomorrow, then have Dr. Marquand refer him to a practicing psychiatrist."

"Why don't we try the government archives in Washington?" Sylvia said. "Don't they have a record of all military personnel?"

"Yes, but I know you can't get at them if the person is still alive."

"But we think he's dead."

"Go ahead and check. I think it'll be a waste of time since we've discovered what the problem is, but it's a good idea to flesh out our research." He actually smiled at her, and she responded with a tentative smile of her own, obviously unaccustomed to complements from him. He'd have to try and ease up on her a bit. She really was brilliant. Not bad looking, either. He turned back to the window, thinking about new lines of research this case had suggested. Time travel psychoses. Hands-off suicide, probably on a subconscious level. The possibilities were exciting. How about...

"Oh, my God!"

He whirled around. "What?"

"Pfc Philip Andrew Osborne from Norwalk, California, eighteen years of age, died in the VA hospital in Honolulu of wounds suffered during the landing operation on the island of Truk in February, nineteen forty-four."

"Good Lord!. Oh, that must be where he got the information to begin with. Of course. There's your answer!"

"No." Sylvia was pale. Her hand shook as she pointed to the computer screen. "No. It wasn't."

"What do you mean?"

Her mouth moved, but nothing came out. She could only point. Maurice walked over to look at the screen himself. In typical military fashion, there was a notice.

FILE LAST ACCESSED........ (no entry)

***

Doctor Ebenstein stepped out of the hotel elevator and rushed down the hall. After what seemed like an endless series of room numbers, he finally reached room eleven-nineteen. He rapped on the door. Nothing. He listened, and it sounded like the TV was on. He pounded on the door. A faint voice from the other side said, "Who is it?"

"Doctor Ebenstein," he said loudly.

The door opened part way, and Tina's puzzled face confronted him. "Doctor. What's wrong?" She undid the safety chain, swung the door open, and stood to one side, wide eyed and frightened.

He entered the room, forcing slow motions and calmness upon himself. "Nothing. I just have a few questions." Jim was sitting on the couch where the two of them had been watching TV. "What are you watching, Jim?" Maurice tried to sound casual.

Jim's face wrinkled in puzzlement. "We ordered a movie."

The doctor glanced at the TV, and saw people boarding a plane. His stomach flipped as fear stabbed through his body. "No!" he shouted. He bounded over, placed himself between the television and Jim, fanning his arms to cover more of the screen. "No TV! Shut it off."

"Why?" Jim looked befuddled.

"Just shut it off. Now!"

"Oh." Trina's eyes widened with realization.

"Okay, okay," Jim said as he pushed the button on the remote. Nothing happened. He held it away from him and pushed again. "You're blocking the remote, Doc. Move aside."

"No. Give it to me." Doctor Ebenstein reached out and Jim handed him the remote. The doctor swiveled his torso, leaving his feet planted, and pushed the OFF button. The screen went dead. "Okay." He felt himself relax a little as he handed the remote to Trina. He walked over to a side chair and sat down.

Trina sat down beside Jim and took his hand.

Jim said, "So you think watching TV might trigger one of my trips?"

"Tell me precisely what you were seeing and thinking just prior to your last visit to Terry Walker." He took a pen and a small note pad from his pocket.

Jim glanced at Trina, then back to the doctor. "I didn't visit him. I became him."

"Right, right. Just tell me. In detail."

After many questions and many answers, the doctor put his note pad away. "In almost every case, except for the time you became D'zeos, the transition is fairly clear-cut. There seems to be a physical trigger. Your surroundings lead from one place to the other. With one exception."

"What's that?" Jim said.

"The time Trina dropped you off at home before she went to pick up a take-out dinner. All you did was get out of the car and walk around it, and it became a taxi at the Honolulu airport. I just don't see any triggering key in that instance."

"Oh, my gosh," Trina said. "There *was* one. I remember now. An ad for a Hawaii vacation package came on the radio just as I pulled in the driveway. I remember because I intended to call about it, and I memorized the phone number. It was one, eight hundred, two Hawaii. Number two, and Hawaii. I never did call."

The doctor looked at Jim intently and said, "Are you still with us?"

Jim glanced at Trina, then at the doctor. "Yes."

"Good. So we have identified triggers, and they are visual and aural both. That's very good."

Trina said, "We certainly can't control all possible stimuli the rest of our lives."

"Of course not. But you must do your absolute best until we get to the real cause and figure out how to suppress or eliminate his reaction."

Jim shook his head, "Suppress or eliminate it? How are you going to do that?"

"One step at a time."

"I don't know how many steps I've got left in me, Doc. How many of those trips I can take."

The doctor nodded. "I can understand that. In the meantime, I've brought you some medication. I want you to take one now. But none in the morning before the testing."

"What is it?" Trina asked.

"A tranquilizer."

"I hate downers," said Jim. "Give me coke anytime."

"Absolutely no stimulants! Not even caffeinated soda." He looked at Trina.

She nodded.

"No TV, no movies, no radio," Dr. Ebenstein went on. "If you have music on your phone you can play instrumentals, but nothing Hawaiian." He looked at Trina. "Use your best judgment."

She said, "There's no way for me to know beforehand what might trigger him."

"I know, but do your best. Censor his magazines and newspapers. Tear out any pictures or articles that you think could possibly trigger another episode."

"That could be anything. We won't have any around."

Jim sagged in his chair, feeling like one of those unfortunate people without an immune system who had to be protected from all contamination. "You may as well put me in a room where you can look in at me through windows."

Trina scowled and shook her head.

The doctor frowned at him, and said, "Be at my office at nine o'clock sharp. And I suggest you use room service rather than going to a restaurant for meals."

Jim said, "You must be the life of the party when you go out."

Dr. Ebenstein actually smiled. "I need to work on that, Jim."

Chapter 11

Nowhere must be somewhere

As Jim and Trina exited the elevator and turned toward Doctor Ebenstein's office they saw Sylvia coming from the opposite direction.

She saw them and said, "Mr. and Mrs. Drake. Good morning! Thank goodness you're just getting here. I was afraid I was late again."

Jim looked at his watch. "Nope. Five minutes to nine."

Sylvia looked at hers. "I think I need a new battery. Mine says nine-twenty."

Jim grinned and said, "Leave it that way."

Sylvia giggled as she opened the door for them. "I think I will."

Dr. Ebenstein stood up from his desk as they entered, one move so completely effortless he seemed to have a power assist. "Good morning, Mr. and Mrs. Drake. And Sylvia, congratulations."

Sylvia just smiled.

"I have a question," Trina said to the doctor.

He headed for the side door. "Talk as we walk."

A few steps down the hall he opened a door and bounded down flights of concrete stairs fitted with steel toe plates. They all scrambled to follow, footsteps resounding through the stairwell cavity. After two flights he turned through a door and proceeded down a concrete tunnel. The trip down had been so fast-paced and dominated by the reverberating sounds of feet clattering on steel and concrete that Trina hadn't even tried to talk. In fact, Jim could see she had to struggle to keep pace with the doctor. He knew this would irritate her, so wasn't surprised when she said, "Doctor Ebenstein, if we must talk while we walk, will you at least slow down? My legs aren't as long as yours, nor am I accustomed to competing in Iron Man competitions, or whatever it is you do."

Dr. Ebenstein actually stopped and turned to face her. He said, with a hint color in his face, "I'm sorry, Mrs. Drake. I was thinking of the tests rather than you. I'm afraid my social graces..." His voice trailed off.

"They're a little sparse at times, aren't they?"

"Yes. I... well, yes. I just never had the time, I mean I never took the time. I mean, I got my Ph.D. at age twenty-one, and never—"

"Twenty-one?" Sylvia interrupted with a look of rapt admiration. She moved up next to him. "Twenty-one?"

"I was so focused, I just never found time for dating or parties or things like that."

Trina said, "That's a shame. You missed a great deal." She looked at Jim. "As opposed to someone else I know, who missed nothing."

"Just because in my year book under hobbies I put vodka."

Trina scowled as Doctor Ebenstein and Sylvia laughed, then she turned to the doctor. "Perhaps we should continue walking. I assume the machine is waiting?"

"It should be."

They resumed at a much more civilized pace, and Jim noticed that Sylvia was right at the doctor's side. "They just got it back up last night," the doctor said, "and we have the first patient time slot. Two hours. Nine-thirty to eleven-thirty, and I pulled every string I had to get that, even going so far as to have Doctors Peter Fillmore and Aubert Marquand—and they're internationally renowned, you know—make phone calls. I probably made an enemy of whoever was displaced, but that's the way it goes."

"This is really important to you," Trina said.

"Yes. But what was your question?"

"I was going to ask which personality you're going to try to induce in Jim."

Jim felt the fires of fear flare up inside his chest and stomach. "Damn it, Trina. I'm not assuming various personalities. This isn't past-life regression."

Trina seemed to withdraw. "I didn't mean..."

Doctor Ebenstein said, "He's right. This is fundamentally different. But to answer your question, I hope to—" he hesitated as he looked at Jim, then continued, "—to induce Jim to assume the life of Talaan. That seems to be, uhh, the most benign."

Trina said, "What's not benign about the one where he's engaged to Maryann? Or that weird one way in the future?"

Sylvia's head swiveled around to Trina, and her face was distorted, silently pleading. Or admonishing. Then she turned to the doctor, obviously expecting support from him. What the hell was wrong? What was going on? The doctor didn't look at either of them as he said, "We don't know for sure." Then he fixed Jim with a penetrating gaze, "Do we, Jim?"

What the hell was he digging for? Jim shrugged. "I don't know what in the hell you're talking about. I'm going crazy, but other than that, I don't see a damn thing to worry about."

Jim saw the doctor raise an eyebrow at Sylvia. He was about to ask what was wrong when they turned into an alcove that framed a large steel door. The doctor pushed on the latching bar, and the door opened with a bang that ricocheted up and down the concrete hall loud enough to announce their entrance to the entire building.

They entered a large gray room. In the center lurked an MRI machine. It seemed to be surrounded by an awful lot of ancillary equipment, far more than at the clinic back in LA. Monitors and instruments, computers and monitors with enigmatic readouts and exotic looking instruments, bundles of cables running every which way. A number of white-robed technicians fussed about taking readings and notes on iPads. A business-like hum filled the room, and it was very cool. Lots of air, probably to keep all the electronics from overheating.

Jim stopped just inside the door and looked at Trina, then at the doctor, and knew without a doubt that he was going to take a trip. He just didn't know to where. Or to when. Or as who.

Before he had time to worry much, he found himself being positioned on the trolley bed. Doctor Ebenstein said to Trina, "Sylvia has made some audio tapes. We're going to play these over his headphones and project visual cues from the surface of the tunnel, somewhat like a planetarium. We shall even cause his bed to move in various ways to try to simulate his description of the starship motion during what he called the boost phase.

Jim felt his bed begin to move almost as soon as he was settled on it, and he was trundled into the bowels of the machine. He hated this. It was claustrophobic. And noisy. But it wasn't so noisy this time. In fact, he could almost hear the name Zeleece, Zeleece, Zeleece, being repeated softly. Rumbling and shaking began, but it wasn't at all like he remembered on the starshuttle, and the name Zeleece wafted through the air again. What looked like stars appeared above him, and he was almost sure he heard the name Zeleece again. Several moments passed, and Zeleece was whispered in his right ear.

Then intense, rhythmic noise arose like a savage tribe preparing for battle. Loud, repetitive and disturbing, with bass notes that he didn't so much hear as feel in his chest. So deep and reverberant they jumbled and dominated his emotions and his innards. Try as he might, he had never learned to like the so-called Velapulse rhythm that shuddered under the discordant, grating Altarian flutes.

"Come on," he shouted as he took her hand. He motioned with his head toward the portal. Zeleece tugged back briefly with a pleading expression, then followed him out of the pulsating club. Her friend Glenoya followed them. They turned off their noise canceling earplants so they could converse more easily. Talaan said by way of explanation, "I hate that pulsar crap."

Glenoya said, "It depends on what drugs you're on."

"I'm not on any."

"I'm not either, but I kind of like it," Zeleece said, twisting her head to the rhythm still doing its work within her. "It awakens something primal in me. I don't have to think, I just let myself feel."

Talaan said, "You don't have a choice. It's too loud to think."

"Don't you feel it?" She pressed her pelvis against him, then rotated it slowly.

"Oh, yeah," said Glenoya as she moved up and pressed herself against his other leg. "That's what it does to me, too."

Talaan put an arm around each of them, but looked at Zeleece as he ran his hand down to her butt and pulled her in tighter. "That's a feeling I like," he said.

They kissed, then she pulled her head back to look at him. She looked for a long time without a word, so long he wondered what was going on behind her big serious eyes, then she said in a raspy whisper, "I want to get married, Talaan."

Her eyes darted over his face, and he was amazed to see they were filled with fear and uncertainty, seeking reassurance, pleading for his acceptance of her even if he said no to her words. And then he saw a hardening in them, and knew she wanted to take the words back; she was afraid he would break off their relationship because of what she'd said. But how could he? That was what he wanted, yet suggesting marriage was the last thing he ever expected to hear from her. Now she was afraid of how he might react, because if he had ever said those words to her she would have run. But he knew, even if she didn't, that it wasn't carefree independence on her part that created this attitude. She fought herself fiercely for what she thought was independence, but it was really fear of rejection. She was scared to death of rejection. He kissed each doe-like eye, and said, "I want to get married too."

She melted against him, then clenched herself to him fiercely. He thought he felt a sob convulse her body, but that couldn't have been. Not her. He drew his head back and tried to look in her eyes, but she wouldn't let him. Instead she buried her face in his neck and began kissing it.

"Yes," said Glenoya. "Yes, yes, yes. Let's all get married. A triad."

"No," said Talaan.

"No triad," mumbled Zeleece from his neck.

"No? Why not?" Glenoya sounded incredulous. "Zang, what could be better? You two better think it over."

"When do you want to get married?" Talaan said softly into her ear.

Perturb

"Let's get married next week."

Terry was surprised and looked away, out the 707 window at the clouds, gathering his thoughts, before he turned back to her. "I wouldn't mind, but your mother's got this plan for an elaborate wedding. There's no way. She'd have a fit."

Maryann leaned her head against his shoulder. "I know we can't, it's just what I'd like."

Terry rested his head against the top of hers and they sat silently for a long time, listening to the drone of the engines. Some buffeting and bumping began. They moved apart so their heads wouldn't bump together.

"I'm going to go to the restroom," he said, and stood up. It was hard to walk up the aisle with the airplane jouncing, but with the aid of seat backs he made it. He had to brace himself against the wall to urinate, then staggered down the aisle like a drunk to get back to his seat. Just as he reached their row, an announcement came over the loudspeakers. *"Ladies and gentlemen, we are experiencing some turbulence. Please return to your seats and fasten your seat belts."* A bell chimed. *"The no smoking sign is on."*

There was a bang and a jolt, as if a giant had swatted the plane. Terry grabbed a seat back. Then the plane settled down with some minor bumping, and he swung toward his seat. Maryann reached her hand out.

Perturb!

Fear whipped through D'zeos, but it was wind over a barren plain with nothing to tug on because nothing existed. He looked everywhere, but everywhere was nowhere. He looked down at his body, and there was nothing there. He didn't exist; his body didn't. He took a deep breath to yell but felt no sensation. He yelled anyway, "Let me go. Send me home!" But he had no voice.

He was not. Not anywhere. Not anything.

Was he dead? He could see, at least he thought he could, but there was nothing to see. The universe did not exist and as this sank in terror roiled, terror far beyond fear, terror that shredded logic and knowledge. He shouted again "I want to go home!" and tried to run, this self without body, without legs, without voice. Nothing happened.

A voice materialized out of the nothingness.

It was Vanqa, he knew, a sing-song voice without sonics. "Come back!" Vanqa had no voice either but D'zeos knew it was Vanqa, and that Vanqa had shouted. He heard without hearing, and felt without feeling that Vanqa was pulling on him. He pulled back to resist, but it was an incorporeal action, nothing pulling on nothingness. He pulled anyway. Vanqa grabbed again, a force less palpable than fingers of fog, no more substantial than threads of imagination. Neither of them were in this nonplace.

"No!" D'zeos whirled, this thing that was himself, and something banged him in the face.

"Come back, damn you!"

He opened his eyes just as Doctor Ebenstein slapped again, shouting, "Come back, damn you! Come back!"

The blow jarred; Jim felt warmth blossom on his cheek. And he knew he was home.

"Thank you."

Chapter 12

Being physical is good.

Jim was groggy from the medication when the alarm went off at five-thirty. He heard Trina call him several times, but he just couldn't wake up. He tried, and couldn't. Finally she took his arm and pulled, and he sat up on the edge of the bed because he knew he had to. She insisted he go into the bathroom and take a shower, and pulled on his arms until he stood up, then walked him to the bathroom. She got the shower going while he urinated, then he stepped in under the hot, stabbing streams. He ran it on the back of his neck for a long time, and that gave him a little life. He washed his hair and his body, then rinsed with ice cold water. He dried himself, but didn't shave. Trina had laid out clean clothes for him, and had he just finished dressing when room service knocked with breakfast. At her urging he forced down some toast and orange juice. He would have liked a cup of coffee, but the doctor had said no stimulants.

As he chewed the toast he remembered what he had been thinking about before the drug took over—could he use meditation to help himself? At one time, before he started his business, he had studied Buddhism and practiced meditation regularly, and had gotten pretty good at it. But that was years ago, and right now he couldn't imagine how that could help.

Trina interrupted his thoughts. "Honey, we really must leave. It's getting late."

"Okay. I've had enough, anyway." He shoved aside the one and a half slices of toast remaining on his plate, took another swallow of juice, and stood up.

They arrived at Doctor Ebenstein's office sharply at seven. The grogginess fled in a surge when he saw Doctor Marquand seated at the table with Doctor Ebenstein and Sylvia, and another man who Jim had never seen. God, was he that bad? Or did they have a cure? Maybe that was it.

Maybe Dr. Marquand had figured out what was wrong. "Doctor Marquand!" he said, "What are you doing here?"

As usual, the doctor nodded his head rather than answer. "Hello, Jim. Hello, Trina. I want you to meet Doctor Peter Fillmore from UCLA—Doctor Fillmore, this is Mr. and Mrs. Drake." He nodded his head again and said, "Peter and I took the red-eye after seeing the readouts from your episode yesterday."

"Why?" Dread stripped away the last of Jim's grogginess. "What's *happening* to me? What did you see?"

Dr. Marquand violently shook his head. "Calm down. It's not that bad. No, no, not that bad."

"That bad?" Jim felt anger rising, and looked the doctor in the eye. "What do you mean, not that bad? Not how bad?"

Dr. Fillmore said, "What Aubert meant was, the results were astonishing, but that doesn't mean they were necessarily bad."

Dr. Marquand nodded energetically. "Exactly."

"Am I in the final stages of insanity? Am I going to permanently lose touch with reality? Am I going to stay in that place that doesn't exist, living in my mind?" Jim felt like he was asking for his own execution, but he had to know what was going on.

Dr. Fillmore raised blond eyebrows and cocked his head as he said, "No, Jim, we don't think that's going to happen." He turned toward the other doctors for confirmation, but that act just confirmed to Jim that it *was* going to happen. He was going permanently crazy. Or existing outside the real world. Both the other doctors shook their head no, but it was sure as hell not convincing. It was obvious they knew something they weren't telling him. "What is Vanqa trying to save me from? And why? Who is Vanqa? How could I even imagine I was in a place that doesn't exist?"

Dr. Ebenstein looked almost angry. "We don't know who Vanqa is or what he's up to, and it doesn't matter. We're not interested in him. How should we know anything about Vanqa? He's your fantasy. You deal with him. We're interested in Terry Walker."

Jim took a step toward the doctor. "You want *me* to deal with him? I thought you didn't appreciate patient self-diagnosis, Doctor. And what do you mean, you don't care about him? He's who I become, he's the one who seems to be pulling on me and interacting with him is the most frightening situation I've ever had to cope with. And you say you don't care? What the hell *do* you care about? It sure as hell doesn't seem to be me."

"Jim," Dr. Marquand said, "This Vanqa, and D'zeos too, seem nebulous at best according to your own description. They're not even in a place. They don't seem to exist in any of your realities. What Doctor Ebenstein meant was, we suspect they may be the manifestation of a subconscious desire on your part to save yourself."

Jim whirled to face Dr. Ebenstein. "Bullshit. Something was on your readouts," he jabbed a finger at the other doctors, one at time, "or they wouldn't be here! And by God, Vanqa is not my imagination. Something else is starting to happen. Something you haven't seen before, and more than likely something that concerns you a lot because you aren't telling me."

"That's not quite true, Jim." Dr. Marquand said, "Sit down, both of you." He indicated the two empty chairs at the conference table.

Jim looked at Trina as they sat, and he could see anger in her face, too.

Dr. Marquand said, "Doctor Ebenstein has made good progress in narrowing down the possibilities, and in quantifying your brain activity." He nodded his head emphatically. "We're closing in on what's happening, Jim."

"Closing in, you say? So you still don't know a goddamn thing, and what you do know you're not telling me."

Peter Fillmore's eyebrows shot up, but Aubert Marquand didn't twitch. He looked at Jim evenly and said, "We know a great deal. We know a lot about the electrochemical manifestations, and some of the physiology, which would not mean much to you. On the other hand, we have no idea why this is happening, or how."

"Well, that makes me feel *much* better. Can I go outside and play now?"

"Jim, stop it!" Trina clenched her fists and slammed them down on the table as she spoke, teetering between despair and rage; seeking control so as to avoid both, tears and fury in a struggle for expression, ready to erupt. She glared at each of the doctors in turn. "Jim's right. You know something you're not telling him, and that's not right."

Doctor Marquand stood up, walked over between them, and patted Jim on the back while he put his other hand on Trina's shoulder. "Actually, Trina, you're right. We're not giving him the answers he needs. He's an intelligent adult, and he wants to know what we can do to help him. I wish we could give him some answers, but we don't have them."

"Hello, folks!" Jim growled, "I'm still here."

Dr. Ebenstein stood up with a scrape of his chair. "This is non-productive. Come, everyone. We have to get going. The helicopter's standing by."

Trina's forehead distorted into a full frown as she shouted, "Helicopter? Where are we going, and why do we need a helicopter?" Her face was red, and she seemed ready to attack Doctor Ebenstein as she shoved her chair back and reared to her feet, but his back was toward her; he was heading for the door. "What are these goddamn secrets you three have? Things you know that have a direct impact on Jim's and my life? Things you have decided we shouldn't know?"

"We're going to NYU Medical Center," he said without turning his head. "Come." He turned down the hall at his usual fast pace, while the others scrambled to follow. He said over his shoulder, "We have a helicopter available that can be used for medical emergencies."

"Medical emergencies?" Trina yelled. She was almost running to catch up with him. "this is a medical emergency now?"

"I have chosen to classify it as one. It's imperative we get to New York University quickly because they opened a time slot for us this morning, displacing some very highly regarded research." Maurice turned into an alcove and opened a door with a loud clank. He began taking two steps at a time up the concrete stairway.

"Good Lord. Everyone's dropping whatever they're doing to attend to Jim Drake?" Trina directed a glare toward the doctor's back. "What's going on, Doctor Ebenstein? Damnit, tell us what aren't you telling us."

Doctor Marquand said soothingly, too soothingly, from behind her, "Nothing has changed, Trina. It's just that the unique nature of Jim's affliction and its rapid progression has become clear as a result of the latest tests. We need to learn more very quickly."

She said hoarsely, "You think he could die, don't you?"

Doctor Marquand shook his head emphatically. "No."

Peter Fillmore said softly, "We don't think so."

Right then Jim knew what the sentence was. "You don't think so, huh? It'll be worse than death, won't it? I'll be alive but not connected with the world. I'll be in that place that doesn't exist."

"No, you could die. We need to learn how to prevent that," Maurice Ebenstein said bluntly, almost antagonistically, as he held open the door to the roof. Jim noticed the other two doctors frown at him, then he added, "We don't want to take any chances, is what I mean. Of you dying."

A big helicopter with a medical insignia on the side was sitting on the pad, a pilot at the controls. A turbine started up as they approached, whining loudly, making a response difficult to hear.

Jim felt he was consigned to a march of preordained events, an observer of his own gradual descent into perpetual confusion and bewilderment. As they boarded the helicopter and strapped themselves in, he thought back over his episodes but could not see why he would die. He might leave reality forever, but die? Yet that was exactly what the doctors feared. He said loudly so as to be heard over the helicopter noise, "I don't see how this could kill me as long as I don't drive or walk in front of a car while I'm in a trance, or something like that. I lose touch with the world and I guess that could become permanent, but how could that kill me?"

Trina looked furious as she said to Doctor Ebenstein, "Yes. How could it?"

Maurice said, "That won't."

That answer pissed Jim off. "Then what the hell will?"

"You tell me."

"You're the goddamn doctor, or at least you're supposed to be. Now all of a sudden you expect me to come up with the answers for you? Or are you playing your stupid little psychological games, trying to get me mad enough to cough up some tidbit that'll solve the problem for you?"

Trina stomped her foot on the aluminum floor of the helicopter. "Jim's right! What do you want of him? How in the world is he supposed to tell *you*?"

Doctor Marquand's soft voice intervened, "A diagnosis is not what we expect from you. Let's all calm down."

Trina turned her glare on him as the helicopter lifted from the roof with so much noise and vibration that they had to stop talking. Trina reached over to Jim, patted his hand and smiled but it was a grim smile, as the interlude gave them all a moment. The helicopter angled into a curve up and around, and the noise subsided considerably.

"I want to know what could kill me."

Dr. Marquand said gently, "What if you had been Philip Osborne when he died? Would Jim Drake have died? He might have. We don't know."

"I've never gone back there."

"That's right."

"So what else could kill me?"

"Maybe nothing. Or maybe another event like that."

What in the world could it be? These assholes knew something they weren't telling him. Was D'zeos really a creation of his subconscious, like the doctors said? If he stayed there, was that a sort of death? Probably more like purgatory. They had no idea what it was like. It was impossible for him to relate the sense of being in a place that was not a place, impossible to make them understand how it was to be nothing. To not exist, but know it. Maybe his brain did stop functioning when he was D'zeos. Jim gave up. And realized the doctors weren't going to let him in on what must be speculation on their part. Goddamn doctors!

He became conscious of the vibrating, rattling, noisy helicopter, the hard metal floor and cold metal walls, and the knowledge that helicopters have a glide ratio like a rock. He had ridden on these things in the past, and hated them. He turned from the window and said, "I hate these things. I'm always afraid they'll crash. Besides that, I don't like heights."

The doctors all looked at one another with expressions that were tense, almost fearful, and Jim felt a surge of panic. Sylvia thrust her hand over her mouth, which intensified his unease. "What's wrong?" he demanded.

"Nothing." Dr. Ebenstein turned his head away and looked out the window. Sylvia dropped her hand and rested it on the doctor's, and he looked at her softly.

Peter Fillmore seemed to be studying his fingernails.

Doctor Marquand said to him. "Nothing's wrong, Jim." He immediately turned to Trina and said, "You wanted to know what we expect of him."

So something was wrong as hell. So much so that Doctor Marquand had to change the subject.

Trina gave Jim a look that was puzzled or uneasy, but went along with the new subject and said to the doctor, "Your darn right I do."

"It's possible..." the doctor paused, took a deep breath, "...it's possible that something in his subconscious may be contributing to these episodes. In that sense, it may be within his power to control them, if we can learn enough to guide him. That's what Maurice was referring to."

Hope and fear yanked at Jim from opposite directions. "So this may be self-inflicted. And if it is, maybe you can teach me how to stop it."

"Well, yes," Doctor Marquand twirled his hair, "that's a possibility."

"Then let's try it."

Doctor Fillmore said, "It's not that straightforward. We need to learn much more before we can reach any conclusion, even a speculative one, let alone devise a treatment or ameliorating regimen."

"Okay." He may as well play it their way. That's the way it would end up anyway. "I assume that's what today is about," Jim said. "What are you going to do?"

"MEG testing."

"MEG?"

Sylvia spoke up for the first time. "Magnetoencephalography."

Trina turned to Doctor Fillmore and said, "I thought Doctor Marquand said you did MEG's at UCLA."

"I do, but the unanimous opinion was that we wanted the results today, and I couldn't gain access to our facility until next month. So we're going to the Center for Neuromagnetism Laboratory at NYU. Mo got us in there, and I'm here to run the tests."

"Mo?"

Doctor Fillmore poked his finger at Maurice. "Maurice. Doctor Ebenstein. Mister personality."

Maurice shook his head as Sylvia squeezed his arm. "They just don't know you," she said to him. Then, embarrassed, she quickly removed her hand from his arm.

"What exactly is MEG?" asked Jim.

Doctor Ebenstein nodded to Sylvia as he said, "This case is going to be the basis of Ms. Maynord's doctoral dissertation, and she needs to participate. Sylvia, why don't you answer Mr. Drake's question?"

Resentment rose in Jim. "So I *am* a research project."

"Oh, no, no," Sylvia said blithely. "That's just a side benefit completely separate from getting to the bottom of your problem. And don't worry. Your name won't be used." She smiled, satisfied that she had settled any qualms he had, then continued eagerly, "As you probably know, when an electric current passes through a conductor, it generates a magnetic field."

"Yeah," he said while wondering how she could be so insensitive.

She was leaning forward, holding his eyes. "Currents in the neurons of your brain obey the same laws. They generate magnetic fields. We use magnetic detectors, in this case over a hundred of them positioned on the scalp by a helmet, to measure those fields. The currents induced in the sensors are detected by superconducting coils in a device called a SQUID."

Jim said, "If I take another trip, maybe your squid can use one of his arms to punch the right nerve to bring me back."

Sylvia giggled, and her intensity softened. "You're so funny. SQUID stands for superconducting quantum interference device. It's extremely sensitive, capable of detecting a single quanta of electromagnetic energy, although in practice external magnetic disturbances preclude that kind of sensitivity."

Trina frowned. "Didn't you get the same thing from the MRI data?"

"MRI has poor time resolution, and even fMRI gives essentially anatomical data. MEG gives us actual brain functional information with time resolutions of a few milliseconds."

Doctor Fillmore added, "We hope to resolve the very onset of these episodes and then track their progression."

"I thought functional MRI did that, except for the time resolution."

Doctor Fillmore said, "MEG goes much further. Doctor Lofiego—Richardo Lofiego is Chairman of the Department of Physiology and Neuroscience there, and has an M.D. and a Ph.D., just as we three do—Doctor Lofiego and others have used it to study higher cognitive functions such as logic, attention and speech. And those are precisely the types of brain functions we suspect are involved here."

Jim shook his head. "I think you're dead wrong."

Five heads swiveled toward him.

Doctor Ebenstein reared back in outrage. "How can you—"

"Hold on, Maurice," Doctor Marquand said sharply, as he held up a finger. "Jim, tell us why you say that."

"I'm pretty sure it involves my mind, not my brain."

Doctor Marquand nodded his head energetically. "I do too."

"Hmmm, ummm," mumbled Peter Fillmore.

Doctor Ebenstein seemed almost belligerent, offended that a patient would suggest that his medical diagnosis was wrong. "What makes you think you can possibly—"

Doctor Fillmore cut him off. "Wait a minute. Let's hear him out."

Jim said, "When I go to another time and place, it's not like a thought or a picture I might conjure up in my mind, a situation with no background or history. I go to a totally different existence. A non-physical part of me leaves and becomes that other person, and since it's non-physical, it can't be my brain. I think it centers in the part of me that transcends your neuronal currents. I think it's the part that is close to the soul, for lack of a better term. The part that exists on a level beyond electrochemical activity. My essence, if you prefer, or my being, the *I am* part of 'I am Jim.' The part that I define as *me* if I meditate. It's not physical, doctors. You're not going to find some nodule you can cut out that's the cause of these episodes."

"How did you arrive at that diagnosis?" Maurice demanded sarcastically.

"Because I experience it, doctor. You don't. All you have is a bunch of sterile numbers and graphs."

Doctor Ebenstein shook his head in disgust. "We need to call in a witch doctor for consultation."

Doctor Fillmore, one blond eyebrow arched, was nodding his head meditatively, seeming to agree with Jim.

Doctor Marquand said, "You sound as if you're not a stranger to metaphysical concepts."

Trina, looking hopeful for some reason, said, "I remember him reading and meditating, back before he started his business." She turned to Jim. "But I had no idea you were so deeply involved."

He and she had never discussed such matters, and now he was sorry they hadn't. He wished he had not stopped the practice. He was sorry about a lot of things.

"Nonsense," said Doctor Ebenstein. "We're going to make measurements and we're going to identify the cause, or at least the region of the brain where it's originating. Then we're going to find out what to do to block it."

"I hope so, Doctor. I truly hope you're right. Because if you're not and I am, you won't be able to do a damn thing, will you?"

Chapter 13

Doom lurking

Jim didn't like this basement lab. It was tomb-like. The walls were metallic gray, unadorned with any esthetic trappings, harshly lit by LEDs which reflected dully from them, as if through a dirty fog. It reminded him of the inside of a huge ventilating system plenum he had built for a chemical plant that had been designed for efficiency with nothing included that was not functionally required for guiding air flow with minimal disturbance. The floor of the room was vinyl, but even that was lifeless and dead-sounding. The room had an inert sort of musty atmosphere and a faint smell of ozone that might be found in a room housing electrical machinery. He said, "This is like being in an industrial equipment room. Or a bank vault."

"That's pretty much what it is." The words had a tinny sound, a deadness to them like a cheap loudspeaker at an airport that cut off the low frequencies. The doctor was busy with a complicated-looking apparatus, but seemingly able to do two things at once. "It literally is a vault. All six walls are magnetically shielded to block outside sources such as power lines and the magnetic field of the earth itself so we can detect the small gradients in the field your brain emits."

"Six walls?" Jim could see the room was square.

"Counting the floor and ceiling," Doctor Fillmore said.

"What are gradients, changes in field strength?"

"That's right. The difference in amplitude between one location and another nearby location. All fields decrease in strength with the square of the distance from the source. The sources in your brain, being at most a few centimeters from our detector coils, produce a field that decreases significantly over those small distances. On the other hand, the external magnetic fields originate far away, so even though they are much stronger they are essentially constant in amplitude over those same small distances. By measuring gradients in the field rather than field strength proper, we greatly reduce their effect." He looked up from his work. "Go ahead, Sylvia, fit the helmet to him."

Sylvia's eyes sparkled. "Yes sir! By myself?"

"Yes, but I want Doctor Ebenstein to observe."

She picked up a helmet-like device with stalks protruding everywhere. Wires of many colors protruded from the stalks. A short distance from the helmet the wires were tied together into a bundle, which draped down onto the floor and disappeared behind a piece of equipment. Sylvia walked over to Jim with the helmet, holding the cable bundle in her other hand, dragging it across the floor.

He looked at the cap. "That looks like a porcupine had sex with a motorcycle helmet."

Sylvia stopped mid-stride. Her mouth dropped, then she and all the others burst into laughter, and she said, "You're so funny."

Trina said, "God, Jim!" but she too was snickering.

Doctor Ebenstein seemed especially delighted. He said, "That's a product of Peter's lab. Makes you wonder, doesn't it?"

Doctor Fillmore said, "Even porcupines need love, Mo. Prickly or not. You should know."

Sylvia, more or less regathering her wits, looked fondly at Maurice Ebenstein. "I don't think you're prickly." The doctor smiled, and their gaze locked for several seconds. Then, as if suddenly remembering what she was doing, she turned to Jim and gestured toward a chair. "Come sit over here, Mister Drake."

As he sat down he said to Doctor Marquand, "I assume you're going to try and induce another trip?"

"Yes. To either Talaan or D'zeos."

Trina said, "What's wrong with Talaan? Or Terry Walker?"

Sylvia emitted a little gasp, and Jim noticed Doctor Ebenstein stiffen and stop what he was doing. What the hell was that about? Again, fear surged with the realization that something was going on, some knowledge they had that they weren't sharing with him. They acted like it was a matter of life or death. He could understand that, but not just with Terry. With everyone. Terry was just some ordinary person living back in the early sixties. Not a drug user or alcoholic, not a criminal, not even particularly intellectual. Not wealthy or particularly talented. There was nothing special about him. So why was he a threat? Just him and not the others?

Doctor Marquand said, "We don't want you going there, Jim."

"Why?"

"Because... we're getting more useful information from your other destinations."

"Come on. Why aren't you telling us?" Jim started to demand to be told, but the moment passed as Sylvia slipped the helmet on his head and began fussing with it and fussing with it. Jim surmised she was adjusting the position of all the sensors, but didn't ask. He was busy. Busy thinking. He didn't want to take another trip, but he wanted the doctors to get the information to cure him. He'd probably take one sooner or later anyway. But why not Terry? They couldn't control who he became, anyway. Could he control it? If he prayed, would that help? He tried, but lost concentration after 'Please, God,' as he began wondering how they were going to induce the trip. They couldn't have much control if it was his inner essence or spiritual self that was involved. But they did get him to become Talaan that one time.

"All right, Jim." He saw that Maurice and Sylvia were wheeling up a video monitor that was nestled in the confines of a tent of black fabric like a photographer's hood, only bigger. Like a black pup tent. They positioned it just in front of him, and Sylvia took something from the monitor table. "These are earphones. They will provide aural isolation and allow us to provide you with audio cues. The hood and monitor will do the same for your visual senses."

She inserted a plug in each ear and the room sounds moved off into the distance, leaving an acoustic void around him. Then Sylvia and the doctor rolled the monitor toward him so the hood enclosed him everywhere but behind. Then they draped the black blanket around the back to close that off, and he was in total darkness. Alone. It felt like suspended animation. The only sensory input was sweat in his armpits. It was stuffy in here. He probably stank, or soon would. Some patterns appeared on the monitor. He tried to make sense of them, but they were ghosts coming and going, flitting and vanishing and reforming. Then he heard sounds, and a voice but no recognizable words. Now another sound was becoming ever more prominent. It sounded a little like running water trickling and gurgling.

He realized he had to urinate. All of a sudden it was urgent. But he'd have to wait until the tests were done. He concentrated on the phantom images and garbled sounds, but the only thing that came through was the trickling. His need was getting worse. This was not going to work.

"I'm sorry," he said loudly. "I have to urinate."

Nothing happened at first, then Doctor Fillmore's voice came over the headphones. "Who is this?"

"Jim. I can't concentrate. That running water. I really have to go bad. I'm sorry."

A long pause, then, "Okay."

Again, nothing happened for what seemed like a long time, and he tried not to think about his need. Finally the cover behind him opened, then the hood and video monitor rolled back, with Doctor Fillmore and Sylvia pushing. Doctor Ebenstein began removing Jim's hood and earphones. The doctor's expression was angry; a frown created a deep gash in his forehead and his eyes were intense. Jim felt guilty, and looked toward Doctor Marquand. Then he relaxed. The doctor's eyes were glistening and his mouth kept puckering as he restrained bursts of laughter. Then he spun around and scurried away where Jim couldn't see him.

Jim glanced over to Trina, and she had an amused smile.

The instant he was freed he scrambled to his feet and started to the door, then realized he needed directions. He turned, and Doctor Ebenstein jabbed a finger. "Turn left, then left again, then the first door on your right."

When he returned, Doctor Ebenstein looked at his watch and shook his head. "All right, let's try again."

The apparatus was re-set, and Jim was once more alone in blackness.

The images and sounds seemed the same. Again, he found himself focusing on the water-like sound. He tried to watch the monitor and immerse himself in the vision. But the trickling. He suddenly realized it wasn't water, and tried to guess what it might be. Lab apparatus percolating? No, probably not. Equipment running? No. Animals? He couldn't imagine what. He began attempting to picture Trina sitting out there in the lab. Wondered if she was tapping her foot. He could imagine Maurice Ebenstein looking at his watch. Pacing. And he smiled to himself. He envisioned the readouts, and could picture flat lines—a dead subject. Wondered what time it was. He noticed a little light seeping in under the black hood where it met the floor. A tiny white feather. He was startled when a voice, Doctor Fillmore's, came clearly over his headset. "Jim, you're still with us, is that right?"

"Yes."

"We're changing the sensory inputs. We're going to try a stick that Aubert brought with him. It'll be a moment."

It was just a few moments. A loud humming came over the headphones. Like being inside an airplane.

Then familiar images swarmed into his consciousness. And a voice of authority. *"Stewardesses, return to your seats. I repeat, stewardesses, return to your seats! We have an emergency!"*

Maryann grabbed his arm. "Terry, what's happening?"

"I don't know. But the engines sound different. I think one or two of them have stopped working."

"Oh, Lord! Are we going to crash? We'll all die!"

Terry looked out the window. There was nothing but ocean. Flat, featureless ocean. Not blue or green ,but gray and somber. They were not very high. He craned his neck so he could look up. Nothing but cloud cover. He looked toward the horizon. Dark clouds merged seamlessly with gray sea to form a menacing unity into which they were arrowing. Lightening staggered between clouds and ocean, like an evil grin with flashing teeth.

He turned to Maryann. Put his hand on her cheek and kissed her lips gently. "I think we'll be okay." He didn't think so. They were going to crash.

She put her arms around his neck and pulled strongly, crushing her cheek against his. "If we crash, we'll die in each other's arms."

Bang!

Something broke. The engines. The sound changed. Was there only one? Terry felt a surge of weightlessness in his stomach.

"You will find flotation devices under your seats. Remove them now. We are going to set the plane down in the ocean as gently as possible."

Horror smothered the cabin in silence. It was a moment that lasted an eternity. Then a scream shattered the massive void, and that triggered a cacophony of screams. Bedlam. Screaming. Screaming! Like a cage of madmen and women, incoherent utterances from the gut and the heart, eruptions of primal fear.

Terry could see whitecaps when he stole a glance out. Maryann clenched his arm. "I love you," she said in his ear so he could hear over the wailing and screaming and cursing. And someone saying the Lords Prayer in a shout as others tried to join in, and someone else shouting that they were all going to hell because they had sinned and they better repent now because Lucifer was among them laughing.

He put his hand on hers and his lips next to her ear. "I love..."

Perturb!

The seat jarred and shook. The scene staggered. Ephemeral glimpses of terrified passengers, interspersed with chromatic swirls and multicolored twists. Passengers; universe; contorted dimensions. The plane. Nothing. The plane. Vortices of gray intertwined ribbons of time in an undulating and churning tornado of eternity. The cabin was filled with twists of black, grotesque, distorted passengers, then torrents of color that screamed up into ultraviolet and rushed down into infrared. Then nothing.

And he was not. One more time.

Then from nothing bloomed light, earthly light.

Awareness gelled in the form of Maurice Ebenstein shaking him violently, shouting, "Jim! Come back!" The doctor's eyes bored into him. "Jim, are you here?"

Jim grabbed the doctor's arms. "That airplane's going to crash, and we're all going to die. Keep me out of it, Doc. Please. I don't want to go back there. They're all going to die."

"Who?"

"Terry and Maryann. They're going to die! The plane's ditching in the ocean, and they're going to die sure as hell. I don't want to be there, doc! I don't want to be there"

"Why?"

"You stupid fucking ass! Why do you think? I'll die. Drug me. Keep me here! Do whatever it takes."

Trina had one of his hands between hers, and Sylvia was holding the other. Doctor Marquand pulled Doctor Ebenstein back away from Jim, stepped between the women and put one hand on his shoulder and the other on his cheek and said, "We won't let you, Jim."

"Don't let me. Jesus, don't let me!"

"We won't," Trina said. "We won't." Her eyes were swimming over his.

"My God, this data is amazing!" said Doctor Ebenstein from somewhere behind Jim. "How is this possible?"

"Tell him to kiss my fucking ass!"

"I don't need to. He heard you." Doctor Marquand flirted with a smile, but it immediately vanished.

"I thought I was dead. Going to be dead. Impact was seconds away. Everyone was screaming or yelling the Lord's Prayer."

"You're here. You're okay. Try to relax."

"No more. That's it. Drug me for life. Do a lobotomy. Do whatever it takes."

"Jim," Trina began, but Doctor Marquand interrupted.

"We need to understand, Jim, but we won't let you go back to Terry Walker. Not if we can help it. I promise, we'll do our very best. I'll never use that set of stimuli again."

"God, I hope not!" He pulled Trina's hand to him and pushed it hard against his cheek. "I love you."

"I love you too!"

"Me too!" said a badly shaken Sylvia.

Jim said, "I don't think they'll be able to prevent it." He looked at Trina as she opened her mouth to object, and he said "How can they? They've been trying and I keep going back anyway. If I go one more time, I'm dead."

"Oh, Jim!" Trina scanned his face in a desperate search for salvation. For escape from this insanity.

He knew she would find none.

Chapter 14

The time of then

Maurice Ebenstein's stern gaze swept around the conference table, first to Peter Fillmore, then to Aubert Marquand, ending with Sylvia Maynord. "I believe you were right," he said to her.

Sylvia said, "You mean that he'll die if he's on the plane when it crashes?"

"Yes."

"What are you talking about?" demanded Doctor Fillmore. "That plane's nothing but a figment of his imagination. If it had actually existed, and had crashed killing someone named Terry Walker back in the nineteen-sixties, then we'd be dealing with a whole different matter."

"We are." Doctor Ebenstein's eyes were black embers, his speech chopped and low. "It happened, Peter. A Boeing 707 enroot from Honolulu to Los Angeles. Everyone on board was killed, including a man named Terry Walker and a woman named Maryann Bethamy Sue Jacobson."

"Good Lord!" Color fled the doctor's face; he probed the expression of each of the others, seeking denial. "You mean Terry Walker actually existed? And died in a plane crash?"

Doctor Ebenstein nodded yes. So did Sylvia.

"You've confirmed it? For sure?"

"I'm afraid so. It's a fact that a real-life Terry Walker died in the crash. And it seems doubtful that Jim could have accessed that information. You remember that Mister Drake was also Philip Osborne that first time, on Truk Island?

Doctor Fillmore frowned. "What's that got to do with it?"

"The information on Osborne's death exists in only one place, as far as we know, and an automatic computer logging system shows that it was never accessed."

"What about Terry Walker? Was that common knowledge, or easily discovered?"

"No. The data are so obscure, scattered and incomplete, that it's essentially impossible that Mister Drake could have gathered all the facts he has. The only reason we were able to find the information is because we started with full names and birth dates, but if Jim Drake were looking he wouldn't have had any of that. There's no way he could have accessed that information."

"Good God!" Doctor Fillmore seemed unable to find additional words. He stammered a moment, then said, "Jim Drake had to have come across the information somewhere."

"He did not." Maurice tilted his head to Sylvia. "Tell him."

When Sylvia finished summarizing her search results, Peter said again, "Good God!" He turned to Aubert Marquand. "Did you know this?"

"No, I didn't." Then he said, "On the other hand, I rather expected that those were real events, events that had actually occurred. I didn't know for a fact, but had reached the conclusion that there's a lot more to this than hallucinations or psychosis. Now I feel somewhat vindicated."

Doctor Ebenstein clamped his mouth into an angry slash, then said, "Good God, Aubert. You don't think he's actually time traveling?"

"Let's face it, no other explanation fits all the facts." Aubert tapped a pen on his knee as he looked Doctor Ebenstein straight in the eye and added, "I think it's a definite possibility, certainly one we must not discard." He turned to Doctor Fillmore. "Don't you agree, Peter?"

"Aubert, I... No. Hell no! That's nothing more than science fiction drivel. Could you imagine trying to publish something like that? You'd be laughed out of town. It violates all the laws of physics."

Aubert sat his pen down and leaned forward intently. "No. It's not against the laws of physics. It's not explicitly included in them, but it's not excluded either. Both sides of the coin are mathematically allowed. Look at quantum physics. Look at string theory. Look at the frontiers of cosmology, and especially the multiple universe concepts posed by some highly regarded physicists. No, Peter, I don't think a prudent man could say it's impossible."

"What highly regarded physicists?"

"Well, Paul Davies, for one, a Professor at the Australian Centre for Astrobiology. He's at Macquarie University in Sydney, and no quack. In fact, he was awarded the Faraday Prize by The Royal Society in England."

"Okay, you found one quack."

Doctor Marquand seemed amused, and said, "We also have David Deutsch, a recipient of the Dirac Prize. He is at the Centre for Quantum Computation at Oxford. And here is a name you may recognize. Leonard Susskind. He and I have met, although he probably doesn't remember me. Doctor Susskind is Professor of Physics at Stanford. He's the man who came up with string theory, of which you no doubt have heard." Doctor Marquand nodded energetically to elicit agreement.

Instead, Doctor Fillmore scowled, and grumbled, "Well, you know more about that than I do. You're the one who'd have a doctorate in physics if you hadn't thought you were going nuts and switched to psychiatry so you could diagnose yourself."

Doctor Ebenstein laughed derisively and said, "It didn't help. He still is. Time travel! That's pure nonsense. Worse."

Aubert, looking at Doctor Fillmore and ignoring Doctor Ebenstein, said, "I did switch majors because of concerns regarding myself. But it was a relief to discover that, as a matter of fact, no one is normal. Normal is only the peak of a statistical curve, and a population is required to fill out the tails of that curve. We off-center folks are a necessary part of the normal distribution."

"We love you anyway, Aubert." Doctor Ebenstein blew him a kiss. "Even if you are nutso."

Sylvia looked fondly at Maurice and murmured, "You're so funny."

"Okay." Doctor Marquand picked up his pen, rapped it sharply on the table, and said, "I defy any of you self-proclaimed sane people to come up with any other explanation. Let's start making a list." He held the pen over his note pad as he looked benignly at the others, waiting.

"Coincidence," said Doctor Ebenstein.

Doctor Marquand wrote it down.

"No," Doctor Fillmore shook his head. "There are far too many concrete facts." Doctor Marquand drew a line through the word as Peter continued, "You yourself said so. We see something extraordinary in the data, and the digging you did into the history of these people is, well, it's an assemblage of facts for which I have no explanation. But coincidence is not a reasonable answer."

Doctor Ebenstein turned to Sylvia. "Did you get a chance to check other databases to see if Jim could have found the details anywhere else? Civil service files, social security administration, Red Cross? USO and other military service organizations? The Who-Where search engines? He *had* to have accessed that information."

"I spent days on it. I couldn't find any other reference to either Philip Osborne or Terry Walker. Hours, Doctor. I had expert librarians help me. I talked to a department head at the Library of Congress for over an hour. I called Boeing and spoke to the Company Historian. The Mormon Church data banks, the largest in existence, and their FamilySearch. The International Genealogical Index and other research sites. I even talked to a nationally renowned private investigator who specializes in tracking people down for inheritances and land titles and so on. Even he couldn't find anything. I have no place else to look."

"I knew you'd do a very thorough job," Doctor Marquand said, then he got up and strode around the table, hands behind his back, speaking slowly. "It's obvious that airplane is within minutes of crashing in the time frame of Terry Walker. Perhaps seconds. If Mister Drake is on it, he could be a dead man."

"You know," said Sylvia, "it seems that we're not the only ones interested in preserving Mister Drake's life. Who is this Vanqa? My guess is he's the one who is giving this 'perturb' command Jim reports hearing, and that's what seems to pull him out of the Terry personality."

"I think that is pretty clear," said Doctor Ebenstein. "But who or what the source of that could be is baffling. But it's definitely the trigger."

Doctor Fillmore said, "I suspect Jim's subconscious is trying to save him. Hell, when he assumes that D'zeos personality he doesn't even have any physical surroundings. He's not anywhere, and he never sees Vanqa. It's got to be a manifestation of his mind."

Maurice Ebenstein nodded grimly. "I agree. It's self-preservation on a subconscious level."

Doctor Marquand was shaking his head, and Doctor Ebenstein scowled at him as Doctor Fillmore raised his eyebrows, awaiting his comments when Sylvia interjected, "But look at the brain activity."

Doctor Marquand's head motions switched from negative to vigorously positive.

Sylvia addressed him directly as she added, "*That's* not subconscious visualization. The Vanqa-D'zeos episodes are dramatic. There is far more unique activity at those times than even during the airplane episodes. Those are the strongest readings of all."

"Let's leave that issue for later," said Doctor Ebenstein. "One thing at a time."

Doctor Fillmore said, "Okay. Without knowing such a plane actually existed I had reached the conclusion that he could die if he thinks he's on it when it crashes. That could occur whether he's time traveling or not. And I'm sure he is not." He turned to Doctor Marquand. "With that in mind, I drew a chart of time passage here in the real world versus the apparent passage of time when he thinks he's Terry Walker. Look." He opened his laptop and pulled up a graph. "The clock times are not well defined for Terry, but as you can see, being generous with the uncertainty, all we have to do is keep Mister Drake sedated for another few hours and enough time will have passed that the plane will already have crashed, with a large margin for error. He won't be able to become Terry Walker, because there won't be a Terry Walker on that time line."

Maurice slapped his hand on the table. "And if he still becomes Terry Walker, we'll know beyond doubt that he's created it in his mind, consciously or otherwise. Good. Knock him out!"

Sylvia lunged to her feet, her chair scraping harshly on the floor in the process, and leaned over the table with her palms resting on it. "What's wrong with you three? This is the most bizarre and challenging puzzle you'll face in your entire careers, and you don't even want to deal with it. You want to deny the facts and hide from them. Why are you afraid to get to the bottom of this? I thought we were involved for the opportunity to investigate something that's never been observed anywhere, by anyone, ever! We should be looking, measuring, probing, and finding answers or at least more questions to ask, not hiding our heads because we don't like the most probable outcome. You're even afraid to acknowledge it as a possibility, and hope that maybe it'll go away if we ignore it. What's wrong with you?" she repeated.

Doctor Ebenstein said with exaggerated calm, "We can't proceed with a dead subject, can we?"

Sylvia didn't bat an eye, but glared at him. "So you lied! You know darn well there's a lot more going on than common psychosis. You *know* that when he's D'zeos, it's not his subconscious trying to save him." She jabbed a finger toward Doctor Fillmore. "For God's sake, you must! It's right there in your MEG data." She swung that finger around to Doctor Ebenstein. "And in your own MRI data! It can't be denied without lying to yourself!"

Doctor Ebenstein seemed taken aback by her outburst. "It is puzzling," he said complaisantly.

"Puzzling? Puzzling?" she shouted. "There you are, using another weasel-word to avoid facing facts. It's more than puzzling, for crying out loud. It's a challenge slapping you in the goddamn face. Kicking you in the ass. It's a data set begging for explanation. For an answer that could significantly expand our knowledge of the human mind!"

Doctor Fillmore said, "Thank you, Sylvia, for injecting some common sense into this debate. We needed that. We had lost our vision."

Sylvia plopped into her chair, exhausted yet tense.

Doctor Fillmore seemed taken aback. "Well said, Sylvia. You're right. We had lost our vision."

Doctor Marquand said softly, "I'm glad you're going for your Ph.D., Sylvia. You've got confidence in your own intuition, and the courage to not be deterred by conventional beliefs." He looked at Maurice. "Especially those espoused by older, hide-bound, and crankier colleagues."

Doctor Fillmore burst into laughter, more in relief at having the tension broken than from Doctor Marquand's comment.

Sylvia relaxed too. Her frown left, and she said, "He's not old." Then she began giggling, then tried to stop, putting her hand over her mouth.

"Damn it, Aubert," said Doctor Ebenstein with his little twitch of a smile, "I'm her graduate advisor. Don't build her up so much. I won't be able to do a thing with her. It's hard enough now."

"Serves you right," he said, then turned to Doctor Fillmore. "Mr. Genius finally got a grad student that can give him a run for his money."

"You mean one that can run circles around him."

***

"You're to take one of these now." Aubert Marquand handed Jim a vial, then turned to Trina. "He's going to be knocked out for a solid seven hours." He looked around the hotel room. "Even when he's asleep, Trina, if you could just read a book or something, rather than turn on the TV or radio."

"Of course."

***

Waking up was a chore, and he didn't open his eyes right away. After a while he felt Trina caressing his forehead and he lay still, half-dreaming, half-thinking about him and her, especially about how he had never fully appreciated her, or really even shown her his love. He wiped at a tickle on his cheek. It was a tear. He wiped the other cheek, and opened his eyes.

Trina said, "Why were you crying, sweetheart?"

"Do you know how lucky we are?"

"Lucky?" Trina blinked, and pulled her head back to study him with her almost-frown. "We are?"

"I am. I have you."

***

The three doctors and Sylvia were once again seated around the little conference table in Doctor Ebenstein's office when Jim and Trina arrived. Jim, still sluggish from the drug, was shuffling along behind her.

After they were seated Doctor Marquand said, "We don't think you will become Terry Walker anymore."

That statement came through clear as a bell to Jim. He said, "He's dead, isn't he?"

Doctor Ebenstein raised his eyebrows, looked at Sylvia, then said to Jim, "What makes you think so?"

"For Christ sake, the plane was going to crash!"

Doctor Ebenstein nodded slowly as he studied Jim.

"That's why you put me to sleep, isn't it?"

"Yes." The doctor continued to study him, then seemed to reach a conclusion, giving a barely perceptible nod, perhaps to himself.

"How do we know I won't go back at an earlier time? Maybe just before the crash?"

"We don't."

"It sure seemed as if something was drawing me there over and over. Why do my visits have to be in chronological order? I know they have been, but if I can go back in time, why can't I go back a little farther next time?"

"We don't know that you can't. All we know is, at least so far there's been a forward time progression between every single trip."

"I'm really scared I'll keep going back to that airplane over and over and over, until I do die. I could keep living the same fate, like in the movie *Groundhog Day,* only nobody is being entertained."

The room was silent. Each face was a strange mixture of pity and thoughtfulness. The silence drug on, until at last Jim said, "You're not the ones who pulled me back, you know." He looked around the table, daring them to contradict him. Doctor Ebenstein frowned, but Doctor Fillmore merely raised his blond eyebrows.

Sylvia said, "Vanqa?"

"Yes."

"Who is he?" asked Doctor Marquand. "Why is he involved?"

"I have no idea. I've never even seen him. I don't even know if he's a person, for God's sake! I just hear a voice in my head, but it feels like he's real."

"I'm not sure we'll ever know," said Doctor Fillmore, "because I think it's very likely he does not exist."

"Why do you say that?" Jim asked.

"Just a guess. But if I'm wrong, I'd sure like to find out more about him. The brain activity for that, umm, for the Vanqa encounters has been extraordinarily pronounced."

"So is this it? Are you going to run any more tests?"

"Absolutely. We're all flying back to Los Angeles. We'll run more there."

Jim felt himself blanch. "No. No flying. I was there just before the crash, even though you put me out. The memory of that plane with the screaming, praying passengers. The yelling, cursing, shouting to God, the anguish. It won't go away. The helplessness, and at the same time the flood of memories—recollections of things that should have been said, things needing to be done or undone, love to be spoken, amends made, fondness or forgiveness transmitted. All impossible, never to happen yet so urgent. And dreams never to be, hopes and plans, children, grandchildren, birthdays, and Christmases. All this and more." He and added, "I really, really don't want to get on an airplane ever again. I don't want to even *think* about flying."

"Don't worry," said Doctor Marquand in a soothing tone, smothering the vestigial images in Jim's mind. "We're going to give you some medication that will keep you in the present for a while."

"Yeah, right. Another one of your fancy pills that don't work?"

Doctor Ebenstein laughed and said, "Too bad, Aubert. He sees right through you." For some reason, Doctor Marquand seemed delighted, chuckling as he twirled his hair. Doctor Ebenstein turned to Jim. "My pharmacological associates have engineered a compound that will disable, temporarily, the part of your brain that has been active in every episode. An unavoidable side effect will be significant loss of memory and reasoning ability, which is probably why Aubert is so pleased. You won't remember his failures."

Doctor Marquand just smiled.

"I'm glad you two are happy, but no way am I going to take a drug that'll wipe out my memory and my ability to reason. I'll just take the bus back to LA. I'll even pay for a couple of bodyguards so I don't hurt myself, or anyone else."

Doctor Fillmore leaned forward earnestly. "No, no, no. The effects of the drug will only last twelve to eighteen hours. We've got tests set up at UCLA for day after tomorrow. You must be there. The lab will be geared up and waiting. My staff is preparing right now."

Doctor Marquand resumed vigorously tapping his pen on his knee as he looked at Doctor Ebenstein. "There's a logical fault in your reasoning, Maurice. It may be impossible for your drug to work, just as mine did not."

Doctor Ebenstein's face tensed up. "Damnit, Aubert. Don't go there!"

"I must. Because if I'm right, your solution is irrelevant."

"Hold on," Jim said. "What the hell are you talking about? Oh shit!"

Trina faced him with her almost-frown. "What?"

"If I go to the future, I go no matter what. If the future says it happened, then it has to happen regardless."

"That's absolutely correct," said Doctor Marquand. "Nothing we do can change future history. If future history says he visited Baltimore today, then of course that's exactly what he will do."

"*If* his mind is actually time traveling," said Doctor Fillmore. "I think that's an absurd proposition, but for the sake of argument let's say he is. Then the brain will patch around your dead zone, Maurice, forming new synapses and pathways, or something else will happen to render your drug ineffective. On the other hand, we do not know what future history will be. In all likelihood the patient will not have visited any past or future today if we give him the treatment."

Doctor Ebenstein looked fierce. "Even suggesting that it might be time travel is ludicrous. Such unscientific nonsense shouldn't even be on the table. The drug will deaden the portions of the patient's brain where this disruptive activity takes place. Period. He will have no episode."

Jim said, "Damn it, listen to yourselves. I'm back to being a goddamn lab animal. Don't I have a say in this? Talk to me, not about me!"

Trina thumped her fist on the table. "At least you could have the decency to stop talking about him in the third person. He's sitting right here."

"I apologize," said Doctor Fillmore. "You're right."

Doctor Ebenstein said, "I'm not accustomed to dealing directly with patients, but that's no excuse. Sorry."

"Besides," Trina continued, "using your own logic, if he's time traveling he cannot have died in that airplane crash. He exists right here and now. As well as in the person of Talaan in the future, and perhaps even as D'zeos."

"That's wrong," said Doctor Marquand. "We know Terry Walker dies eventually. Philip Osborn died too, yet Jim is here. The only concern we had, Jim, was that if you were a passenger on that plane when it crashed, not only would Terry Walker die, but so would Jim Drake, because at that moment you would have been one and the same, at least on some level. On the other hand, if you are not one and the same at the time of death, the death of one would have no effect on the other."

"I agree with the logic," said Doctor Fillmore, "but not the supposition."

"Even if I didn't die in that airplane, it doesn't mean I don't go crazy in this existence. And if your little wonder drug is permanent instead of temporary, I may as well be crazy as to have no memory and no reasoning ability."

"I promise you," said Doctor Ebenstein, "it will be broken down by the body within hours. You will regain full mental function. And you'll still have some of your reasoning ability even while under the influence of the drug. Just nothing too abstract."

"Well, doctor, I may not remember that promise, but Trina will. And I would not want to be in your shoes if I don't come out of it."

Doctor Ebenstein gave his little twitch of a smile, then looked at Trina very soberly for a long time, eventually saying, "That will not be the case."

Chapter 15

Numbed Out

Jim was on the couch with a book in his lap, but he was not reading. He felt detached from life, a wanderer, and could not remember, well, much of anything. He was an uninvolved observer of events that involved him. He had been trying to reconstruct the details of the last few days but they seemed distant and unreal. He aware of the things that had happened, and that he had been frightened, but now the fear seemed like someone else's fear. It was a dusty telling about a series of events that had been filtered through a mildly interested third party.

Then a name came to him. Talaan. Talaan was a person he had become, some sort of engineer or computer scientist. Jim definitely felt an affection for the guy even if he was a little naïve and too submissive in his dealings with women. Jim mulled over the unusual name, dragging out the a's in his mind. He was pretty sure it could be spelled Tala'an, and wondered if it was, with the a's separated rather than slurred together. No, Zeleece had gotten in two a's when she said the name, but they came out as one sound with a slight drag in the middle, almost like a Southern drawl. He mouthed the name, "Tala'an. Talaan. Talan." He didn't like 'Talan' at all. A harsh sound like a bird's claw. Tala'an, though, he liked. "Tala'an," he said.

Trina looked up from her book. "You're memory's coming back, I take it?"

"I guess. I'm talking to myself, thinking about this guy I became. Talaan or Tala'an. I like him."

Trina gave a little chuckle, then said, "That's good. Since he was you. Or you were him." She laid her book on the end table, got up from her chair, and came over to sit next to him on the couch.

He put his arm around her shoulder and she snuggled close and that was nice, but it didn't seem right to just be sitting here in the afternoon. Shouldn't he be doing something? He was constantly doing something. He always had more to do than there was time for. But what? What was not getting done? He had no idea, and that was bothersome. "Isn't there something at the office I need to take care of? I can't remember a damn thing about what's going on."

"Abby has it under control. She's very competent." Trina lifted her head from his shoulder and looked into his eyes. "At first I didn't like her. I thought, I was afraid something was going on between you."

"I know. Are you sure there's nothing I need to do?"

"I'm sure."

Then another thought occurred to him. "Why wasn't I able to take time off before?"

"You could have."

"I guess. I never realized it."

"You should have. I asked you often enough but you always said you couldn't. Too busy. This to do or that to do."

He did? Damned if he could remember. He frowned and said, "There must have been a good reason."

"Huh-uh. You just obsessed over work."

"If I wasn't needed then how come I was so busy? Whatever it was, it must have needed doing." He slammed his hand against his thigh. "Damn, I hate this feeling!"

She reached over and patted his stiffened-up hand. "Just relax and enjoy the time off." She took his hand in hers and unwrapped his clenched fingers, then held it between hers. "You'll return to normal soon."

He looked at her beautiful face. The play of the oblique lighting crested her high cheekbones with bone-china highlights which accentuated the hints of mascara under eyes, and that drew his focus to them. They were arresting eyes, clear, translucent, a startling golden brown with sharply delimited pupils. It was as if they had an inner source of light drawing his attention like magnets while radiating interest and intelligence. Her pixie-like nose had an upward tip at the end, a puckish, impish little twist that seemed to be embracing the humor in life. She could easily have been a supermodel. He caressed her cheek. "I think I was stupid."

She almost smiled, but not quite. "I'm not going to argue."

"We'll see, when I get my mind back."

"Yes, we'll see." She snuggled back against him, then raised her head and reached for his book. "What are you reading?" She picked it up and read aloud, "*Awakening the Buddha Within,* by Lama Surya Das." She flipped through some of the pages. "Judging by the dog-ears and underlines you've read it before. Studied it."

He felt himself scowling. "I don't remember any of it."

"If it doesn't come back, it's never too late to start over."

"You know Trina, part of me wants to do that sort of thing, study and improve myself, and the other part wants to party, party, party and another part feels I should work, work, work. It seems appealing to alter my consciousness with meditation on one hand and with chemicals on the other and with business on a third. Drive fast cars, hop a plane to Vegas, go to concerts. Or become a living Buddha."

"You've more or less done that wild stuff for years, at least before you started working compulsively."

"Wasting a perfectly good life."

Trina raised her eyebrows. "This doesn't sound like you."

Jim pointed to his head. "This misfiring has caused me to think about what's really of value. I'll tell you what's not. The stuff I just said. Exotic cars, money, and party friends. There's not one thing there that I want to take with me into my insanity. Or my grave."

Trina searched his face. "Is that the drug talking?"

"Probably. But it's what I've been thinking. I've had time, you know, and I can even remember some, now that the drug's beginning to wear off."

"What would you take with you?"

He brushed her cheek with his hand. "Having loved and been loved. And having helped others find peace and love."

"I like this guy. Who are you?"

"The name's not important. You won't remember me in the morning anyway."

She nudged him with her elbow, then lay her head back on his shoulder. "Read your book."

***

Trina drove Jim to his office, arriving just after ten the next morning. The doctors had called early and were still fussing with their apparatus, so they had her give him another half dose of the memory-blocking drug. When they entered the office Abby was there, of course, and looking so sexy that fear and envy made Trina hesitate. Fear that Jim would find Abby too alluring to resist, that something had happened in the past, and envy because Trina couldn't bring herself to unselfconsciously and naturally cause men to desire her without seeming to try, the way Abby did. Why couldn't she be carefree and sexy too? Flirt without flirting. Lure without fishing. Attract without trolling. And be sexy with style and class. The woman was smart, too, and ten or so years younger. Why did Jim have to have such a good looking assistant? She knew the answer. It was because she was the best applicant. But darn her, she was so doggone likeable, so nice, so thoughtful, that Trina couldn't help but like her in spite of not wanting to.

Abby broke into a radiant smile. "Jim!" She scrambled to her feet. "And Trina." She looked closely at Jim. "It's so good to have you back. Are you okay?" She glanced at Trina for confirmation or denial as she gave Jim a hug.

Trina said, "He's medicated."

"They've broken me, Abby. I'm defanged and declawed."

Abby giggled, then embraced Trina. "Are you okay?" Her eyes radiated genuine concern, searching Trina's face, and Trina knew she would do anything she could to help her.

"I'm okay."

After a moment Abby drew back but held Trina's hands, silently offering support. "You look tired."

Trina tried to smile. "It's been a strain, Abby, but I'm okay."

"God, I've missed this place." Jim wandered into his office and over to his desk, absently riffled the small pile of papers on it, then walked to the drafting table he used for spreading out blueprints to bid on jobs. There were two rubber-banded rolls standing on end on the floor next to the table, each with a bidding slip attached. He bent over to read them and realized they all had a completed bid package.

Abby had actually bid on both of them, probably with Salvador's help, and left them here for his review. He picked one up and unrolled it on the table, setting the bid package aside. It was a large bundle, a big commercial project with a lot of heating, ventilating and air conditioning requirements. He began flipping through the sheets to get to the HVAC details.

As soon as Trina saw that Jim was absorbed in the plans she pulled Abby away from the open door and quietly filled her in on what had been happening. Then she said, "Just keep him busy looking at plans, or whatever. He won't remember much, so don't count on that. But keep him busy. He's got all day. The doctors thought he'd be better off here than at home so his mind is kept occupied."

"We've got two big jobs I bid on that he needs to review. Can he do that?"

"Probably, as long as he doesn't have to keep things in his mind very long."

Abby put her hand on Trina's arm. "What if he, what if he seems to be off on another trip? How can I tell. What should I do?"

"You can tell because he won't be here. He won't respond. He won't be working. He won't be doing anything. And what you do is..." she looked around. "You take that notebook, and hit him on the head with it."

Abby frowned, then got a half-smile.

"I'm serious. Or hit him on the shoulder, or yank on his arm. That's the sort of thing that brings him back."

"Well, okay."

"I mean it. Don't hesitate. That notebook's not going to hurt him, and neither is your hand. But leaving him somewhere else in his mind could. Promise me you will."

Abby's smile faded as her expression folded into something more than concern. Probably fear. "I will."

Trina looked at her watch. "I'll be back around twelve or twelve-thirty and bring lunch."

Abby started to go into Jim's office three different times but was so unsure what to say or do or how to act that she backed away each time. Hit him? Why couldn't she just call his name? What did Trina mean, he was elsewhere in his mind? She said they thought maybe it was something outside him that was causing it, that maybe it was some sort of time travel. That was crazy! Why couldn't Jim realize he was hallucinating, or whatever it was? Time travel? That was stupid. Why would Trina even say that? She must be under an awful lot of strain. When Jim thought he was somewhere else, couldn't he see where he really was? Surely he could. He had eyes. This just didn't make sense. It was probably good for Trina to get away for a while. Why hadn't she called her sooner? She could take a shift with Jim. She peeked in a fourth time, but Jim saw her and said, "Come on in, Abby. I have a question."

She walked over to the drafting table where he was standing with blueprints unrolled. She walked to his side and he ran a finger along a section of the plan she had prepared the bid on. "When you did the material take-off, did you plan on double wall ducting here in this main feed section over the offices, or just insulation?"

"Double wall. Salvador said that's what you'd want."

"Good!"

"Jim, I..." She moved close to him and rested her hand on his arm, looking deep into his eyes. "Are you going to be okay? Are they going to fix you, whatever it is that's wrong?"

"That remains to be seen." He put his hand on hers. "Keeping my mind occupied seems to be the best medicine. I can't remember from one page to the next, but I can do one page at a time. It looks like you did a great job."

"Can I do anything to help?"

"Abby, you already have. You've done a fantastic job. I really appreciate it. Thanks."

"You're welcome."

He turned and hugged her, and she hugged back. They stood silently, bodies pressed against one another, for a long time. He obviously needed comforting, and she inwardly scolded herself for feeling a certain amount of arousal. What was wrong with her? This was a sick man, and he needed her support. But she sensed that he seemed to be reacting that way too. Was that bad? Would it cause one of whatever it was he experienced? Should she back off, or respond?

Jim must have realized his emotions were coming alive. He dropped his arms and stepped back. "Sorry."

"There's nothing to be sorry about, Jim." She studied his face, and he seemed okay, so she said, "You seem a lot mellower than the old you, and I think I like that. I guess I am too, or I probably wouldn't like you being that way. We both used to be more emotional and intent."

"Maybe it's the drugs. I'll probably come to my senses later."

"Don't. This new guy seems to actually be a lot more sensitive. I like him better."

She smiled, and it was sunshine flooding the room, warming him, telling him the world was all right and so was he. He realized she was right, that they both seemed to have mellowed out. "I had to visit hell to realize that having fun has little or nothing to do with being truly happy in life. But you seem to have moved in that direction on your own."

"Don't put me on a pedestal, Jim. You and I have been close for years, and we were always on the same page."

"Yeah."

"If you need help, Trina said to yank on your arm or something. If you can, please let me know. I'll do anything."

"Abby, I never could've imagined myself saying this to you or any beautiful woman, but after Trina, you're my best friend."

She turned away and hurried from the office, and he knew she was crying.

***

Trina was curled up in her chair wearing her fuzzy pink slippers. She had been reading a book but was now looking off to the side, thinking or daydreaming. Jim was in his own chair with his computer in his lap and a game of solitaire up on the display, but he didn't remember how long he'd been playing. This damn drug had immobilized him mentally, but at least it seemed to be preventing his trips. He looked blankly out the window for a few minutes, then back to Trina. She seemed comfortable, but he could tell she was tense. There was even a line in her forehead. She looked tired, almost haggard.

She glanced over and saw that he was looking at her. "Jim? Are you okay?"

"Yeah, I was just thinking."

"About what?" She laid the book in her lap.

"About me. About us. You know, it's weird, I can remember our past together, but not many names or places. This morning I couldn't even remember where I filed the pricing data on my computer."

"What were you thinking about us?"

"I just realized today at the office. I told Abby. You're my best friend."

"God, Jim!" Her eyes filmed with tears as she scrabbled from her chair, dropped her book on the seat, and hurried over. She sat on the arm of his chair and kissed him all over the forehead and cheeks and pressed her face against his, smearing him with tears. "And you're mine, and have been for a long time."

"I'm going to try and treat you like you are."

"Jim, I—"

The phone rang. Trina started to get up, then settled back down, then got up and hurried to the phone, saying over her shoulder, "That could be the doctor."

She came back while talking. "Tomorrow? One PM? Okay—wait," she said when she saw Jim waving his hand. "Jim wants something."

"Tell him that it will be day after tomorrow. That you'll give me another dose tonight." Trina's forehead wrinkled with questions, and he added, "Tomorrow you and I are spending the day together. We're driving up the coast, lunch in Santa Barbara, spend some time on the beach. Tell him day after tomorrow, first thing in the morning."

Trina blinked several times, held back the tears, then broke into a smile as she said on the phone, "Jim wants to make it day after tomorrow so he and I can spend the day together driving up the coast and sitting on the beach. Is that all right, if I give him another pill?"

After listening for several moments, she said, "Thank you, doctor."

"What did he say?"

Trina brought the phone with her to his chair, took his computer and set it on the coffee table, and settled into his lap. "He said it might actually be better. It would give them more time to conduct the tests on the apparatus."

Jim nodded.

"You really have changed. I'm just wondering how much is due to the medication."

"Probably all of it. But we won't know for a couple of days, will we?"

Chapter 16

A jumbled lattice called Jim

Jim eyed the box in the lab technician's hands. It reminded him of the urn the crematorium had put his cousin's ashes in, the one the family had carried up to the mountains where they scattered his remains in a landscape he loved. "What's that? An urn for what's left of me after my mind crumbles?"

"Not quite," Doctor Fillmore said with a grin, "Not yet, anyway. It contains a radioisotope. We're going to inject you with a tracer compound. This particular radioactive chemical is designed to accumulate in areas of the brain where we have identified abnormal activity taking place."

"Will I glow in the dark?"

"No, but you'll glow in our images. We're going to run a PET scan. That will give us metabolic information, actual molecular function. It will complement our other data."

"What was that you injected me with earlier?"

"A compound to neutralize any residual neuroblocker."

"You mean the anti-memory drug."

"That was just a side effect. But yes, that one." He pointed to Jim's left arm. "Hold your arm out."

The doctor took his wrist and turned his arm over. Jim watched as he swabbed it with an alcohol swab, then the technician who had been carrying the box handed the doctor a syringe. As he eased the needle in, Jim wondered aloud, "Is this the ticket for my next thrill ride?" He raised his voice. "Hello, fantasy land! Here comes Jim-boy."

"You're so funny," Sylvia snickered.

"Jim, for God's sake!" Trina almost-frowned.

The doctor removed the syringe and pressed a cotton ball against the puncture. "Hold your finger against this." Jim pressed the cotton against his arm. "Actually," Doctor Fillmore continued as he bent Jim's arm at the elbow to hold the cotton in place, "it's not your ticket, it's our ticket. It's going to let us ride along with you." He looked at Trina. "No offense, but it will allow us to watch the activity that results from any trips he may take."

Sylvia nodded enthusiastically, "We'll see the actual chemical changes in his brain at the same time he's experiencing his time travels." She glanced at Doctor Ebenstein, and said in a more subdued manner, "If he does. Or whatever it is he's going through." She continued to look sheepishly at the doctor, silently asking forgiveness. He scowled and turned away.

Jim turned to Doctor Marquand. "As my travel agent, Doctor Marquand, where are you sending me this time? Tahiti in the eighteen-nineties surrounded by naked ladies? That would be interesting."

Trina just turned her head away, but a tiny smile tweaked the corner of her mouth in spite of herself. Sylvia and Peter chuckled, and even Maurice seemed amused.

Doctor Marquand smirked. "That was our second choice."

"And the winner is?"

"Your friend Vanqa."

"You're a strange dating service, Doctor. Setting me up with an invisible person that doesn't exist, and a man at that."

Doctor Fillmore picked up a virtual reality helmet that was sitting on the table and fitted it over Jim's head. The goggles were still up but room sounds faded as it was settled into place.

"What are all those wires connected to the helmet, Doctor? It looks something like your porcupine offspring."

He laughed, and said, "It is. They're EEG pickups. We're going to record electroencephalographic data at the same time as the positron emission tomography. That'll give us good time resolution as well as additional information." He motioned to Sylvia. "Set the pickups."

He noticed Trina biting her lower lip. She knew he wisecracked more when he was nervous, and his being nervous made her nervous. On top of that, he knew that she was concerned about whether they could bring him back. He was too, for Christ sake. More than concerned. And what about that airplane? Had it crashed by now? Or would he go back there anyway but at an earlier time? Trina had to be thinking the same sort of thoughts. No wonder she was upset. He was glad it was him and not her. That would be even worse. Trina saw him looking in her direction, although he wasn't actually looking at her, he just happened to be staring her way—or maybe he was, trying to imagine her thoughts, put himself in her place—so he smiled and gave a wink. She smiled back, but there was no humor in the expression. Mostly resignation. And hope. And what was supposed to be support.

"All right, lie down and in you go. These radio isotopes decay fairly fast."

Jim stretched out on his bed and was no sooner settled then he began moving into the machine. This device was not at all like the hulking MRI machine. It had a similar bed and trolley tracks, but the torus itself was less than a foot deep. It wasn't even a tunnel. Just a donut. Almost harmless looking. When the bed stopped Jim's head was near the center of the torus.

The doctor said, "You know the drill, Jim. Just relax."

"No problem. Maybe I'll take a nap. Dream about Tahiti." He started to ask the doctor why he was hoping he would meet Vanqa, but realized it was too late when the goggles were lowered. The time for conversation was past.

The bed rocked slightly, then a gentle rushing sound came, and barely visible wisps of coral and gold and green light appeared, swirling like strands of ribbon carried by invisible dancers. But that was all. After what seemed like a very long time, Doctor Fillmore's voice came over the headset, "Jim, are you still with us?"

"Yes."

"These stimuli aren't working. We're going to try something else."

"Got him, but the set is incomplete. He's metachronal and indeterminate."

D'zeos felt a surge of fright. This was not good. Metachronal and indeterminate? That implied they could lose him, scatter him irretrievably through a higher-dimensional web.

"That strong resonance. Quench it at once."

"We can't, it's a primary entanglement loop. He dissembles through the seven-mesh and actualizes at that four-well with high probability."

"Then leave Him metachronal."

Panic rampaged through D'zeos. No room for reason. Thoughts came too fast, jumbled, fear on top of other thoughts too fleeting to register, to be meaningful, to make sense. Blasts of red surged through whatever sensory receptors were assembled, overlaid by cankers of black pierced by numbing flares of white.

A frantic need to act emerged—yet he knew his mind and body were incongruent. Emblazoned to take action, yet catatonic.

"That is an unstable cusp."

D'zeos enfolded his avalanching thoughts and the bursting colors. Smothered them, shut them down. Took a moment of naught, then slowly let consciousness seep back in and realized, yes, he was scattered. He listened—felt—with his senses at the lattice points for orientation, for a grasp of condition and substance. There was very little. Nodes came and went. How the hell did he know this stuff?

"Try to maintain the balance until you get better coherence."

He felt like an eavesdropper listening in on plans for his destiny, and he did not like anything he heard. Actually, the conversation did not have an aural component. It was something else, but he could not describe it. They had him dissociated and dispersed over an extremely large higher-dimensional lattice, higher than four, for sure, if he was metachronal. But again—how did he know all this? They had pulled him here from Jim Drake. This was preposterous—how could they presume to do this? And it was dangerous! They didn't even have him locked, and they had been unable to amalgamate his fields to a convergent cluster. He had to do something to stop them. What? Nothing, not without being; he was formless and impalpable and there was no way he could cause himself to precipitate out and become coherent in a space of three dimensions and one of time.

"This balance will only be temporary. I told you, he's indeterminate, so we have random entanglement of strands.

We have the sevenfunctions and sixfunctions under control, but some fivefunctions are warping the geometry quite badly. He may actualize into fourspace at an undesired timeplace."

It was true. D'zeos could tell by the fluttering disquiet and ephemeral palpitations of his consciousness, the lack of unity, the flashes and a vagueness about his sense of self. But at least it was just fivespace that they had screwed up. The higher ones, which were far more difficult, were now under control they said. In fact, he felt cohesive enough to tell he was not tending toward a familiar timeplace, certainly not one where he belonged. Where he could exist. Apparently he had been attached to a divergent solution. It might be like before with Vanqa, perhaps worse. He again tried to stir, to make his presence known, to be extracted. His efforts were like trying to run in a nightmare with legs that would not respond, mired in a rubbery gel.

"The resonances are not converging to critical at the lattice points. But when they do lock, he's going to actualize."

"You already said that."

"It may be as Talaan. He has a primary entanglement with Talaan."

"Of course he does."

"It's starting! His wavefunctions are beginning to convolve and synchronize. The patterns are converging. He is going to actualize soon, but that timeplace will be your herenow with only a thirty-one percent probability, and it is fluctuating. Thirty-two percent. Thirty. Twenty-nine.

"This is too hazardous. Force an actualization right here, right now, with what you have."

"It might be incomplete."

"Do it! Now!"

"Hello!" A shimmering mirage shimmered amidst swirling silver fog. It consolidated into a small round man with a face-wide smile. He strode across the silver, semi-lustrous floor toward him, hand out. "Welcome, D'zeos. Sorry you were unplaced."

Panic surged. He knew it was Vanqa without being told. "Who are you, Vanqa? Why are you doing this to me?" He looked around wildly, and realized that nothing existed except the floor and he wasn't sure about that. It probably didn't either. But at least Vanqa was actually here, a strange looking little man with a round face and bright gold hair that stood straight up. He reminded D'zeos of Cupid in old paintings, except that he didn't have any wings. "I don't want to be here. Who are you, anyway? Are you an actual person? What are you doing to me?"

"I am Vanqa. Your friend."

"No, you're not. I know you're Vanqa, but you're not my friend. I don't know who you are." Yet he did know him. Knew him well. "Am I suffering from amnesia? Have I missed something?"

"Oh, no. No, no. Well, not really. Not amnesia."

He was right. It was time-related. "I've undergone a major time displacement. That much I know."

Vanqa grinned with his mouth that was too wide, the grin extending from one side of his cherubic face to the other, which caused his chubby cheeks to puff up nearly to his eyes. "Excellent! Yes, you definitely have. Welcome, my friend. Come with me."

D'zeos didn't comment on his use of the word friend again. Vanqa took his hand—and D'zeos could feel that hand; it seemed real, tangible, warm. It had texture; he squeezed, and it resisted just like a real hand should, yet Vanqa seemed—what? Prosthetic. Not truly human.

He led D'zeos toward some laboratory apparatus which had not been there a moment ago. But it was here now, and fear surged again. "What do you—"

"I don't mean to be brusque," Vanqa interrupted, "but I want to measure some of your parameters before you deconvolve."

Panic roared through him at new levels. Was he some sort of a madman's experiment? A metastable standing wave pattern in five or more dimensions? Yes. Of course. And they wanted to be able to grab him next time more completely and more easily. They needed parameters. Why? What was Vanqa up to? Who was supporting this work? D'zeos pulled back. "No. I don't want you to make any measurements. I don't want to come back here, Vanqa. Ever. I don't want to be time displaced. I want to be Jim Drake. I don't want you experimenting with me. Let me go!"

"This is very urgent, D'zeos, very very urgent. Please."

"No—"

Vanqa did something to the device—

Creation erupted. D'zeos was immersed in a rapture of light and color and glory. And terrifying infinities.

For an instant he experienced the universe! All of it. But it was incomprehensible even though it lay before him just beyond his five senses, beyond six, all right here. He could reach it but not, be part of it but not even though he was as it swirled in a jumble of dimensions and times tumbling and cascading. Obvious, logical and imponderable. He understood but could not.

Panic surged anew in the face of this power, this might. This infinity of infinities. "Stop!" He tried to flee, and a maelstrom of foggy tendrils swarmed over the multidimensional snarl. Grayness began to churn amid the colors, grayness that entangled him, obscured the display of creation and dirtied it.

Then the fog was gone. Whisked clear.

"Hello!" A shimmering mirage-like figure amidst swirling silver and gray fog consolidated into a small round man with a face-wide smile. He strode across the silver, semi-lustrous floor toward him, hand out. "Welcome, D'zeos. Sorry you were unplaced."

D'zeos was close to panic again. "Who are you, Vanqa? Why are you doing this to me?" He knew it was him without being told. He looked around wildly, and realized that nothing existed except the floor. But at least Vanqa was actually here, a strange looking little man with a round face and bright gold hair that stood straight up. He reminded D'zeos of Cupid in old paintings, except that he didn't have any wings. "I don't want to be here. Who are you, anyway? What are you—"

D'zeos froze with the realization he had already experienced this event. Then the scene wavered as if he were looking through a transparent shower curtain, and Vanqa evaporated into the fog.

D'zeos stared into it intently and thought he could make out a form, but no. It was a phantom of his imagination. Was he alone? Was he abandoned in nowhere? Could they retrieve him? Could he be reconciled? His mind seemed to be coherent. Then again there was motion, and a materialization from the vapidity. "Hello!" A shimmering mirage amidst swirling silver fog consolidated into a small round man with a face-wide smile. He strode across the silver, semi-lustrous floor toward him, hand out. "Welcome, D'zeos. Sorry you were unplaced."

What the hell was going on? He said, "Did you back up time?"

"Back up? No. I don't back up time."

"But we just did this. More than once. You really screwed something up. You're not in control, are you?"

"We had a little kink in the strands, that's all."

D'zeos decided it would be best to calm himself as best he could and decided to try a different approach so as not to upset whatever balance Vanqa and his friends had over this situation. So he said, "Vanqa, when did we meet?"

He studied the stiff golden hair, only about an inch long, the golden eyebrows with the pronounced arc, and the full red lips, almost pouting. He seemed almost like a holographic projection. Made-up, a mannequin, a composite, an actor. But he was solid.

"Relax, D'zeos. All is well." Vanqa put his arm around D'zeos's shoulders, a friendly gesture, and D'zeos felt a fleshy yet solid arm, a real arm, one with body warmth. Vanqa continued in his sing-song voice, "Of course you're confused, you have to be. We met now and millennia ago, D'zeos. In the twenty-first century and at this moment. Always and not yet."

"I hope that's a colloquialism."

"Of course it's not. You know better. It's a closed inequality."

D'zeos twisted away from Vanqa's arm and turned to face him. He needed answers. "Who am I, Vanqa? I'm not complete. I have no history, no self. I simply exist, yet somehow I know you and I know about Jim Drake and Talaan and the others. But nothing about myself." He gestured in an arc with his hand. "This isn't even a place. It doesn't exist, I know that much. I want you to quit playing games with me. Why am I here and why are you here?"

Vanqa said, "Since this is where you are at the moment, this is where we are. And these are not games, believe me."

"Who is we? All you have is riddles! Non-answers! Damnit, let me go."

"You have no idea how much effort this required. How many centuries."

"Fuck you!" D'zeos spun away; yet even as he did he wondered where he came up with that archaic term and realized in the same instant that it was from Jim Drake.

"Come back!" Vanqa shouted.

"No! Go create another plaything."

D'zeos had a groggy feeling, as if he was on the verge of deep sleep yet aware of his mysterious in-between state, unable to control which he would fall into. Colors swarmed, tumbled and gyrated across his senses, then faded and collapsed. He looked back, at Vanqa and the silver floor, and he and the floor seemed impalpable, at once opaque and translucent and diaphanous and solid.

"I'm teetering on a brink." He put his hand out for balance, and blinked to bring things into focus, to stop the underwater smear. The view snapped back. But then several little crystals of Vanqa and the floor and the silver fog fell away, just a few small pieces, then more, then many then a rush into a heap of shattered bits. The scene crumbled like a pattern in a child's kaleidoscope. Timespace folded, twisted and agonized as it writhed in eddies. He grabbed into the void for something solid.

"You're hurting my hand, Talaan." He relaxed his grip and she yanked her hand away and shook it, frowning. "What the zang's wrong with you?"

He looked around wildly, then realized the scene was complete. He was complete. Everything was real and—how did he get here? He was in the mining robot control room complex. He didn't remember arriving. He looked at Zeleece, and she was waiting for an answer. "Sorry," he mumbled. "I was... zang, Zeleece, how did we get here?" He turned toward the door, and there was no memory of entering through it, or of walking over to here. Not even of landing on the company pad. He was just suddenly here. What the zang was going on?

"What do you mean, how'd we get here? We took the company lander from that shuttle."

"I don't remember. I'm blank."

"Are you having some sort of attack? Do you have chest pains?"

"No. It's just that I'm blank on how we got here and what we're doing." He took in his surroundings, trying to get oriented. "Is it just you and me?"

"Brenicia is with us, you know that. She's waiting out in the visitor lobby so we can go with her to study those talking plants when you're through here. The Talal'a." She took his hand and lifted it up. "Are you dizzy?"

He shook his head. "No. It's just, I don't know. For some reason I've blanked out the recent past. What were we doing?"

"You're *not* alright." She moved closer to him, then hesitated. "We were going to softwire your robots some new psychocircuits," she said slowly and uncertainly. "What's wrong, Talaan? Are you afraid to do it now? Is that it?" She put her hand on his forehead, frowning. "You don't seem to have a temperature."

"That's not it. It's... I'm... Haven't we done this already?"

Zeleece's expression hardened, between puzzlement and anger. "What the zang is wrong with you?" she said again. She looked him over from head to foot. "Do you need a medibot?" He hand hovered near her communicator.

"No. But I feel like I've been here. Done this. Like you and I... Zeleece, did you ask me to marry you?"

"You *are* crazy!" She backed up, taking little steps away from him. "Zang, no! I *never* want to get married." She seemed ready to run. "Is that what you're thinking? That we should actually make that commitment? Talaan, don't even—"

"No, no. It's just, I don't know what's wrong. It's like déjà vu. I must have blacked out or had a dream or something. It seemed so real, like you'd asked me. But I had no thought of marriage." He stepped up to her and took both hands in his. "I must have dreamed that you asked me."

"More like a nightmare."

Then he lied, "Yeah, it probably was. I've never had any thought of marriage."

"Good. Then we can still be lovers." She relaxed a little. "As long as you're not crazy." She felt his forehead again, then his cheek.

"I don't know what it was. It was like my mind left me and was elsewhere. I would have sworn we already did this, that we reprogrammed the robots. But now, things are falling into place."

She leaned back to look into his eyes. "Have you been experimenting with the psychoslaps those young Andromean fools use to resonate with their so-called Velapulse rhythm? Or some of whatever it is those out-of-time freaks use to make themselves think they're from another era?"

Talaan shook his head vigorously. "Outtime freaks. They're called outtime freaks. Zang, no. Those people are crazy! I don't use drugs, you know that. I don't know what it was. I feel fine now."

Zeleece relaxed. "If you're sure, then let's go enhance your robots and give them a chance to evolve."

"Let's go." He knew where he was, knew what they were doing. But it still seemed as if he'd lived this entire sequence before. He shook off the feeling. Or rather ignored it, and said, "We'll start with the master control. His name is Ron," and as soon as he said it he knew what Zeleece would say. He knew it, because he could remember it happening. She was going to laugh, and then exclaim about him having a name, an old-fashioned one at that, and then say she 'loved the shit out of it,' her favorite expression.

Zeleece laughed. "Ron? He already has a name? And it's Ron? How quaint. I love it! Ron." Her face squished up in a grin as she chuckled again. "I love the shit out of it, Talaan. Ron."

He took a breath, almost afraid of himself, and concentrated on her. On her beautiful dancing eyes. And let that weird déjà vu feeling pass. They knew each other so well they could predict responses. That's all it was. He gathered his composure and said, "Giving him a name made it easier to direct instructions to him. What I mean is, it made it easier for me. It seemed more like I was dealing with a human."

Zeleece couldn't stop grinning. "You aren't the uncaring yanko you put on to be. I knew you had something else inside you. Some shred of humanity."

"To tell you the truth, Ron has actually evolved a personality. Much more than I expected him to, and faster. He even cares about the slave robots. Sometimes he acts more like a father to them than the central computer."

"Talaan, I feel good."

"Let's go put in our programs. I'll let Ron know what we're doing." He turned and headed for the control room.

"Wait a minute!" Zeleece grabbed his arm and pulled him around so they were once again face-to-face. "Much more than you *expected him to*? And *our* programs? You've been doing psycho updates all along, haven't you, you yanko? Trying to make them more human. You didn't *tell* me?" She hit him in the shoulder. "You... you..."

"Well, I did a little. Actually, I've been adding a little at a time for quite a while now. That's why they're evolving."

"So! It's because of you! You just didn't want me to know. You were afraid I might go too far and the corporate peek-a-boos that reside in the master program would detect it." She hit him again.

Perturb.

"Damn!" He rubbed his shoulder, then felt as if he was going to pass out. The world faded to gray. Then his mind snapped back into focus. He said, "I'm back, I'm back. Stop hitting me."

Doctor Fillmore raised the goggles, took his arm and helped him sit up, then removed the helmet. "You probably didn't need to hit him, Trina. He actually slipped back quite easily, according to the data. Those lit-up areas of his brain just seemed to suddenly quench themselves."

"I was scared." She looked at Jim, then bent over and kissed him. "I'm sorry, honey."

Doctor Marquand took the other arm and helped him stand. "How are you, Jim?" He held the arm tightly. "Can you stand okay?"

"For some reason I feel less traumatized than usual. Like it was easier. What I mean is, the return. It just happened, bam!"

"Was something different this time?"

"Was it ever! Everything was different. And it makes me wonder if I might go back to the airplane."

The lab came to a standstill as everyone snapped their heads around to look at him. Sylvia, Jim noticed, had her hand over her mouth.

Doctor Ebenstein frowned as he asked, "Why?"

"At first I was D'zeos, but not fully materialized, and then I seemed to become partially real, and Vanqa actually existed. He was there, I saw him and talked to him, but before that, when I was immaterial, I heard him and someone else trying to get me there. But even when I was materialized nothing existed except me and the floor and Vanqa. He tried to make some measurements on me, and I think he did, but I struggled, then suddenly became Talaan. *But I was out of time sequence!* I was Talaan at an earlier time than the last time."

"Damn!" Doctor Marquand's eyes stabbed into Jim's "F-ing damn!"

"Yeah. I know. Zeleece and I were back on Ektar, and were about to modify the psychoprograms on those mining robots to increase their social inclination. Brenicia was nearby, waiting for us. But we'd done all that before. You got the report from me."

"Damn!" said Doctor Fillmore as he pounded his fist into his palm. He continued hitting it. "Damn! Damn! Damn!"

"Vanqa made measurements?" Doctor Ebenstein pounced like a lawyer. "Tell us all about it. How did he do it? What kind of measurements? What did the equipment look like? How'd he hook it up to you?"

That guy didn't seem to give a damn about Jim or what he went through.

Sylvia reached out to Jim, putting her hand on his arm. "How could you be out of time sequence?"

"Sylvia, wake up!" Doctor Ebenstein's voice was a stinging, brittle slap. "Why is that any more preposterous than believing he's actually time traveling in the first place? If you insist on believing that, what law of physics says his visits have to be in chronological order?"

Sylvia looked at him blankly, shaking her head. "I don't know. It just seems reasonable."

"Ah. Reasonable. Time travel is reasonable if the visits are in sequence. Otherwise it doesn't make sense."

"Well," said Doctor Marquand, "it would certainly be more orderly if that were the case." He turned to Jim. "Tell us everything. Go through every detail." He rummaged in his briefcase and pulled out his memory stick and iPad. "Come over here." He walked toward a desk against the wall.

Chapter 17

Why? Why not?

"I'm going to have you do something different," said Doctor Fillmore. "You said you've done meditation in the past. I want you to try and meditate for me. I want to see if there's any correlation with your other brain activity."

"It's been a long time." Jim looked at Trina, who almost-frowned, then he turned back to the doctor and said with a shrug, "What the hell. I'm willing to do anything to get to the bottom of this."

Trina leaned toward the doctor. "What if he takes another trip? Mediation might induce one, and it seems to be getting more dangerous the way he was tossed around in time when he became D'zeos and Talaan, repeating things that had already happened, not materializing, being dispersed, and all that. Is this really necessary?"

Doctor Fillmore gestured with a helpless shrug. "It's possible, but I don't see why it would. We have to try something. We may not learn anything new, but we'll take whatever we can get. We have absolutely no diagnosis now, and therefore no treatment. Any additional insight no matter how small might help us piece together a more complete picture. And who knows? Meditation might offer a path to control it."

She slumped in her chair. "I know. It just seems so futile."

The doctor compressed his lips.

Jim stood up. "Let's get on with it."

"Right." The doctor ushered them into a quiet little alcove off his laboratory, an office of some sort with a big window that looked out on the lab. He placed the EEG helmet on Jim's head. "Do you need anything? Dim lights, music?"

"A serene mood," said Jim with a shake of his head. "I really don't think I'll be able to do much for you. Not what you want."

"Just give it a try. We know what the meditative state looks like in typical subjects, we've got maps in various data banks. I want to see what areas are involved in your brain, if they're different." The doctor wheeled an upholstered desk chair over next to where Jim was sitting on the edge of the desk. "Make yourself comfortable."

Jim sat. The chair squeaked, and it had a brittle feel and that faint, just at the edge of the senses musty aroma of decades-old office furniture. It had no doubt been used by generations of students and professors. Been witness to many events. It was a little lumpy, but not bad – who had sat in it? How many people? Where were they now, what were they doing? How old were they? He scooted his butt around and maneuvered himself back in the seat so that his lumbar was supported as well as possible, and found that it fit him fairly well.

"We're going to leave you alone."

"Yeah." Jim closed his eyes, placed his hands loosely in his lap, took a deep breath, and consciously relaxed. Relaxed his shoulders, his brow, then his scalp. He tried to stop thinking, to isolate himself from the world and from his body. He wondered what the doctors were seeing, then realized he was thinking and stopped the thought. He willed himself to float in a silent place. And found his mind active, wondering about Abby at work. He stopped that thought and sought inner silence again but felt a prickling on his forehead. He was able to stop paying attention to it and retreat again to a state of emptiness. Huge, deep stillness. Even though he was immersed in silence, in the absence of thoughts, he had to be sure not to think about that. He rested there where everything was serene, where the infinity was peaceful and the silence profound, and watched himself, and he became overwhelmed with terror.

Perturb.

And he was Jim. What if he became D'zeos permanently? And lived in that crazy world that was not a world? And never saw Trina again! Terror swarmed, and he opened his eyes. Doctor Marquand was standing in front of him. "Jesus! Don't ask me to try again."

Doctor Marquand removed the EEG helmet, and Doctor Fillmore's voice came from somewhere out in the lab proper, "You did very well. It even looked like you took a trip for a brief moment."

"I became D'zeos. But only for a second. I shoved him away before I even saw any surroundings and grabbed myself back."

"It's amazing," said Doctor Ebenstein, also from the lab. "From this cursory look, for a very brief time you did about as good at meditation as I've seen. I think I need to apologize."

Jim turned around so he could see him, then stepped out of the alcove and into the lab. "Apologize for what?"

"You actually have amazing control. I expected the opposite because of the ease with which you flitted from one personality to another during your so-called trips."

Jim felt a surge of anger. "You expected the mind of a witless moth attracted to bright objects?"

"No, I—"

"Should I thank you or give you the finger?" He was already giving him the finger mentally.

"Jim!" Trina said. "What in the world's wrong with you?"

Jim looked at her for a moment, then said, "Nothing in *this* world, dear."

She shook her head and turned to Doctor Ebenstein, but then when Jim looked at him he saw a big grin, actually a friendly one. "Probably both," the doctor said. "No, on second thought, just the finger."

"That sounds right," agreed Doctor Fillmore.

Jim looked in Doctor Fillmore's direction, but he had moved behind some lab equipment. "What did you find? Anything?"

"We've got many channels of data. But from a quick look there doesn't seem to be anything unique about the physiometry of your meditative state compared to our baseline of other subjects. The overall patterns and intensities do not seem to be connected to your trips, although many of the same areas of your brain are active. Except for a period of about two hundred milliseconds. You say you were D'zeos?"

"Yes."

"I can see it. Dramatic, dramatic changes in the patterns, but very fleeting. Like flashbulbs in a football stadium."

"Does that tell you anything?"

There was no answer from Doctor Fillmore, and when he looked at Doctor Ebenstein the doctor gestured helplessly, so Jim turned to Dr. Marquand, who said absently, “If it does, I don’t know what.”

“That I can get away from Vanqa?”

“He didn’t even see you, did he?”

“I don’t know if he saw me, but I do know he didn’t latch on to me.”

Doctor Fillmore arched an eyebrow.

Jim continued, more or less thinking aloud, “It kind of seems like maybe Vanqa always has been involved. Or at least watching.” The last time he had been D'zeos, he had known that Vanqa was in control, or at least trying to be. “In my earlier trips there, there was no evidence of Vanqa, but gradually he’s become more and more prominent and the last time there was no question that I visited him. I don’t mean just now, he didn’t have me, but he sure did the last time. I overheard him and his cohorts deliberately manipulating spacetime in several dimensions higher than four.” He thought about the experience. It really had felt like it was a wild experiment of Vanqa’s, that they were learning as they went, practicing on a live subject. Surely this sort of thing would be illegal. Aside from the ethics issue, what government would allow its citizens to manipulate past history and run the chance that they would change it enough that a different government was in power? Manipulating history would be absolutely forbidden. So either Vanqa and his partners were part of an outlaw nation or independent planet, or they were a big corporation engaging in illegal activities. “There’s no question in my mind that he’s doing it, and he’s getting better, and what he’s doing is sure as hell illegal.”

“Come on, you people.” Doctor Ebenstein was glaring at no one in particular.

Sylvia gestured very intensely to Doctor Marquand, "I bet the reason Jim went back as Talaan out of time sequence is because Vanqa didn't have a good lock on him, and they messed up whatever it is they're perturbing. The spacetime lattice, or something. Vanqa's assistant, whoever was talking before Jim materialized as D'zeos, said as much. It sounded as if they were desperate, and settled for just part of him." She looked at Jim. "You said the place felt like it didn't exist."

Just thinking about the experience brought quivers of apprehension scrambling over Jim's back. "It didn't. It was like a virtual reality simulation where they haven't done the background yet. It was me and him, and he didn't feel real. It's hard to describe, but it was surreal or dream-like." He took a slow deep breath and tightened the muscles across his shoulder blades to chase away the quivers.

She continued, "Whatever they're doing with spacetime and some higher dimensions, it was all messy. When they grabbed you, part of you was elsewhere. So when D'zeos left, the Jim-you was flung toward the nearest convergent point, and that was Talaan at an earlier time."

"Sylvia, do you have any idea what you just said?" Doctor Ebenstein sounded like a parent scolding a child.

Sylvia did not back down. "Yes I do, Doctor. I was mimicking their jargon, and I bet I got the general idea. They didn't have a solid connection, and Jim fell away to the nearest energy minimum in higher-dimensional spacetime. A four-well, they called it. To me that means a location in real space and real time." She looked at Jim, and he nodded yes, and she continued, "A minimum in the energy field in some sort of timespace grid, or whatever."

Doctor Ebenstein closed his eyes and shook his head vigorously as he turned away. "Dear God."

"That's pretty much the way it felt, Sylvia."

"I think you all need medication," Doctor Ebenstein growled, still with his back to them. "I have some of Jim's pills left over. Form a line to my right." He poked toward the floor to his right, repeating the motion several times. "Right here. Ladies first."

Doctor Marquand wagged his finger at Doctor Ebenstein's back. "Wake up, Mo. Vanqa told D'zeos that the twenty-first century was when they met. He knew that." He looked at Jim.

Jim nodded.

Doctor Ebenstein whirled around with a ferocious look. "For Christ sake, it was Jim who knew that. Those people don't exist. They're a product of his subconscious mind!" He held out his open palm toward Jim. "They're a delusion in our patient."

"Telepathy?" mused Sylvia. "Could he be using telepathy to make the connection, Jim?"

"God!" Doctor Ebenstein slapped his hand to his forehead. "Isn't time travel enough? Do we have to add telepathy? How about psychokinetics while we're at it so we can make things fly around the room. Teleport me that pen, Sylvia." He held his hand out while he looked away.

Sylvia threw the pen that she had been gesturing with, and giggled. In spite of himself, the doctor laughed aloud as the pen clattered on the floor near his feet.

Jim said, "Vanqa hasn't tried to put thoughts in my mind, and he doesn't read my mind. It doesn't seem like it, anyway. I mean, when they were talking to one another I heard them without sound, I don't know how, but I did. But I was overhearing them, it's not like they were putting thoughts in my mind. And there wasn't anything like that when we were face-to-face."

"I don't know about that," Doctor Fillmore said, rubbing his chin, "but it's a fact that your brain activity is different when you become D'zeos than when you're anyone else. The regions of maximum brain activity are also more sharply delimited."

"It worries me that you were out of time sequence," said Doctor Marquand. "But as you said, maybe Vanqa was not getting the solid connection he wanted. You said you were confused at first when you became Talaan."

"Yeah. I was just there, with no recollection of arriving." He looked at Doctor Ebenstein. "Like when I'm coming out from under your damn drug. But then after a while Talaan got a grip on reality. I think Vanqa let go so I would be all there. Like you said, Sylvia, he didn't have everything under control. Until the end. Then everything made sense, and Talaan knew where he was and what he was doing, and he didn't know anything about Jim Drake or D'zeos."

"Let's assume," said Doctor Marquand, twirling his hair, "that Vanqa really does want you there as D'zeos. Just suppose. Now the question is, why would he want that?"

"Nobody in his own time likes him," snapped Doctor Ebenstein. "He's trolling spacetime for a friend." Everyone smiled, surprised at his change in attitude. Sensing their confusion, the doctor added, "Since not one of you will be reasonable, I figured I may as well be stupid too." He made a goofy face and stuck his tongue out.

They all laughed, and Jim said, "The guy does want to hold my hand a lot."

Doctor Ebenstein displayed a full smile, and Sylvia took his arm and squeezed it. "You're so funny, Maurice."

"Call me Morrie." He beamed at her. "When we're away from faculty and other students, that is." He glared at the other two doctors. "You can ignore these characters. Just assume they're not here. They may as well not be."

"Can I call you Morrie, too?" said Doctor Fillmore, struggling to keep a straight face.

"No, Peter. To you, I'm Doctor Ebenstein. Or Sir."

"Whatever you want, Morrie." Doctor Fillmore turned to Doctor Marquand, and as quickly got serious. "All right, Aubert, let's play your game. Why would Vanqa want Jim there?"

Doctor Marquand tapped a pen on his knee, looking off in the distance. Eventually he said, seemingly to himself, "I wonder if physical contact helps Vanqa lock D'zeos into his spacetime?"

Sylvia answered, "It seems like he's experimenting, trying to discover how to materialize Jim as D'zeos. To develop some sort of time travel for his personality so he's solidly in that far future."

"No." Doctor Ebenstein shook his head emphatically. "He'd pick someone closer to him in time, at least to start with. No experimenter would try to take a huge leap at the beginning. If you were developing the first radio, you'd try to transmit across the lab first, not from here to China."

Sylvia nodded in agreement.

"I'm not sure it would be any easier to accomplish," said Doctor Fillmore, "but it would certainly be easier to verify the results if the subject came from the recent past. Like last week, or an hour ago."

"The more I think about it," Doctor Marquand said, "the more unlikely it seems we'll be able to deduce the reason he wants Jim there. At least not with the data we have. On the other hand, if we take Jim's reporting at face value it's certain that Vanqa wants him there very badly. Very badly, indeed.

Doctor Ebenstein raised one finger in the air. "That much I can agree with. *If* we take it at face value. But that's a huge if."

"But why?" persisted Sylvia. "Why would he?"

"Whatever it is, said Doctor Fillmore, it has to be of tremendous importance."

Doctor Marquand continued to twirl his hair. "Peter, I suspect it's of importance to many more people than just Vanqa. It's obvious that they're having a f-ing hard time accomplishing what they want. He said they've been at it for centuries. That's a huge, almost incomprehensible undertaking, which means there's more than one scientist or scientific team involved. It's had continuity and funding for a long, long time."

"We have no way to know."

"Here's another set of questions." Doctor Marquand began counting on his knuckles, resting his finger on the first one. "Was Jim chosen, or was it a random selection?" He moved to the next one. "If he was chosen, why him? What is it that's special about him?" He tapped the next knuckle. "If it was random, then how and why do they keep coming back to him? He's not all that willing a subject." Then he tapped the knuckle of his little finger repeatedly. "If they chose him, how could they possibly have located him, one specific individual out of the entire population on earth, one person who will live for maybe a hundred years at most, from Vanqa's position thousands of years in the future?"

"Unanswerable," said Doctor Ebenstein. "But if any of this time travel crap is true, there has to be something about Jim that makes him susceptible to whatever mechanism they use for locking on to an individual. Of course, there could be others. Many others. People from the present time, and people from other times." Suddenly he frowned and swept the others with a glare. "I'm just playing along with your silly game. I don't believe any of it for one second."

Doctor Fillmore said, "If any of our suppositions are true, then I agree that whatever the reason it has to be of major significance to future humanity. In fact, it must mean the very survival of human civilization."

"You know," said Doctor Marquand, "if Jim has been chosen deliberately, we're chasing the wrong quarry."

There was silence as everyone tried to follow his reasoning.

He continued, "If that's the case," he waved off Doctor Ebenstein, "I know, I know. There are a lot of ifs—but *if* they chose him, then there is nothing wrong with Jim. He's perfectly normal. The answers we're seeking, or should be seeking, are who they are, and why they are connecting with Jim and transporting some aspect of his mind to the future."

Trina had been following intently, and now took a step forward and said, "Doctor Marquand, do you think that's a real possibility?"

He shrugged. "I don't know, but it's all I've got."

"If that's correct," Doctor Fillmore said, "then Jim's trips to the past where he became Terry Walker and Philip Osborne before that, and also the ones to Talaan, were misguided efforts. The experimenters were trying for D'zeos but didn't have enough control over the parameters to prevent him slipping into some deeper or stronger fourwell, as they call them. Or maybe the ones earlier in time were just much easier. Perhaps those fourwells were where the parameters matched those of Philip, Terry, and Talaan."

"Good God!" Doctor Ebenstein slapped his forehead again. "If you guys keep this up I'm going to get a headache from slapping myself. I think it's time for a reality check. You should hear yourselves."

"All of you, stop!" Jim thrust his hand up. "Just hold on a damn minute. For some reason I'm still concerned about my welfare. I'm the one who's going back and forth becoming other people. Can we focus on my condition?"

Doctor Marquand said, "We have been, although I guess it didn't sound like it."

"No, sure as hell it didn't. I slipped into the future and back a lot easier this time. Yet now you say maybe there's nothing wrong with me! Are you trying to cure my condition, or are you playing scientist games while my sanity dangles by a thread? It seems to me you're more concerned about publishing papers in scientific journals and getting your names in the news than curing me. He glared at them one by one and decided, to his surprise, that Doctor Ebenstein was probably the least guilty of them all. They locked eyes for a long moment, then Jim inclined his head ever so slightly. The doctor's expression relaxed, unspoken acknowledgement.

The doctors glanced at one another, silently selecting the one who would respond. Doctor Marquand said, "Jim, we see astounding activity in your brain. We know that you are not a bystander, that you are the one and as far as we know the only one who is so intimately involved. One of the many things we don't know is whether it's caused by internal or external stimuli. If you are truly visiting the future, the initiating agent *could* be external. In that case, you are probably perfectly normal, at least in most ways." He paused and waved his finger upward, toward the heavens. "It's entirely possible there's nothing physically or mentally wrong with you. You're being manipulated by an external agent. But the important thing from your perspective is, it may not be a problem within your mind."

"Oh. I see. If it was something in me, maybe you could fix it. If it's not, if it's caused by some intelligence that exists in the future it's totally our of your control and…" He could not finish the sentence. There was no need anyway, to say that there could be no cure. He stared at Doctor Marquand, and the doctor nodded grimly.

Then he had to say it. "That would mean I'm not crazy, but you doctors can't stop my trips or do anything to help me."

No one responded.

How could they? What would they say?

Finally Doctor Marquand said, "That could be the case. But it may not be."

Hoping—fruitlessly he knew—that they would gain some crucial insight if only he could shed more light on it for them, he repeated some of what he'd told them right after the experience. "Vanqa did do that scan on me. And when he did, things got really weird. I told you, it was complete déjà vu afterward. We recycled the exact same event twice more, like a hiccup in time with Vanqa striding across that silver floor welcoming me. So it's absolutely a fact he was doing some major timeplace manipulation, at least at that time, which means at least some part of what was happening was controlled by him. His number one priority was to measure something on me."

"Some of your parameters," said Doctor Fillmore.

"Yeah. I'm no doctor, but that seems to verify that they're trying to improve their ability to zero in on me and make me become D'zeos. If that's true, then it really is me they're after."

The doctor nodded slowly. "Exactly."

"Then why do I need something to set me off? You know, a sound or a picture or something?"

Doctor Fillmore twisted his lips like he had something sour in his mouth, then said, "Maybe it's them who needed something extra, and perhaps now that they've made measurements on you, they don't."

"Our stimuli may have made your mind more compatible with whatever it is they're doing, or at least with what they're probing with," said Doctor Marquand. "In a way, like meditation alters your state of consciousness."

"You people have gone off the deep end." Doctor Ebenstein began pacing. "You've completely accepted time travel and aren't seeking the real answer."

Sylvia scowled at his back.

Doctor Fillmore said, "You're ignoring the evidence so as to hang on to a conventionally acceptable answer. But there *is* no conventional answer."

"Bull poop."

But Jim noticed him give a sly wink to Sylvia, who smiled proudly. The doctor was merely prodding the others to think of alternatives. He said, "The only way to get answers to these questions is for me to go back and become D'zeos again. I sure as hell don't want to, but I don't see any alternative. You doctors can't do anything, you don't really have a clue, and this has to come to an end one way or another."

"No!" yelled Trina. "It's too dangerous. That Vanqa wants you there. One of these times he'll just keep you. It gets easier every time. No, please don't. You won't be able to function."

"I functioned okay last night, didn't I?"

Trina turned a frown on him, a real frown with creases. "You jerk!" Her fists were doubled up at her sides.

He stepped over to her and put her clenched fists around his neck, and put his own arms around her waist and pulled her to him. He said softly, "I've got to, Trina. If there's ever going to be any sort of resolution to this, if this is ever going to come to an end I've got to. There's no solution here, that's for sure, but maybe, just maybe, there'll be one there." He turned his head to Doctor Fillmore and said, "Just make sure that I don't go back to Terry Walker and that airplane."

The doctor said, "Jim, I don't want you going anywhere tonight. We need to plan. We need to think. And we need to monitor you. Peter has overnight patient facilities here." He turned to Trina. "You too. We'll have food sent in."

"No," Jim said. "I've had enough of medical labs. I don't need to sleep in one too, and eat hospital food. I'll come back in the morning, but I don't want to spend the night."

"Just the one night?" Trina asked the doctor, ignoring Jim.

"No," Jim said

The doctor held his hands out in a helpless shrug. "I have no idea what tomorrow will bring."

"We'll stay as long as necessary."

Jim said loudly, "I may as well talk to the damn wall." He turned his back to them and said loudly, "Hello, wall. Why don't you just stay put like a nice wall? I'll bring you some paint tomorrow. It'll make you feel real pretty."

"Jim, stop it!" Trina stomped her foot. She didn't have the creases but was frowning anyway, as the others chuckled.

Peter said, "I want you to wear an EEG cap all night. I've got a modified one with a neck support that will allow you to sleep with reasonable comfort."

"I can just imagine. But at least that's a good reason for me to spend the night here at your hotel. If I have another trip I want you to get whatever data you can, even though I don't think it'll help. And more importantly I want someone to see what's happening and pull me out of it."

Trina said, "I know we should be grateful for all this expert attention, all these facilities dedicated to Jim. But it's a terrible strain."

Jim bowed his head to the doctor. "Jim, the lab rat. At your service." He held his hands out, drooping them like paws.

Even Maurice got a grin. He came over and put his arm around Jim's shoulders. "That's a good little rat. Now go spin your wheel."

Jim decided he liked him.

"I wish you wouldn't do this," said Trina with more than a tinge of desperation in her voice. "It's just too dangerous." She turned to glare at the doctors, one after the other, her clenched fists on her hips. "I don't want him to."

Jim gently brushed his fingers against her cheek. "Trina, I may as well go willingly. I'm sure Vanqa is the one behind it, and if that's true we can't control it anyway. He'll keep pulling me there no matter where we are or what I'm doing. I'll go sooner or later no matter what. Maybe we can learn enough to stop it once and for all. It's for damn sure we won't if we don't try."

"I know," she said faintly. "I know." She squeezed him harder. "But what makes you think they'll be able to find out anything this time?"

"I doubt if they will. Vanqa hasn't been very cooperative. But what's our alternative?"

"I don't know. I know you're right. I'm just scared, honey. Really scared."

"I am too." And he was. His fate, his very life was being manipulated by persons in the future, by means and for reasons he could not comprehend, at times of their choosing. —No, not entirely. The doctors had been able to induce trips in him, but it seemed as if the only thing that had done was make it easier for Vanqa and his cohorts to latch onto him. Like fishermen sitting there waiting, poles out and lines extended in the waters of time, watching for the float to bob. If only he knew what they were up to maybe he could do something about it. But what? Refusing to cooperate didn't work. Maybe cooperating would. The best defense was often a good offense. But a good offense required a plan and some power, and he had none. He would be going in blind. And afraid.

"I still don't buy it," said Doctor Ebenstein. "Some guy seven thousand years in the future reaching across all those centuries, finding Jim out of billions of people, and then causing some part of him, something that identifies itself as Jim, to inhabit a body called D'zeos in his own time? It's preposterous."

"Don't think about it," Jim said. "It'll drive you crazy."

The doctor smiled and tilted his head, and Jim and he again experienced a bond of sorts, an unspoken understanding, a joining of spirit.

"Let's all take the rest of the day off and sleep on it tonight, and see what tomorrow brings," said Doctor Marquand.

"Sleep on it?" Jim said. "By 'it' I take it you mean that cushy little helmet of Doctor Fillmore's."

Chapter 18

Introductions

***

The pilot's voice crackled over the PA system, "Put your head between your legs. We are ten seconds from impact."

"I love you I love you I love you."

The plane responded with ominous shuddering and rattling, then an impact so conclusive, so overwhelming that it yanked a shroud of blackness over all his senses. Thought sight sound was erased, and the present too.

"Shang it!" Vanqa snapped. *Perturb.*

D'zeos swiveled his head to look at him. "What?"

"That jolt."

"What was it?"

"This shanged air car. The thing's going to tear itself to pieces. It's the approach program, and believe it or not it was just serviced. It's impossible to find qualified technicians anymore."

"No, it was that airplane. It just crashed. I was in it."

"No you weren't. Do you really think so?"

"Yes. But how could I have been there? I thought that had already happened on this timeline. Damn it, I'm scared! You know damn well I was in that plane when it crashed!"

Vanqa was staring straight ahead. "You did not experience the crash. You were extracted at the moment of impact."

"Then what was it I felt?"

"A reverberation."

D'zeos leaned forward to force eye contact. "It was real."

"Just let it go. Your mind was in a confused mode. You weren't there. It was a strong reverberant shadow caused by a dimensional kink."

"It was more than a reverberant shadow, goddamn it!"

"Believe me, it wasn't the actual you or you wouldn't be here. You're D'zeos, and D'zeos experienced a little flicker. You were not Terry Walker. He is inaccessible to you. He no longer has a presence on this time thread."

"You're sure?"

"I'm sure."

D'zeos thought a moment, then said, "If I accept that, then D'zeos must be real. So why don't I have a history? Am I mentally deficient?"

"No. Your memory will assemble itself."

D'zeos tensed as a realization dawned. "You screwed up and damn near killed me."

"D'zeos, you're here. Let it go at that. The strand is severed."

"Then tell me, where did we meet? And when? I asked you before, and I think you told me, but I can't remember."

Vanqa smiled. "That's understandable. It was now and millennia ago, D'zeos. In the twenty-first century, and also at this moment."

"That's not an answer. It's also a huge gap."

"Yes and no. You see, those moments are the same at one or more points of the multiverse. What matters is, you're here now. There have been many failed attempts, and the intersect still has some ephemeral fluctuations and discordant strands, but it's much more stable than before, and you're here solidly."

D'zeos still had a groggy feeling. He said, "I feel as if I'm teetering on a brink of reality. No, that's not it. I don't know how to describe it, but it's like I'm barely me. Like this person D'zeos is only partly real. I don't know myself."

Vanqa looked at him intensely as he said, "Try and hold on." Vanqa took his hand. "Here. Keep this reality. Hold on to it. Grip it. Squeeze it."

He squeezed. "But how could I not know myself?" D'zeos felt panic beginning to roil. "Who am I, Vanqa? Why don't I know me?"

Vanqa smiled and said, "Are you holding a real hand?"

D'zeos felt himself frowning as he looked at their hands, and felt the pressure and warmth, and even moisture from perspiration, and said, "It seems like it. But I don't have a history. I seem to exist at this moment, but it's like I didn't exist in the past." Anxiety continued to tumble, churned in his stomach. "Why? Who am I?"

"Many of us spend years finding out who we are. Some never do. But you are yourself, D'zeos. No one else. The rest will resolve with time."

"Damn it, you're deliberately avoiding my questions. I want to know why I don't remember an existence before now. How do I know about Jim Drake and Talaan and the others, but not myself?"

"I told you, it will come. It will develop." The aircar jerked and shuddered, then experienced a sudden drop of several centimeters, jarring every bone in his body. "Shang technicians," swore Vanqa.

But at least D'zeos knew he had bones. That jolt was real; they were definitely his bones and his muscles.

The aircar walls dematerialized, and the two of them arose and stepped out. "Shang technicians," repeated Vanqa.

He looked at D'zeos. "Are you feeling more self-aware now?"

"A little."

"Good. Your mind should be starting to coalesce." Vanqa released his hand. "Come, follow me."

D'zeos, trailing Vanqa through the transit port, realized what was causing the knot in his stomach. It was fear of death. That airplane crash centuries ago. And not feeling complete as D'zeos. He said, "I thought that airplane had crashed. The one with Terry and Maryann."

"It has. Jim Drake was having a dream, which you experienced. The plane is at the bottom of the earth-ocean called Pacific."

"Bull shit! That was no dream!" It had been stark. The face of death, and Vanqa saying it was a dream was a damn lie. Anger boiled, and he said, "And you know it. It was not a dream! Stop lying to me."

Vanqa tried to smile, but that too was a lie. He stopped and turned to face D'zeos. "Alright. You're right. Here's what happened. You did partially experience the airplane crash. Some time-like seven-dimensional sheets became twisted due to an error in our manipulation. It was something akin to a dream to you, or a vicarious timespace experience because that event is over and will not affect Jim Drake or you, D'zeos. In that sense and in those dimensions, the most logical label to put on it is a reverberation."

D'zeos felt his tension soften somewhat. "I won't go there again?"

Vanqa shook his head. "It has crashed on Jim Drake's vector, and that is not reversible. It cannot happen again, and could not have happened again in his sevenspace, and therefore not in yours, and therefore did not."

"What about on a different vector? Can't we have multiple vectors?"

"It was an error that will not occur again." He turned and began walking. "Come."

D'zeos followed, taking several fast steps to catch up, but could not shed the sensation of crashing. It had been so far beyond fear—doom crushing his perceptual senses into a black ball, an irresistible thrust by forces completely beyond endurance. No way out. No alternative. No second chance—yet at that precise instant he had been plucked from the abyss to become D'zeos in the year ninety-three fifty-three. He shuddered and said, "If I had been Terry Walker when he died, Jim Drake would have died too, wouldn't he?"

Vanqa gestured with his hand in annoyance and said, "Yes, and no. That's a valid question but it does not have a closed answer."

"What are you talking about?"

"I mean," said Vanqa, looking him in the eye for a change, "that realities are multivalued. On that vector, Jim Drake would have died. But that was not his primary vector. On the other hand we are unable to label any one event as *the* reality because there is no preferred observation point, that is, no master reference timespace from which to compare or calibrate realities and say that one particular timespace experience is complete reality. From any one individual's perspective they are determinate. But from a more general, multiphasic view, they are often either indeterminate determinate or not unique. Furthermore, they are co-contingent." Vanqa broke eye contact and picked up his pace again.

D'zeos lengthened his stride to keep up. "Co-contingent on what? And what do you mean, multiphasic?"

"There is no way you can understand. We have a scientific gap of seventy centuries, for shang sake!" Vanqa glanced at him impatiently, then his stern look faded as he smiled slightly, and said more softly, "But don't feel inadequate. Most people, including myself, don't have a good understanding of timespaces. Now, let's change the subject."

All right. He was D'zeos and he was here. He had no personal history, yet he remembered Philip Osborne and Terry Walker and Jim Drake and Talaan. All the details. He knew all their pasts without even trying, the same as everyone does with their own life. He looked at Vanqa, deciding how to open the matter again, and said, "I really need to know this. How is it I know these other people and not myself?"

"All right. Here it is. You are not allowed to know yourself, D'zeos. You cannot. You may not learn anything that could be carried back to Jim Drake that would change the events of future history. Just accept that those people whose existence you briefly shared, each of them, are part of your multiversal past. That's your history, D'zeos. That's who D'zeos is."

"Jim Drake was seventy centuries ago."

"How many times do I have to tell you? It is also now. The multiverse lattice for you and Jim Drake, and also the other individuals you mentioned, intersect at certain timeplaces in the higher dimensional universe. At least one place in most instances. This is one rare and unique multidimensional point where these all meet."

"I know that's how I *can* be here. But how *did* I get here?"

Vanqa stopped again, turned to him, put a hand on each shoulder and said, "I would not tell you if I could. You know, future history. You cannot learn about any of these things. We can't fiddle with realtime. But I will tell you that yes, we did it, and by we I mean my associates. I will also tell you that such a feat is very, very complex. I couldn't come close to explaining it even if I wanted to. Intellects far greater than mine cannot do so. The actual feat involved nonbiological and semi-biological and fully biological mechanisms. Even so, it's been exceedingly difficult effecting this. There have been many false starts and several near calamities in which you participated, and even now the confluence is metastable and the lock tenuous. Now, enough! That's all! Come along and stop asking such questions. We must hurry." He released D'zeos and resumed walking.

"So you *have* been doing this deliberately."

Vanqa did not stop, but confronted him with a frown. "Stop! No more. There are many things you must not learn or this will not have happened. You'll ruin everything."

"Where are we going?"

"I want to introduce you."

"To who?"

"Everyone."

D'zeos shook his head in frustration and gave up. For the first time he looked where they were heading, and saw a low, circular platform about two meters in diameter. The surface looked like etched or frosted glass. Vanqa stepped onto this platform, and D'zeos followed. As soon as they were both in the circle, walls and ceiling suddenly encircled the platform. Walls that had not been there when they stepped on. Then they wrinkled and a swirl of multicolored fog encased them, and it or something held him firmly. Which was good, because he lost all sense of orientation. There was no up or down. No direction. Not even any solidity. He was starting to panic when it came to him. They were in a dissociation chamber traveling elsewhere. D'zeos had no idea how he knew this, or if he had been in one before. But he knew.

As quickly as it had vanished, up and down returned. The semi-vaporous restraints evaporated as the fog was whisked away. And they were on a stage of some sort in front of a large crowd of people. He looked at Vanqa in puzzlement.

Vanqa turned to the crowd and, with a sweeping gesture said, "This, ladies and gentlemen, is the First Great Confluence."

A murmur surged from the crowd, then slowly died out and there was silence. Total silence. Not even echoes. The background was poorly lit and hazy; D'zeos could not see walls or furnishings of any kind. Nothing. Just the surface they were standing on, and a background of faces looking at him. Like the rest of the universe didn't exist. To make matters worse he had the uncomfortable feeling it did not, at least from this vantage point.

Vanqa continued, in his peculiar sing-song voice that stretched out the sibilants and smoothed the consonants in a most relaxing and reassuring manner, something like a child's rhyme, "This is where it all began, where it leads, and where it ends."

Another murmur swirled from the crowd. D'zeos didn't know whether he was awed or afraid. He decided it was mostly fear.

Vanqa looked at D'zeos. "This event is being cast multiversally to all settled star systems, so everyone may bear witness." He turned to the audience. "I am Vanqa." He turned back to D'zeos. "And this," he said with a catch in his voice, "is D'zeos." He paused. "The Drake." He paused again, then his voice quavered as he said, "The One."

The audience gasped, and for a moment seemed on the verge of applauding, but refrained except for a few tentative little claps from somewhere far away. Rather, they bowed their heads in silence. This was too much for D'zeos. Who the hell was he supposed to be? Whoever they thought he was, they were wrong. What did they expect of him? Who were these people? "Enough!" he shouted.

The scene dissolved; time shrugged.

And they were elsewhere. D'zeos expected to face the wrath of Vanqa, but instead he simply said, "Yes. It was enough for this time. Now they know."

D'zeos looked around in puzzlement. A group of perhaps twenty people had stopped and were staring at him. He turned to Vanqa, and he seemed different somehow. More full-bodied. More physically real, to have more presence. But at the same time D'zeos's mind was leaping among a swirl of disconnected thoughts, almost unbalancing him. Now they know? Who? Know what? He said to Vanqa, "Who knows? They know what?"

"Not now."

"Don't tell me not now! I'm tired of your games, and I don't like being treated like a specimen or captive. I don't belong here, and I'm not sure you do either."

Vanqa merely smiled as he continued walking, then looked at him with a confident nod and said, "Oh, but you do. So do I, but especially you."

"Why? Why am I even here? How do you know anything at all about Jim Drake? How do I know anything about Jim Drake? I seem to be him, but I'm not."

Vanqa looked at him sharply and hesitated, but only briefly, before saying, "I think you know that I am not prepared to answer such questions. Now, I insist we change the subject. You may not learn and retain anything that would change Jim Drake or his knowledge of any details. That would create an incompatibility with us being herenow under these precise conditions. Obviously, you have not learned anything yet that would make a noticeable change. Let us keep it that way."

D'zeos was feeling even more unsettled. "I want to go home."

"Where is home? And when? The answers are multivalued."

"Damnit, enough of this crap. I want to be Jim Drake! Twenty-first century earth Jim Drake." He clenched his fists at his side and shouted, "I want to go home."

Vanqa nodded, an almost imperceptible motion.

Perturb.

Trina was sleeping in a chair, a book in her lap. The door knob clattered, and Doctors Fillmore and Marquand burst into the room.

"Are you back?" Peter said loudly.

"Yes." Jim looked at Trina, who was suddenly wide awake, scrambling out of her chair. "Good Lord, Jim!" She rushed over to him. "Did you have *another* episode?"

"Did he ever," said Doctor Marquand. "Off the charts."

Doctor Fillmore said, "Fortunately we had that EEG cap on him. I don't know what we'll learn, but we have data. Christ, do we have data!"

"Oh, you poor thing!" Trina caressed his forehead, then leaned over and kissed it.

At that moment Maurice and Sylvia rushed in. "Thanks for the text," Doctor Ebenstein said. "He had another one, I take it."

"Yes." Doctor Marquand had his ever-present note pad, and sat down in what had been Trina's chair. "We need to get the details while it's still fresh, Jim." He crossed his legs and took out his pen. "Who, where, and when were you?"

"D'zeos. With Vanqa. Ninety-three fifty-three."

"Ninety-three fifty-three?" said Trina. "Good Lord!"

"Good," said Maurice. "We've got a date."

"Yeah, double check it. See if I'm right."

Trina got her wrinkleless frown. "Jim!"

Jim looked at Aubert Marquand. "The people there that Vanqa and I were talking to, I think they were a hologram, or some sort of projection. And I'm not so sure about me and him. It didn't feel... I wasn't complete, but I don't know what was missing, and Vanqa didn't... I don't know how to describe it, but he seemed artificial. He just didn't feel like a real person. It was like he was missing a life-force. You know how you can feel when another person's in the room? Or you can sense their mood just by being near them? That was missing, but maybe it was just me. He said I needed time to... I forget. Reassemble, or something."

"Back up. Start at the beginning. Where were you?"

"I have no idea. But let me tell you what's *really* weird. Both me, that is D'zeos, and Vanqa, we both knew about Jim Drake and Talaan and Zeleece. We both not only knew about them, we both knew I had been them. Now how in the hell could that be? And I, D'zeos, didn't even know myself. I just was. No sense of self, no life experiences. No me. I knew everyone's history but my own,"

Doctor Fillmore said, "I'd say you were dreaming, except we know you weren't." He thrust his arm toward the wall, indicating some place down the hall. His lab. "We have data."

"I'd say the data is garbage," said Doctor Ebenstein, "except we know it isn't. Not entirely, anyway." He turned to Jim. "Something major is happening in your brain. It's not like you're lying."

"Well thank you, doctor!"

Trina frowned at him, but didn't say anything.

"Morrie," said Sylvia, "why do you keep regressing to non-belief? It's impossible to verify future events, but we *have* corroborated his version of what happened in nineteen forty-four, and also in nineteen sixty-three, and concluded that he could not have had pre-knowledge of those events. Certainly not the details he's given us. He had to have lived through those experiences."

"What!" gasped Trina. She turned from Jim to face Sylvia. "It's real? He actually became those people? You know for sure? It's not just his mind?"

"Yes, we know," said Sylvia. "No question."

Jim felt a flash of anger. So the assholes did know beyond a doubt! Why hadn't they told him, instead of letting them believe, almost, that he was hallucinating or something? Letting him fight the fight alone? It had felt like him against the world, even including his own wife. He had thought they all agreed he was crazy, but they were just afraid of sounding crazy themselves. "You assholes!" he growled. "You didn't have the guts to come out and tell me it was real, so instead you let me fight this thing alone?"

"It's real but we don't know what 'it' is," Doctor Marquand said. "And your assessment of us is true as well. We were afraid to accept such an unconventional answer and kept looking for something else. Anything else." He looked at Trina and said, "He knew things that he could not possibly have known had he not been those persons, but even so we kept looking for another answer. We still are. There may be one, but I'll be darned if I have any idea what it could be."

Trina turned to Jim, brushed her hand over his forehead. "You poor thing! You really, really *were*, you weren't crazy. I mean you weren't, you know." She looked at Sylvia. "How long have you known that he's... is he actually time traveling?"

"So you didn't believe it either," Jim said. He felt betrayed. Let down by his wife and best friend, coddled out of sympathy. He didn't know whether to be mad or hurt. "Not even you."

"I'm so sorry." She put her arm around his chest and turned her head to Sylvia. "How could you let him suffer alone when you knew... *is* he time traveling?"

Sylvia reached out toward Trina, then dropped her hand. "He's, at least I believe he's... yes, his mind is going to those places and those other identities."

"Listen to that, Peter," said Doctor Ebenstein to Doctor Fillmore, "she has the same problem I have. She can't even say the words time travel." He turned to Sylvia, but his voice softened considerably, "We have to be missing something, honey. There just has to be some other explanation. There has to be!"

Jim noticed Doctors Marquand and Fillmore exchange brief raised-eyebrow glances and little smirks at his use of the word honey, but it was only a momentary interlude invading the seriousness of his mangled feelings.

Trina seemed dazed as she slid her hand from his shoulder to his cheek, "Did you know too?"

"Of course I knew. I was there."

She bloomed with anger and shoved on his chest as she demanded, "Why didn't you tell me?"

"I did."

She put her fists on her hips. "You most certainly did not!"

"Trina, I told everyone. I said I knew I became those people. I said I visited those other times. I said I really was them."

Her anger melted as she realized what he was saying. "I know you thought. I mean, when did you know they knew?"

"Just now. The same time you did."

"You didn't know they had facts about Philip and Terry?"

"So now you believe me. You didn't when I was the one who told you, but now when someone else says the same thing, you believe it." Jim was both angry and hurt, but simultaneously relieved to discover that the doctors knew he wasn't making it up. And now he felt guilty for attacking Trina.

She looked at Dr. Fillmore. "Why didn't you tell us? That wasn't right, making him think he's insane. And me too."

"Because we didn't believe our own data. We're still not sure. There might be some other explanation that makes more sense. To tell you the truth, I hope there is. Something rational and plausible. This is too crazy."

"It sure is. Time travel? How could that be?"

The doctor said, "I'd pay someone every cent I have for an answer to that." He turned to Dr. Ebenstein. "I agree with your reservations. But I also agree with Sylvia. The facts support time travel better than any other explanation we've been able to come up with. And yes, I feel foolish saying that. Damn foolish. I'd never utter those words in public."

Doctor Ebenstein said, "Don't feel bad. Maybe we can publish our findings in one of the supermarket tabloids, alongside a story about an alien mummy."

"Right." Doctor Marquand fished his mini iPad out of his pocket. "Let's get on with it, Jim. Start at the beginning."

After they were through Jim said, "You've got a ton of data, plus the detailed descriptions from me about what I experienced. And now you agree that maybe it's time travel. Do you have any new ideas? New plans? New cures?"

Doctor Ebenstein tugged on his lower lip, and Doctor Marquand stirred his hair with his finger. Eventually Doctor Fillmore spoke. "We know your brain activity is becoming more spatially focused, and more intense with each episode."

"What does that mean? Is it good or bad?"

"I don't know. I truly don't know. I'm beginning to agree with you that it's out of our hands, that we're merely observers. In fact, that *is* what I now believe. It seems pretty evident to me that your mind is not the cause of these trips to the past and the future. Vanqa actually said so. He said they had screwed up and made mistakes, some of them near fatal. I now believe that every time you took a trip, right from the very first time at the ball park, it was Vanqa and his cohorts who were causing it because they were trying to get you there with him in the ninety-fourth century."

"Thank you." Jim felt immense relief jostling for space with helplessness. Defeat too. He wasn't insane; his mind was okay. Yet he was unable to remain Jim Drake, and that was insane. He was a sane person who traveled to the future. "It's good to know I'm perfectly normal," he said to no one in particular. "I'm not insane, but I'm doing something that's totally insane. You doctors need a new word."

"Bewildered, befuddled, and bamboozled would be a start," grumbled Doctor Ebenstein. "Take your pick."

"See my effect on the world's leading psychiatrists?" Jim said to Trina. "They've undergone total meltdown. Ain't I good?"

Doctor Ebenstein actually burst into laughter. "Good? You're more than good. You're the best I've ever seen."

"Oh, God, Jim." Trina laid her head on his shoulder, and slid her arm back across his chest. "What are we going to do?" she murmured.

Chapter 19

A view from nowhere

They were all gathered in the lab again.

Sylvia placed her hand on Doctor Ebenstein's. "This situation with Jim is not the only thing that is illogical. A lot of science seems illogical. Just look at quantum mechanics."

"This is different. No one in their right mind would consider this whackadoodle crap as remotely scientific."

"So the fact that a particle acts like both a solid speck of matter and an immaterial wave, and can be in many places and no place at the same time, and instantaneously communicate its state to another particle no matter how far away, all that is okay?"

Doctor Ebenstein smiled at her. "Yeah, but this is insane. Let's see if the other kooks have anything new."

Sylvia hiccupped a chuckle as she glanced at Doctor Fillmore, then smiled fondly at Maurice. "You're so funny."

He smiled and looked at Doctor Marquand. "Have you consulted your Tarot cards today?"

Sylvia didn't even try to suppress another giggle.

"I've thought about it a lot," said Doctor Marquand softly, ignoring the comment. "It seems that Vanqa, whether he's a real person or a subconscious construct, wants Jim to be at the time and place where D'zeos is. It's urgent and very important. One of the other things is that Vanqa has many characteristics none of the others have. He's the only one who is aware of the time displacements. He knows D'zeos is Jim Drake. He knows about Talaan and Zeleece. He knows what year Jim is from, and the same for the people Jim has become. And perhaps even more intriguing, he seems to be the one causing it all."

Maurice raised his heavy eyebrows. "And what is your diagnosis, Doctor, since you apparently have concluded that Vanqa is not a manifestation of Jim's subconscious?"

Doctor Marquand shook his head. "I don't have one." He began tapping a pen on his knee. "I don't have one," he repeated quietly, as he stared off into the distance. "But it sure is f-ing weird."

Doctor Fillmore said to no one in particular, "I'm intrigued by what happened during Jim's attempt at meditation." He turned to him. "Last time you slipped into the D'zeos personality almost immediately and effortlessly. It was like you opened a door for Vanqa. In this bizarre world we're investigating that's actually logical, since many of the same areas of your brain are activated and suppressed during meditation and your trips. I'd like you to try it again."

Jim's eyes bored into the doctor. "Exactly what I don't need. An open door to insanity. I'd rather close the fucking thing, not open it."

"Jim!" Trina unleashed a disapproving scowl at his profanity.

Doctor Fillmore waved sideways to indicate to Trina that it was okay and said to Jim, "That's the only thing we've done that seems to be directly related to your trips. I think we should follow up. I suspect that approach has the best chance of leading us to some answers. Will you try?"

"Last time I did it scared the crap out of me."

"Jim," Trina said, "I hate to say this, but you said it earlier yourself. We'll never get to the bottom of this if we don't do everything possible. Maybe you should."

Jim sagged with a big exhale, "I know." He closed his eyes and dropped his chin onto his chest. "I know. I just... Damnit. Of course I'll do it."

"Good!" said Doctor Marquand. "Let's get started."

***

Jim reached up to his head to feel the EEG helmet. "There's a tornado going on up here, and it's slinging shit around like someone doing their job in in front of a fan."

"Jim!" Trina frowned, but her eyes had a slight glint of humor.

Doctor Ebenstein got his little twitch of a smile and he said, "It also applies to the conclusions these guys are arriving at. Just toss some crap in the air and see if any of it sticks."

"Oh, God!" Trina turned her head away. "You two are a pair."

Jim had to laugh and said, "Just medicate me, Doc, so I don't feel the pain.

Doctor Marquand said, "Using tranquilizers to attain a peaceful mind would not be the same as a meditative state."

Jim nodded. "I know. It's an inside job. Okay, let me see what I can do. Do you want me to do it right here, right now?"

"In just a minute," said Doctor Fillmore. "I need to make sure the EEG system is up." He got up and hurried out the door. It seemed like only a couple of minutes later that he called from down the hall, "All set here."

Jim scooted his chair back from the table, closed his eyes and quenched his thoughts. Shifted so as to sit upright. Placed his hands in his lap and relaxed. Stillness came, but almost at once he began thinking of the airplane. He yanked the thought away, sought stillness once more, and his mind went to his episode back at the Mexican restaurant. He closed those thoughts. Tried to imagine himself immersed in a golden glow, a golden field generated by a force that came from within himself. Or from the universe. A peaceful golden glow. Huge emptiness. Immense silence. Total awareness of profound emptiness and silence of the infinite universe, at one with it, of it.

"Ah, D'zeos, that was *much* easier."

"Yes, I'm afraid it was." He and Vanqa were strolling along a path in a park. A serene lake on the right was separated from the path by green grass. Glints of slivery sunlight sprinkled the lake surface, reflections from wavelets stirred by the gentle breeze. There were no watercraft and no water birds, but D'zeos saw a circle of ripples that was almost surely caused by a fish flicking the surface. The lake appeared clear and pristine, but alongside it the grass was ragged and unmowed, more than ten inches high in places. D'zeos wondered if that was deliberate or if the city was short of funds. There was litter in the grass too, as if the area had been untended for some time.

He looked to the left where there was a forest of trees ranging from seedlings to stately, mature ones that looked like pines, the higher limbs swaying slightly in the breeze. But they weren't pines. They had needles like pines or firs, but the needles were much fatter than pine needles. He looked up higher and the sky was blue, just as it should be. And suddenly he realized he was grateful for that. Was this earth?

He had no idea. He scanned the sky, and it sure looked like an earth sky, deep crisp blue with two billowy white clouds. Thank God it wasn't violet or orange like in some of those science fiction movies. Then another realization occurred: movies were of Jim Drake's time, not from now, so how did he know about movies? So the same question as before arose. How did he know about Jim Drake? And about immersiums from Talaan's time. He knew these things, yet was still vacant regarding himself, devoid of all the recollections one accumulates in life. He was now, yet he had no self. No "I," as in "I am D'zeos."

He looked at Vanqa, who seemed to be enjoying the stroll, immersed in the tranquility of the outdoors. Vanqa felt more human now in spite of that absence of a sense of him being a person. Maybe this increase in acceptance was his mind beginning to, what? Become normal? Adapted? Or was it being conditioned by Vanqa and his friends? Who were Vanqa's friends? He had only overheard conversation. He didn't have the vaguest idea of even who Vanqa was, where he came from. Or how they met. As a matter of fact, he could say the same things about himself. Exactly the same things. D'zeos said, "I still don't have any memory of my life up to now, or even a sense of who D'zeos is. I thought you said it would come back. Who am I, anyway? What's my history?"

"You are assimilating a history now. We're going to dinner."

"Why do I need to assimilate one? Am I even human?" He sure as shang wasn't a complete personality, not in his own mind anyway. Vanqa was still. Vanqa didn't *feel* like he was here, the way the presence of a person feels. Like the way you sometimes know a person is next to you before you see them. Vanqa's essence was missing, or else D'zeos' sense of it was. Maybe that was it. Maybe it really was just a matter of time. He asked, "Are you human? You seem sort of… absent a life force."

"Don't be so negative." Vanqa pointed to a path that branched off to the left, up through the forest. "Come this way. We'll take the transpath so we'll be among the crowds. That should help."

They climbed up a steep pathway, up as high as the treetops, higher, then down a little, another fifty feet or so, and D'zeos found himself looking at a busy city teeming with people and aircars. He stopped and turned around to look back, but the park was not visible from here. It was over the rise they had just descended, and some distance below them. Maybe a few hundred feet. He was out of breath, that was for sure, and his legs burned from the exertion. At least that part of him felt real.

He turned back to the cityscape. They were near one edge of a transit corridor that was four hundred feet or more across and on three levels. It was filled with pedestrians, transpaths, and transtubes, a mélange of motion and activity that at first was very confusing, but after a few moments he discerned an order and logic. He let his gaze rove upward where aircars flitted silently following invisible highways, packing the airspace like electrons moving in a crystal lattice or particles in a flowing fluid. But wait—how did he know about crystal lattices and flowing fluids? How could he know all these things, and nothing about himself? As a matter of fact he knew many things, and many more were coming back to him. Except for anything about himself. He glanced at Vanqa, then begrudgingly decided to do what he knew Vanqa would tell him to do anyway. See if it started coming back to him.

He looked across the corridor to the buildings on the far side. They were of an architectural design that looked like abstract art. Compound curves and arcs swooped and soared to the heavens in graduated pastel colors like a series of convoluted and interlocked rainbows drawn with a French curve. He looked up and up, and the tallest ones were literally in the clouds. It was a breathtaking spectacle, yet along with the sense of awe it felt familiar. Mundane. Even old. He realized they had been constructed centuries ago. He looked at Vanqa and tried to formulate a question, but Vanqa merely smiled and took his arm, directing him toward the transpath, which on this side of the corridor was hustling people to their right.

They stepped on. Nothing was moving except them and the people, faster in the central part of the twenty-meter-wide surface. In fact they were moving quite fast, too fast, and D'zeos thought he was going to fall, but some force seemed to support and steady him. Like fingers. Like a web. Something similar to when they were in the dissociation cube. Finally he realized this was much more sophisticated than the transwalk he rode as Talaan. This one was not only much faster, but he knew, somehow he knew, that it would detect his fear and provide additional support to compensate for it. Realizing he knew these things D'zeos managed to relax a little, confident he was stable, hoping he was beginning to assemble his memory, and began trying to take in things around him.

He glanced up and became intrigued by a blob of colored fog that appeared to be following them. It spread out when he looked at it and assembled itself into a scene of humans enjoying a beverage called Zinamine. He looked ahead and back, and realized that cloud-blobs were everywhere, but only one or two were organized into a three-dimensional vista, and those were ones someone was looking at. He couldn't see what those were displaying, though. Then he remembered; there was a point-of-focus detector in each of the blobs that determined when someone was looking at it. These three-dimensional panoramas were highly directional constructs, with content tailored to the individual. 'His' would promote a different product to someone else, even to Vanqa who was next to him. He glanced at 'his' cloud, and as he knew it would be, it was now behind them and had collapsed into its quiescent, minimal-energy globular shape, monitoring the crowd for another looker.

He looked at the people and was reminded of a circus with acts everywhere—above, to the front, behind, beside them. Colors and visions and blurs of motion, totally unexpected visual displays or out-of-context clothing. Skin and hair colors of every hue and tint. Many bodies were brightly colored and others reflective, and a few were illuminated from within.

The aircars glided silently above the commercial fogs. Some were single passenger, others carried two and four, and some were much larger. They, too, were of a variety of colors and luminosities.

Most astonishing of all were the people. Maybe he was beginning to gain a sense of belonging, because the only astonishing things were the people. Many of them appeared perfectly normal, going about their business, but some were in outlandish attire. One just in front of him was wearing a hat with green and orange bands and a dozen or more brightly colored bead necklaces. He was carrying what was probably an alcoholic drink in a fancy glass. Another, considerably farther ahead, had glowing pink shoes. Another was wearing athletic shorts and track shoes, jogging in place on the transpath while facing backward. They passed a man concentrating on performing what looked like feats of magic at a table that was somehow levitated without legs.

D'zeos said, "It looks as if some of these people came right out of an insane asylum, and others from the Cirque

Du Soleil. But then, you wouldn't know what the Cirque Du Soleil is."

"I do."

"You do? Is there anything you don't know?"

"A great deal. Far more than I do know."

D'zeos glanced over his shoulder, and with a surge of terror saw that the woman behind him had huge, panic-filled eyes, and he was struck with the notion that she was ready to attack him. He turned away quickly so as not to antagonize her and said, as he edged Vanqa between himself and the wild-eyed woman, "What's wrong with these people?"

Vanqa shrugged, "With some, nothing. Depends."

"Thanks again."

Vanqa merely inclined his head.

D'zeos noticed a change in surroundings. They were passing through an area where the buildings appeared deserted. A transpath that intersected their own was inoperative. As they passed, D'zeos looked down its length. There were only a few people about, and those seemed to be derelicts, or lost. He caught a glimpse of a face peering around the corner of a building, but it quickly darted back out of sight. An overway that had once been suspended above the non-functioning transpath had fallen and one end rested on the ground like a toppled Roman column made of a shiny, silvery plastic-looking material, crumpled on one end.

"You still have slums?"

"I guess you could call it that. They are referred to as The Abandonds."

"As in unoccupied buildings?"

"Not quite. They are occupied, but most of us never go there. The owners have abandoned them, and they are not safe places to visit."

"I expected that sort of situation would be a thing of the past."

"It used to be."

"There you go again."

"No. There you go. I gave you a fact and you jumped to an erroneous conclusion."

"You—" A bright flash of light blinked and was gone, and D'zeos swiveled his head to the left. It had been in the dissociation tube, translucent tubes above and on either side of the transpath. The tubes were continuously active, seeming almost alive as clusters of luminescent gas flashed in flickers of motion. It reminded him of an old fashioned fluorescent light tube that is wearing out and has bands of fog or light propagating up and down the length of it. Only these blobs were immensely faster. He pointed and asked, "Those are dissociation tubes, right?" He knew the answer, but maybe the question would stir Vanqa to give up some additional bit of information.

"Excellent! Your brain is beginning to function better. Yes, those are trantubes. The gaseous-appearing bundles are people, dissociated inside a protective field. They aren't ionized, but that's the way it looks. I have no idea of the science behind it. All I know is, the departure gate disassembles the person, the arrival gate reassembles them, and something else transports what was, and will again be the person. But you know about them. You traveled in a dissociation cube, which uses the same technology. It is a much faster and safer way to get around the city than these transpaths, but in them you are completely removed from human contact. I wanted you to experience life here firsthand to help you assimilate."

"I sure need to. What was that bright flash in the tube a moment ago?"

"That was a large group that insisted on being transmitted as one. Maybe business people or politicians."

"Why would they want to go as one entity?"

"Probably security when they reconstitute at the arrival point."

"I thought you said they were safe."

"They are, but some terminal points may not be, and they want their security team reassembled right with them."

"That does not seem like an advanced civilization."

"Personally, I don't consider this to be one."

After a moment it became clear to D'zeos that Vanqa did not intend to continue, so he said, "Quite a few of these people look and act very strange, to say the least, and many seem like foreigners. I don't understand a lot of the languages."

"Nor do I."

"Then they are foreigners."

"Well, that's an archaic word, but if you wish to use it then yes, some are foreigners."

"Speaking of foreigners, why aren't there any aliens? I mean non-human aliens? Surely you have encountered other races in the part of the galaxy you've explored."

"Oh, yes. But we no longer interact with them."

"Why?"

Vanqa looked at him intently, then turned away and said, "Diplomatic reasons. They decided that was best."

"Why? What happened?"

Vanqa shrugged. "The situation changed."

D'zeos was puzzled. "It doesn't make sense to withdraw from the rest of civilization."

"It does make sense. It's best for everyone. But I am not allowed to discuss that subject. Please drop it."

It sure seemed that something was wrong with civilization. D'zeos was beginning to feel very, very uncomfortable. He said, "This doesn't feel like a nice place to live." A man who had been several places in front of them moved aside to a slower section of the transpath and now he crumbled to his knees, whimpering, his head almost touching the surface. D'zeos stared in amazement as he and Vanqa whisked by, and like everyone else, Vanqa ignored him.

"What's wrong with him? Why doesn't anyone help him?"

"It's not necessary."

D'zeos twisted around and saw some people in uniform lift him into an aircar. "Was that the police?" he said to Vanqa.

Vanqa said while looking straight ahead, "No. But he'll be attended."

"Vanqa, I don't belong here. I'm not comfortable in this timeplace."

"Of course you belong."

"What year is it? Is it still ninety-three fifty-three?"

"Yes." Vanqa looked at him steadily and very seriously, then added, "Until next month."

D'zeos didn't know why, but something about that date seemed ominous. He tried to place it, but could not. Finally he said, "Then Talaan and Zeleece were a couple thousand years ago."

"Yes."

"What happened to them?"

"They are in their timeplace."

"Ah-ha! So you know them."

"Of course. As do you."

"How do we happen to know them, out of the billions of people before and since?"

"If I told you, then it will happen that this conversation did not occur."

"I love Zeleece. Talaan does. Will I ever be him again?"

"Of course, and of course not. It will be as it is, and it is as it must be. Otherwise it would be different."

"Shang it, anyway!" D'zeos exploded. He was getting more and more frustrated. "All I get is non-answers. I want to know how I remember Talaan and Zeleece and Jim Drake, but not myself?"

Vanqa smiled grimly and merely shook his head. D'zeos started to press for an answer, but gave up. Vanqa had not answered anything. Everything in its time, he always said, or something to that effect—wait to reassemble your memory, or a crazy riddle-answer. If I told you, the present would be different or not exist.

"Let's eat." Vanqa motioned toward a restaurant they were approaching, and D'zeos followed him off the transpath. They entered and were seated at once, and just as D'zeos was beginning to adjust to the dimmer light he heard Vanqa order, speaking into the table. "Delta Boo Beta soup without the estuans, Achird beels in green sauce, Klanis omfruit gratin, and Fomalhaut-Three pudding. For two."

D'zeos looked around at the other diners and was overwhelmed with a feeling of unease. He was in the midst of something threatening or alien—or wrong. It was much different than a claustrophobic attack, more a surge of anxiety. He had to get out of here. "I've got to get out of here. I need to go back. Right now."

Vanqa looked at him intently, and after a moment nodded, and said, "I'll be waiting."

Perturb.

Chapter 20

A view of the end.

Jim said, "What did he mean, 'I'll be waiting'?"

"Darn good question," said a subdued Peter Fillmore. "This whole development puzzles me."

"Me too," said Dr. Marquand. "The situation there seems to have taken on a whole new aspect."

Sylvia looked at Jim, "It seems like Vanqa was trying to show D'zeos how bad society had gotten."

"Maybe," said Doctor Fillmore. "It sure doesn't look like I would have expected society to be seven thousand years from now. From your description, Jim, it was rather unpleasant, almost ominous."

"Not almost. It was. Parts of it." Jim felt himself frowning in his disappointment of future humanity. No, it was more than that. He felt let down by it. Betrayed—by who? The politicians? The corporations? Probably both. Whatever the cause—how could it be? After seven thousand years! That was outrageous. "I guess I expected some sort of Utopia, but nothing could be further from the truth. I mean, good God, they're seven thousand years in the future and at least as bad off socially as we are right now in the twenty-first century. What happened to progress? What happened to that great civilization we all expected would evolve?"

On the other hand, maybe it wasn't as bad as he imagined. He'd seen less than a five kilometer long stretch of just one city. Hell, someone from the thirteenth or fourteenth or fifteenth century could be taken into a back street in any one of dozens of countries today, say Uganda or Haiti or Zimbabwe or Belize, even sections of LA or Detroit, and see the place littered with desperate junkies and mentally unstable homeless people. Those visitors from our past would probably assume that the plight of the common man in the twenty-first century was as bad or worse than it was in his or her own time. Maybe that's all it was. A snapshot from the ninety-fourth century, and a bad one. Typical of some areas, but not of others or even most.

Yet he didn't think so. He had been taken there deliberately. To see. But to see what? And why? Surely Vanqa did not expect Jim, or D'zeos, to cure the ills of the era. So what the hell was it all about? What was the point? He would conclude there wasn't any if it weren't for the fact that it had taken such enormous effort and centuries of work to enable them to get him there. Could it just be that was the sought-after goal? Maybe he was the final experiment in some huge scientific effort.

The proof of concept.

The more he thought about it the more sense that made. He was the beta test, the demonstration of their theory of spacetime. Incontrovertible evidence of the correctness of their equations, their hardware, their software and their encephaloware or psychoware or whatever the hell it was that screwed with his brain. "I think I'm the guinea pig in a stinking experiment! Me appearing there as D'zeos is the final proof that their theory and their apparatus works. Now they can go do what they've been wanting to do. Predict the stock market. Rule the universe."

Doctor Ebenstein had been standing with his back to them, looking out the window. Now he spun around and thrust a finger at Doctor Marquand. "There! You couldn't come up with a logical solution, Mayfield, but Jim has. If this absurd time-travel hypothesis of yours has even a shred of truth to it, that's the one thing that might make sense. I think your patient has solved that part of the problem for you, Doctor!"

Doctor Marquand chuckled and chuckled and chuckled as he twirled his finger in his hair. He looked at Jim with eyes dancing, sharing a joke. But Jim did not get. "I like it," the doctor chortled. He added, "That answer suits you, Mo. It's very good. It's one of the best specious arguments I've ever heard. It almost gives you an out. Not quite, but it comes close."

The glimmer of triumph that had been lighting up Doctor Ebenstein's eyes faded as if a curtain was drawn, and his outthrust arm slowly dropped as he mulled this over. He frowned, and eventually said, "What do you mean?"

"If Jim, appearing in the ninety-fourth century as D'zeos, was a demonstration of the correctness their theory, then when Vanqa made his holocast to all the civilized star systems that would have been all the proof they needed, the final report. *Finis coronat opus.* But that was not all. There was more. Even more importantly, if what Jim said was correct they would never, never let the universe know they were able to do that. It would be the most closely guarded secret in the galaxy."

"Damnit!" Doctor Ebenstein glared at Jim. "What a stupid idea. Time travel!" He whirled around and began pacing, head down. "Stupid!" He stopped, turned around, and as he headed back he began reasoning aloud to himself,

"Vanqa's not parading D'zeos in front of scientists, is he? He's not showing him off, except that once. He's trying to acclimate him to their society. He's educating him by letting him observe and reach his own conclusions." He turned again and paced back. "Why? What the hell's he up to?" He turned again. "The son of a..." He hesitated, glanced at Sylvia and shook his head grimly, then resumed pacing. Up and back, then he stopped in front of Jim and spun around to face him. "You're going back. You've got to find out what he's trying to teach you or guide you into discovering. Otherwise we'll never resolve this goddamn thing. Sitting here it's like trying to listen to a radio station without a radio." He glared at Jim, all but daring him to refuse. "He's going to make you go back anyway, so we may as well learn what we can on our own schedule with our apparatus."

Jim began laughing. He couldn't stop, and the more he tried, the harder he laughed. Almost immediately Doctor Marquand joined in, then Sylvia and Trina did too. Now Doctor Fillmore began roaring, and even Doctor Ebenstein smiled uncertainly before saying, "What's so damn funny?"

At first all Jim could do was point, but eventually he managed to get out, "You," between spasms.

"Me?" He was partially laughing, half-smiling, totally puzzled.

Jim, his laughing spell beginning to abate, held his hand out, wordlessly asking Doctor Marquand to explain. Doctor Ebenstein turned to Mayfield quizzically.

Doctor Marquand stopped laughing, more or less, but couldn't wipe the grin away as he said, "My dear Doctor Bull-Poop, you, sir, are the very one who insisted time travel was absurd, kooky, and irrational. Now you demand that our patient visit the future again, which you say he cannot do, so he can come back to the present and enlighten us, which we don't need because Vanqa is a product of his subconscious."

Doctor Ebenstein smiled in spite of himself. "I guess you've sent me off the deep end, haven't you?" He actually laughed and said, "I think I need a psychiatrist. But I have no idea where to find a competent one, or who to ask for a referral." Then he pointed to Jim, suddenly dead serious again. "You must go."

"I know." There was no longer any question. He had to go for himself if nothing else. He knew or felt that he was close to getting some answers. If he wasn't, at least he seemed to be making progress, and that was the only thing he could think of that seemed to hold any hope. It was obvious that if there were to be any resolution to their questions they lay with Vanqa and D'zeos. They would not be found here.

It was for damn sure the doctors couldn't do anything, although not for lack of trying. The answers were seventy centuries away.

***

D'zeos and Vanqa heard the footsteps of a jogger coming from behind and they moved to one side of the pathway so he could pass. It was a man dressed in shorts and a shirt, and as he drew even with them his panic-filled eyes stabbed them. "Have you seen Martha?" he panted as he slowed his pace, still jogging but moving at a walking pace.

"No, we don't know Martha," Vanqa responded.

His eyes still locked on them he said, "What have they done with her?" The man turned his head toward the forest, releasing them from the entreaty like a rope snapping. D'zeos felt as if a burden had been yanked off him. Then the stranger, having moved ahead, looked into the forest and yelled, "Martha, where are you?" He disappeared around a bend, but they could hear the shout being repeated over and over. "Martha. Martha, where are you?"

D'zeos asked, "Shouldn't he be under a doctor's care?"

Vanqa merely nodded slightly. "He'll be attended."

As they made their way around the bend themselves they saw a woman standing with her hands on a tree trunk. As they drew near she glared at them in utter hatred. "What have you done with the squirrels, you bastards?" she demanded. "Where are they? Where? There were so many before. What have you done?"

Vanqa smiled a gentle smile, then took D'zeos' arm and pulled him along. "She'll be all right. Come."

"Why are you showing me this, Vanqa?"

Vanqa raised his eyebrows and said, "Why D'zeos, it's part of your education."

D'zeos felt anger struggling with curiosity. "All right, educate me! I have four identities in four different placetimes. Terry Walker in the nineteen-sixties, Talaan in the seventy-three hundreds, Jim Drake in the twenty-first century, and here as D'zeos in ninety-three fifty-three. And that's not counting Philip Osborne in the nineteen-forties. What's going on? Which is me? Which is real?"

"All of them."

"Yes I know. But which is really home for me? It seems that Jim Drake is, but so do the others when I'm there. Except for this one. Which one is where I really belong?"

"All of them."

"You can't even answer a single question."

"What do you want to know?"

D'zeos took a deep breath, then another, and felt his rage subside enough to let him speak. He said slowly, "Which one is happening right now? Really, actually happening?"

"This one, of course."

"Okay. Good. Then—"

"So are each of the others. As well as many more. Each in their own timeplace."

"Are you trying to drive me crazy?"

Vanqa raised his eyebrows and shook his head slowly. As Vanqa continued to look at him, D'zeos had a flash of insight. "Shang! Is that what's happening with these people? They don't know where or when they are, or who? Are they lost in time?"

Vanqa nodded grimly. "You knew something about them when you were Talaan. You used a derogatory term, but also a very descriptive one. You and Zeleece called them outtime freaks. There are many of them. It's an epidemic. And you have only seen an isolated, comparatively sane section of the planet."

"Good God! Is the entire human race going insane?"

"Yes," said Vanqa softly. "It is."

"What is it? Why can't the doctors fix it? They can grow every organ and bone in the body, every piece of it! New limbs! Even brain parts!"

"Come, sit down." Vanqa sat on a bench under a tree a short distance from the walkway. He patted the bench next to him. "Sit. We need to talk."

D'zeos sat. After a long period of silence, he said, "Everyone?"

"Maybe sixty percent."

"Shang! How can the world even work? How can the government function?"

"It can't. The infrastructure, from transportation to finance to trade and manufacturing and health care varies from being in shambles to nonexistent. The food and water supply is collapsing in many locations. And the power and communication systems."

"It's getting worse, then?"

"Rapidly. The experts predict that soon the human race will no longer be able to function as a civilization."

"What is causing it?"

"The specialists have a fancy name for it. Temporspati paresëns, or TSP. Those so afflicted are not insane, for the most part. They just don't live in any one time and place and most no longer know which timeplace they originally departed from. So they think they're insane, and act the part."

D'zeos frowned. "Can't the doctors do anything? Or the scientists? Surely there's an antidote for the drug they're using, or a detox protocol, laws to prevent its manufacture. If they can build an entire human to order, and transport me across time, surely they can stop this addictive madness."

"It's not a drug addiction."

"It's not?"

"No. The term 'outtime freak' is a misnomer based on ignorance. Those people were not using drugs. The affliction is the result of a genetic abnormality."

"And you're telling me that today's scientists, who can grow and replace any part of a human body, who have eliminated all diseases, can't cure this?"

"That is correct." Vanqa slowly shook his head. "They can't. If they try to treat someone, that person invariably slips off to a different timeplace. But even that, as annoying as it is, isn't the main problem. The disorder is based on a defect that is dominant in the germline and is so intertwined with the chromosomes required for life that correction is impossible."

"You seem normal, Vanqa, except for the fact that you know about all my other existences. How is it possible for you to know those things?"

Vanqa paused for several moments before saying, "You are correct. I am not afflicted by this defect."

"You didn't answer my question. How do you know so much? How do you know about Jim Drake and Talaan and the others? And how is it you're always here when I become D'zeos?"

"You may not know those things. All I can tell you is, the gaze of my consciousness is very long. Very long indeed."

"The gaze of your consciousness is very long? What the shang does that mean? What about mine? I can recollect all the way back to the twentieth century." Then a thought occurred to him. "But my timeplace experiences are sparse, just three or four over seventy centuries. Is your memory continuous?" The more D'zeos thought, the more questions he came up with, and every one of them were unanswered. Just as these would be. He knew Vanqa would not answer a single one. Yet the man had a purpose. These meetings were far from accidental. D'zeos caught Vanqa's eyes and held them. "I know you are forcing our meetings, Vanqa. Does this, your presence and mine, have anything to do with that disease, TPS or whatever you called it?"

"It's TSP. And I am not permitted to answer that question."

That infuriated D'zeos. He shouted, "You're not permitted? Who says you're not permitted? And why are you not permitted?"

Vanqa put his hand on his shoulder. "I believe it is safe to tell you this: you must reach your own conclusions and find your own answers. If I tell you, I am in essence telling Jim Drake something about the future that could possibly change future history, in which case this conversation may not occur. If you are to find any answers, D'zeos, they must come from within yourself."

"How can I answer questions if I don't..." Then the truth hit D'zeos. He grabbed Vanqa's arm and said, "I have this disorder too, don't I?"

Vanqa turned a steady gaze on him, a fatherly gaze, one filled with love and empathy. "Yes, D'zeos. You do."

"Shang!" He felt himself wilt, his energy, his determination, his will. "I want to go back while I still know were home is."

Vanqa nodded. "I'll be waiting."

Perturb.

Chapter 21

A very dim view

Doctor Ebenstein arose with a harsh scraping of his chair and walked away from the table, then whirled around and said as he flung an arm toward Dr. Fillmore, "What, you think the human race is coming to an end? This crap we're hearing from Jim is no better than tabloid psychic predictions. It will never be proven wrong because it's seven thousand years in the future so we can make any claim we want. This is just great big steaming piles of bull poop, and every one of you has bought into it hook, line and sinker. Talk about suckers, you guys win the prize. Just count me out from now on. I'm through with this project."

Sylvia's mouth dropped open as she blanched, eyes wide, seeking guidance from the other doctors as her gaze darted from onc to the next. Trina grabbed Jim's hand, her face taught in fear.

Doctor Marquand twirled his hair and smiled at Doctor Ebenstein. "I'm glad you've finally come full around, Mo. We need your help."

Sylvia wrinkled her forehead and was about to ask what he was talking about when Doctor Ebenstein said to Doctor Marquand, "I'll help, all right. I'll quit playing games with you. We'll debunk this garbage straight away."

Trina leaned toward Doctor Marquand, and was just starting to speak when he said to her, "Mo wouldn't be so upset if he didn't believe it was true. To use his phrase, he's bought in to the fact of time travel, hook, line and sinker. And he doesn't like it because it doesn't fit any common-sense scientific explanation."

"Really?" Trina stared at Doctor Ebenstein, who shook his head angrily and paced around the table. Then she turned to Doctor Fillmore. "Why are all of you so worried? I mean, more than before?"

Doctor Fillmore said, "Vanqa said that D'zeos has this genetic defect. That almost surely means Jim has it too. And if it's something they can't cure, it's for doggone sure we can't."

Trina went slack. "Oh, my God! You're right!" Then she gathered herself and her eyes bored into the doctor's as she stretched her hands out toward him on the table, unconsciously beseeching him to correct her thinking, seeking reprieve and release. Deliverance.

Breaking the dense silence, she said, "Then he's going to keep doing this time traveling. There is no cure."

The doctor nodded grimly. "That does seem to be the case."

Jim stared silently out the window, then turned to Doctor Marquand and slammed the table so hard with his palm that Doctor Marquand's pen clattered. "Son of a bitch!"

Everyone jumped except Doctor Marquand, who was nodding in agreement. "My conclusion too, Jim," he said.

Trina frowned and demanded, "What in the world are you talking about? Knock off the fucking riddles."

Jim had never heard her use that word, and it drove home the depths of her fear. But there was nothing he could do to soften it, no way to make the conclusion any more palatable, and he said to her softly, "I'm the one"

"Don't even go there," growled Doctor Ebenstein.

"He has to." Doctor Marquand kept his eyes locked on Jim.

Trina looked at Doctor Ebenstein. He had his lips cinched and his head down, shaking it in defeat. "What?" she said. She faced Jim and demanded, "What?"

Jim said softly, "I'm the first." His eyes roved over her face, and he said so softly it was barely audible, "I started this whole goddamn epidemic."

"Lord!" Trina reached for his hand.

Silence descended over the room like a hood until a gasp escaped from Sylvia. She reached for Jim's other hand. "You mean the genetic mutation that's destroying human civilization? It starts with you? You can't mean that!"

No one answered.

After many heartbeats Trina's scream shattered the interlude. "Noooo!" Tears streamed down her face. "That's crazy! That can't be. I won't let it." She turned to Doctor Marquand in unrestrained fury. "Do something, damnit! Say something! Tell him no, it's not so. Fix him, goddamnit."

Jim removed his hand from Sylvia's and reached over to put it on top of Trina's. "He can't. I've been there. I've seen the future. The entire race is going insane. It happened. And since it happened, I can't change it, and neither can he."

"Hmmm." Doctor Fillmore was in deep thought.

"Jim's right, yet maybe not, and at the same time maybe so." Doctor Marquand energetically tapped away with his pen. "Even Vanqa said as much. Physical reality is multivalued, perhaps even nonconvergent on some timethreads. But it's also determinant. Paraphrasing, he said that our experiential manifold has innumerable outcomes, but the future cannot alter the past."

"As you can tell," growled Doctor Ebenstein, "Aubert has been anticipating this all along with that genius mind of his."

Doctor Fillmore ignored him said, "If the future is set, Aubert, then why is Vanqa connecting to Jim over and over, insistent on bringing him there? Why is he going to all this trouble, and it's obviously been incredible trouble? Good Lord, he said it took centuries to learn how, and it's apparent they just got it down, sending Jim to the D'zeos personality rather than Talaan or one of the others. If they didn't think there was a possible way out they wouldn't have undertaken such a massive effort."

"That's bull poop, not science!" Doctor Ebenstein kicked his chair out from the table and sat down. "Reality is reality, and that's it. It's determinate, not iffy. You can't change it to suit yourself."

"Mo," said Doctor Marquand, "as I pointed out in the beginning, and even you have to agree, our minds are physical systems. Why should they have preferred status under the laws of physics, particularly quantum physics, which allows the occurrence of what we normally consider mutually exclusive events? In every other physical system we allow a multiplicity of realities, such as a particle being in two places, time disappearing before the big bang and at the event horizon of a black hole, or the phenomenon of quantum entanglement. How can you exclude the mind from these same physical laws?"

"Those are all effects at the limits of size."

"A single helium nucleus diffracting like a wave through a pair of slits is not near the limits of size. Time stopping at a black hole is not subatomic. The superconductivity used in your SQUIDS is based on quantum mechanical phenomena, and that is certainly a macroscopic device."

"Okay, so I didn't study physics. But you're still talking garbage about time travel."

"I no longer think so." Doctor Fillmore's gaze was unwavering.

After a long pause, Doctor Ebenstein said with a ferocious scowl, "Damnit, I know it. I hate it, I hate the crap out if it, but I don't know what other explanation fits. Even so, I refuse to stop looking for a reasonable answer. I absolutely refuse! In the meantime, on the stupid-ass assumption that this really is time travel, it means we are dealing with nothing less than the fate of the human race." He looked at each of the others in turn, glared at them in fact, as he said slowly, "Don't ever breath a hint of this to anyone else, but apparently it's in our hands. At least to some extent. But we have no idea what we're doing, or even if we can do anything at all. The only reason I hold out any hope is because of the involvement of Vanqa. He obviously thinks there may be a solution so maybe we should keep looking."

Doctor Marquand leaned back, crossed his legs, and began tapping a pen on his knee. "Let's presume that's correct. Then what options are available to us? What steps might we take?" He moved the tapping pen from his knee to the table. Tap, tap, tap.

"None," said Doctor Ebenstein. "We're too stupid. Or at least too ignorant."

Jim put his hand on Doctor Marquand's pen to stop the tapping and said, "You're right, Doctor Ebenstein. You don't have any options. I was there. I saw rampant insanity. Whatever you did, you did not stop it."

"No, we don't know that," said Doctor Fillmore. "If we accept the assumption that reality is multivalued, that we live in a multiverse with many more dimensions, then it seems there is no singular, predetermined future, at least in some sense. We need to play out our hand." He turned to Doctor Ebenstein. "Also, there's the fact that Vanqa is involved and he's got to have a powerful reason to be involved. That wouldn't make any sense if there were absolutely no solution. If that's true, then it follows that Jim is a necessary element. A crucial element."

Jim got up and held his hand out to Trina. "You play this hand out, Doctors. I'm folding. I'm going home with my beautiful wife and talk about what matters in life, then decide how to maximize that. Unlike you, I've seen the end."

Eyes glimmering with moisture, Trina darted a glance at the others, then stood up and clasped his arm. "I think that's a perfect plan."

"Wait," said Doctor Fillmore as they headed toward the door. "Let's try gene therapy."

Trina tugged on Jim's arm to stop him, then turned to the doctor. "You didn't listen to what Jim said. If something as relatively simple as gene therapy would work, don't you think someone would have done it ten or twenty years from now, after this thing started to spread? Or fifty years, or a hundred, or a thousand? But they did not. No one did. That, gentlemen," she paused as she turned to Sylvia, "and lady, is why nothing you do is going to work. Because nothing *did* work. Jim's idea, however, of seeking the things in life that are truly of value, will at least make the remainder of our time more meaningful. And that's why we're leaving."

Aubert Marquand cleared his throat and held up his hand. He glanced at the others, then said, "Would you mind if I join you?"

Trina glanced at Jim, and he gave a slight shrug. She said, "I think I'd like that, Doctor."

Doctor Ebenstein said, "I'm going to Peter's lab to analyze the data we gathered. We've got a ton of it." He looked at Sylvia with a raised eyebrow.

She did not hesitate. "Me too."

"So am I," said Doctor Fillmore. "Besides this new stuff, a lot of the older data hasn't been looked at from this angle."

Doctor Marquand stood up and said to the others, "I have my phone."

Doctor Ebenstein scraped his chair back as he stood up and frowned at Jim. "At least stay in the damn hotel across the street so if something comes up we can get to you in a hurry."

Jim looked at Trina, who gave a brief nod of agreement. "Okay." Then, for a reason he could not explain, he smiled, and felt more relaxed than he had in a long, long time. He turned to Doctor Marquand. "Come on, Aubert. Let's go find what's right in the world."

Chapter 22

Things that matter

Doctor Marquand went with them to their hotel room. After some small talk he said, "Why don't we have lunch?"

"Why don't we just eat here at the hotel?" Trina looked at Jim with concern.

Jim realized he had started to frown, and made himself stop. "Alright," he said, "but not in the room. They've got some good restaurants here. Let's go spend some of that money I don't need."

Trina looked at the doctor, who shrugged. "I don't see what it matters. Vanqa's waiting for him anyway, so when it's time to go, he goes."

"Finally you're making sense," said Jim.

"About time," the doctor laughed.

They chose the finest restaurant in the place and were seated at once. Jim looked around at the other diners, the few there were, and hoped there wouldn't be any embarrassing episodes. Then, as Vanqa ordered in his soothing sing-song voice, D'zeos relaxed.

Vanqa turned to him. "You seem to have something on your mind."

"Yes, I do. With the entire race heading into schizophrenic madness, why is it that no one from the future came back to fix us?"

"No one from the future can change the past. If they tried to, then because of those changes they would not exist in the future, or their situation would be different enough that they wouldn't go back into the past and make those changes. They couldn't change anything because as soon as they did, everything would be different."

"So humanity sinks into madness and oblivion."

"I don't know, D'zeos."

"What do you mean, don't you know? You can go to the future and find out."

Vanqa was silent for a long time. Finally he said, "I just told you. No one from the future can come back and give us information about the future that would change the future, and such information might do that. On the other hand, I do know this: no one has ever gone to or come back from further in the future than January of the year fifty-three fifty-four. Just a few days from now."

"Is there a reason?"

"Of course there's a reason. We just don't know what it is."

"Oh, my God!" D'zeos felt himself blanch. "The human race ends."

Vanqa nodded ever so slightly. "Probably not, but human civilization may. Either that or something else happens that changes future history. But I suspect humanity self-destructs. Suicides are increasing exponentially. Local governments and even planetary ones are collapsing, and entire continents are already reduced to roving bands of insane, starving savages."

"That answers another question that's been nagging me," D'zeos said.

"What's that?"

"That's why there aren't any aliens around, isn't' it? Humans are crazy, and none of the alien societies will mingle with us."

"That is correct. There are two other starfaring species that we know of, plus several non-starfaring ones. Both of the starfaring ones cut off all contact with humanity over two hundred years ago."

D'zeos nodded. "I don't blame them. Only two, huh? I would have thought there would be more."

"I'm sure there are. But we've only encountered two. On the other hand, we no longer explore. We haven't for several centuries."

"What were the others like?"

"They aren't much different than us. Bipedal, humanoid. Actually, there's a third species, and they actually do maintain interstellar communication with us, but they're not humanoid. They are a cyberspecies that evolved over the last twenty centuries from man-made robots, and they use a man-made communication system for contact with us."

"Really!" He immediately thought of Talaan and Zeleece and the robot Ron, and wondered—

"You know them, D'zeos. They evolved on the planet Ektar in the Delphia system but now inhabit three other nearby stellar systems. They are not considered interstellar though, because they never developed a means of circumventing the laws of relativity."

"Why? Why haven't they developed star travel? We did."

"They can optimize an existing system far faster and better than humans can, but they have no... no imagination. No intuition. Apparently not even any curiosity. No tendency to understand why things are as they are. They can't come up with completely new concepts other than by chance. They can only improve on existing ones. They're computers, basically. They can run iterations and permutations based on existing devices, or use stochastic processes to see if anything useful results, but using such a method to try and develop anything that is totally new is excruciatingly slow and very unlikely to occur. But the main reason is, the human method of star travel involves the mind as an integral part of the system. The robots have brains, but not minds that at times can seemingly transcend the physical universe."

D'zeos said, "Talaan's robots. Him and Zeleece helped this race evolve."

"I know."

"Why do I remember that? How do I know that?"

Vanqa just shook his head.

"Shang it!" D'zeos banged on the table with his fist. "Why can't our scientists fix it? Your scientists?"

Vanqa looked at him steadily, then said softly, "We've discussed that before. The original gene is dominant rather than recessive. It is needed for many essential functions, and it affects the germline cells, which are passed to the offspring."

D'zeos was not going to let him off so easily. "So? So what?"

"Early in the evolution of this condition, it could have been corrected. However, the technical capability was not available until somewhere around the thirtieth century. The doctors of that time could have used a new technique to correct the condition, but they had not realized that, nor the cataclysmic nature of the disorder."

"The outtime freaks," D'zeos muttered. He remembered Talaan and Zeleece discussing them. Whatever caused it was considered a mystery drug. Many people purportedly used it, but no one ever seemed to be able to find a source for themselves, although not for want of trying. It came to be looked upon as a subculture with very restricted entry. Super secret with mysterious sources. Exclusive and therefore highly desirable. Frequently they heard of someone being tortured or even murdered without ever divulging their source of supply, and those events only served to increase the aura of intrigue surrounding the supposed drug. But unbeknownst to them, it wasn't a drug at all. It was a genetic disorder.

"Widespread awareness of the true nature and seriousness of the condition was realized only later, but by then it had spread too widely to treat. On top of that, over the generations it evolved almost like an independent organism, becoming ever more intertwined with other bodily and mental functions. It is now so complex that it permeates virtually the entire body and affects nearly every metabolic function. It involves many proteins and the action of many, many enzymes which perform millions of functions. An intervention would render the human organism unable to function."

D'zeos began thinking how far the human race had come, how many steps it had taken since the spread out of Africa, and eventually to the stars. He said, talking to himself more than Vanqa, "So, after this long journey, the human race ends. What a disappointment we must be to God."

"Hmmm." Vanqa was looking at him intently.

"What do you mean, 'hmmm?'"

Vanqa didn't answer.

"Oh!" D'zeos understood now, and it was a relief; an obvious and welcome solution. "I kill myself. Jim Drake does. That solves the whole thing."

"No. Jim Drake lives, at least for some time. That we know. We don't know what happens next, though. Except that no one comes or goes from further in the future than a few days from now."

"Then Jim won't have any children. That's it! That's what I'll do. Get a vasectomy. Jim Drake will."

Vanqa remained silent for a long time, looking away, but eventually turned to D'zeos and said, "I don't think this knowledge will cause any changes in the present, so I'll tell you. Jim Drake does have offspring, and his offspring have offspring. We know he lives at least that long."

"If I don't kill myself, and I have offspring who are afflicted, and they go on to have offspring of their own, that causes the end of the human race."

"That would seem to be the case. But there is no way to know. Minds are physical systems, and as such they are ruled by the laws of physics. You know that, you knew it in Jim Drake's time. Temporspati paresëns, or TSP, is a result of a quantum entanglement among the manifold of experiential possibilities, a high order multiplicity of physical reality that results in the simultaneous existence of distinct experiences. But in quantum theory, doing anything to precisely define one state renders all other states nonexistent. Just as in simple quantum mechanics, questions such as you asked are not answerable by yes or no. The human race may both cease to exist and not cease to exist. No answer is possible from this timeplace. What we do know is that early January of the year ninety-three fifty-four is the furthest anyone has ever visited. And this is ninety-three fifty-three, my friend. Late December. So either human civilization does not exist after next month, or some major event occurs that precludes anyone going to or coming back from the future beyond then."

"Maybe this piece of the multiverse implodes, or whatever universes do."

"In one sense there is a multiverse, but it's not clear whether it's physical. Even if it is, there's no way to access it. Separate universes in fourspace are mutually unreachable and unknowable, and in higher order spaces we cannot function because our minds are inadequate to make sense of that world. But on the other hand human minds and technology do, in a sense, connect with a higher dimensional reality and it seems that is what we use to access those higher dimensions to circumvent the limitations of relativity. That's how we can flit from one star to another, or from one time to another. There is quite often at least one point where distinct points of fourspace are at the same timeplace in one of the higher dimensions. But we have no way to know if there is any other intelligent life form in some other parallel universe. We we're stuck with the one we're in."

"So we're doomed."

Vanqa nodded. "Apparently."

Another thought struck D'zeos. There was still something vaguely vacant about Vanqa. "Are you human?"

"Does it matter?"

D'zeos looked down and realized their meal was on the table. "I'm not hungry."

"Jim, you've got to eat."

"The human race ends in ninety-three fifty-four. January."

Aubert said, "It doesn't necessarily end. Not if we find a cure."

"You don't. I was just there."

"Just now?"

"Just now."

"Good Lord, Jim" Trina reached for his hand.

Dr. Marquand said, "But the universe perceived by any one mind is not..."

"Bullshit!" Jim stopped himself for a moment to calm down, then continued. "Sorry. You don't know all the facts. Here they are. Over half the race is schizophrenic, governments are collapsing, anarchy reigns in many places, and other starfaring species have banned all contact with humanity because we're insane. And, no one travels to or from any further into the future than early in January, ninety-three fifty-four. That, I'm sorry to say, is the way it is. Vanqa just told me."

"Let's go back to the lab," said Doctor Marquand. "I want to make one more type of measurement on you."

"No. No more. It's no use."

Trina said, "You've got to help, honey."

"Help? There's no way to help. I've seen how it is." He stood up. "Let's go home." He took the money clip out of his pocket and tossed a hundred-dollar bill on the table. "Come on."

Trina looked at the doctor, who shrugged in helplessness. "He's not our prisoner," he said.

She put her hand on his shoulder. "Honey..."

"No. I'm through." He held out his hand to her. "All I need is a taxi driver."

She sighed, looked at the doctor one more time, took his hand and got up from the table. The food had not been touched.

***

Trina came over and stood at the end of the couch. "What are we going to do if you have another trip?"

"Nothing."

She sat down next to him and he put his arm around her. They sat quietly for a long while, then he said, "I don't know if I'm going to have any more trips."

"Why do you say that?"

"Vanqa was pulling me there, and I don't think there's anything else left for him to do. He showed me what happens to the human race, which seemed to be his objective, but I don't know why. Maybe he was hoping something would present itself, or that just my being there would solve the problem, but it didn't. No ideas, no epiphany. So I have the feeling that's it."

Trina pulled his head around to look in his eyes. "It's not like you to be so fatalistic."

"Realistic," he said. "The word is realistic."

She closed her eyes. Soon a tear formed, a tiny one. The droplet grew into a sphere glistening in the corner of her eye. He could see light and dark places on the surface of it. He couldn't make out anything, but supposed it was reflections of the room. Maybe they would shield the universe inside it from the turmoil of the outer world. Jim imagined the drop filled with the miracle of life, a miniature universe isolated and complete unto itself.

Then the drop, that world, surrendered to the force gravity and skittered down her cheek leaving sheaves of itself to mark the path, a lonely trail of woe peeling from that little universe that was now reduced to just a streak on her face. The remains of the drop hung a moment on her jaw, then gave up and plummeted onto her chest and dissipated, an evaporating spot of moisture, a brief reminder of a universe forever canceled.

Jim thought of William Blake's haunting verse in *Auguries of Innocence,* a poem he hadn't read in years.

He said aloud, "To see a world in a grain of sand and a heaven in a wild flower, hold infinity in the palm of your hand, and eternity in an hour."

Trina sobbed, an emotion that came from the depths of her soul. She wrapped her arms around him, clenched him to her, convulsing in sobs that wrenched his psyche. It was all he could do to keep from weeping too. In fact, he couldn't. He blotted his own tears with the back of his finger, then he leaned over and kissed her eyelids. Each one. Pulled her head to him, and held it tightly. Silently. Finally he said softly, "You are the greatest blessing I have. And the only one that matters."

She broke into a series of heaving, gasping convulsions.

He fought against his own tears again, angrily brushed away failures with his hand, and returned to caressing her head. Finally he said, partly to himself and partly to her, "Everyone must die eventually."

She shook her head no without raising it. "New people are born. Life goes on," she mumbled from the pillow of his shoulder.

He blinked to clear his vision. "Whose laws are those?"

"God's."

She was right. God created the universe and man and saw to the propagation of the species, according to many religions. "Those *are* His laws." He put his hands on her shoulders and moved her away so he could look into her red-rimmed eyes. "That's all we have now, isn't it? Faith."

She raised her chin and sat up straight. Latched onto his eyes with hers and held them. "No. It's not all. It's the most important thing, and it supports everything else, but it's not all. We have each other, Jim. We have friends. We have people we love. And if we allow it, we can still have joy in our lives."

He studied the red veins webbing her eyes, the darting focus as she studied his face for a response. His chest tightened, a tingling tension inside. And remorse. But that was soon followed by a resolve that surged through his veins. "Yes, we can have joy. At least moments of it."

"More than moments! We've had moments here on the couch. Even though I've been crying, I've been filled with joy. Because I felt your love."

"I felt yours, too. You know, I have! God, I love you."

"I know. For only the second time in all these years, I truly know."

"I'm not sure I really know how to love. I mean, I feel it now, but during the day. During life. If I'm really honest, my concerns are always about myself, what will make me happy, what I want."

"It may be that neither of us knows true love. But together, I bet we can learn."

"It's pretty straightforward to talk about it and philosophize about it and agree that it's right. I don't know about living it, though. I don't think I can. I know I never have."

"Sure you can."

"My whole way of thinking has been the opposite of love. I've spent all my life trying to make other men envy me or fear me, and women desire me. That's what I thought a man was. And as we just said, it should be the opposite. It takes a lot more courage to love than to hate. I'd have to do a one-eighty."

"You've already started, my dear." She kissed him gently on the lips. "The only thing is, now I'm going to have to change the whole ending to my book. I had the betrayed wife killing her husband and getting away with it."

"I always figured it was an autobiography."

She laughed and kissed him again. "I wanted you to think that."

Chapter 23

Looking back from the end

"I think I'm going to sell the business. You didn't know this, but Boyd Ackersen Construction has offered to buy me out several times, and I did everything but close the deal last time. In fact I signed the papers and had Abby witness them. I just didn't give them to him. If anything happens to me, the papers are in my desk. Bottom left-hand drawer. Just take it to the lawyer and sign it. He'll take care of the rest, and you'll never have any financial worries."

Her eyes widened. "Do you know something I don't? About what's going to happen? Have you seen our future?"

He frowned, then realized what she meant. "No, I haven't seen anything about us. Only about humanity. And that's thousands of years in the future."

Her mood lurched into anxiety. "Jim! Why are you telling me..."

The doorbell rang.

Jim said, "If that's one of those doctors, I'm going to shoot the son of a bitch."

Trina said, "Good idea. That'll fix everything." She got up to answer it.

"Abby!" She opened the door wide. "And Jeff. Come in."

Jim stood up as Abby came rushing over. They hugged until Jim became uncomfortable, then he self-consciously released her.

She said, "Oh, it's so good to see you. How are you feeling? You remember my fiancé Jeff, don't you? We're getting married next month. Are you okay now?" She brushed his forehead with her hand.

"At the moment I'm perfect. Hello, Jeff." He reached out and shook Jeff's hand. "Congratulations."

"I hope we're not intruding," Jeff said.

"Absolutely not!" said Trina. "We were just talking about friends, people we love, and how important they are." She turned to Abby. "And you're at the top of the list. He'd never say this, but I think you're the best friend he has. He's closer to you than anyone."

Abby put her hand on his cheek. "Oh, Jim. I love you, too." She looked at Trina. "Is he really okay?"

Instead of answering, Trina said, "Come, sit down. Can I get you anything?"

"No thanks." Abby looked at Jim as she settled herself next to Jeff. "Are you going back to UCLA tomorrow?"

So, the doctors had sent her. "What makes you think I'd do that? How did you know I was here?"

"Oh, I just... I don't know. Someone told me. You, I think. Anyway, I called to see how you were, and they said you went home. That's all."

"The doctors sent you over here, huh?"

"No. Well, sort of."

"Good." Jim stood up. "I have a message you can take to them. Tell them that for the first time in my life I'm going to do what's right just because I know it's right." He went to Trina, put his arms around her, and kissed her gently. "I love you so much. Know that forever. Now," he said as he went toward his office, "I need to be alone a few minutes. I'm going to meditate."

He entered the office and closed the door. Went to his desk. Dropped into his chair, unlocked the bottom right drawer and hefted his Ruger three-fifty-seven magnum. Made sure a bullet was chambered. Pulled back the hammer until it latched into the cocked position. Stuck the barrel in his mouth. For some strange reason he was acutely aware of how cold and hard it was, and metallic tasting. He'd never realized that metal had a taste.

He pointed it toward the top of his head. Tightened his finger on the trigger and felt it meet the resistance of the latching mechanism. He continued to squeeze, then felt the sudden absence of pressure as the hammer was released. He saw the hammer start down, watched it move as if in slow motion. Just like that fly ball so long ago. The fly ball that started it all. Slowly, slowly the hammer traced its mechanical curve. The serrations on the hammer formed an arc like a bird's feather as it moved toward the firing pin. Slowly. Slowly. Inexorably.

And stopped.

A hand took the gun. Removed it from his mouth. Reset the hammer to the rest position and set the gun on the desk while Jim's mind went blank in a flare of stupefaction.

Then he realized Jeff was standing next to him. "What... how'd you do that? How'd you... Damn you! Now you've fucked up everything. You just killed off humanity. What the hell are you doing?"

Trina and Abby rushed in the open door wide-eyed, open-mouthed, horrified. Then they froze, comprehending but not wanting to.

Jeff said in an odd, sing-song voice, "Well, well. If it isn't The Drake, in person. D'zeos. The One."

Jim tried to respond but just made a croak, his mouth suddenly dry, then managed to get out hoarsely, "Vanqa?"

"Imagine meeting again at precisely this moment."

"Vanqa? How'd you get here?"

"Lovely home you have." He turned around. Looked at Trina and bowed his head. "And Trina. An honor." He turned a penetrating gaze on Jim, seeming to peer right into his mind.

Trina's hand flew over her mouth.

Jim said, "What the hell are you doing with Jeff?"

"Vanqa is a temporary guest of Jeff."

"If you're Vanqa, why did you turn on me? I was saving the human race in the only way possible. I was going to make it happen in spite of your future history. No wonder we die in ninety-three fifty-four. You stopped that hammer from coming down. Why? Are you even human?"

"You must get to the lab at UCLA quickly." He turned to Trina. "Zeleece, call the doctors while you are on the way there. Have them meet us in Peter Fillmore's lab. Hurry! I have very little time. Abby will accompany you. Take Jeff with you. Hurry! I can't linger. I will rejoin you there."

"Zeleece?" Trina almost stumbled as she took a step backward.

No sooner had he stopped speaking than Jeff's eyes rolled up and he crumpled drunkenly to his hands and knees, then looked up at Jim. At first blankly, then with shock. "Good God!" he stammered. He put a hand on the edge of the desk and struggled to pull himself to his feet.

Abby rushed to his side and pulled up on his arm. "Jeff! What happened? Are you all right?"

Jeff shook his head and blinked his eyes. "I had to let him take me over. I don't know how I knew how important it was, but I knew without a doubt. I had to. I had to let, to let whoever it was, damn, I don't know. Let him use me or something. Whatever it was, it's gone, but I know we must hurry. It's really, really urgent."

"Then let's go," Jim said. "Trina, you drive."

"I intend to."

The traffic was unusually light, and they made it to UCLA Medical Center in record time. Trina swung her Mercedes into a spot reserved for doctors and they all began piling out before the car was completely stopped. They scrambled into the building, half-ran down the hall, and burst into Doctor Fillmore's lab.

Four startled faces swiveled to face them.

Doctor Marquand scanned Jim from head to foot and said, "What's wrong?"

"Va... Vanqa was here!" Jim twisted around and jabbed a finger at Jeff. "He took over Jeff's body."

"What?"

Trina said, "He stopped Jim from committing suicide."

"What?"

"I had already pulled the trigger. And he stopped it. He stopped it in midair."

"And he called me Zeleece."

Abby grabbed Jeff's arm. "Then Jeff collapsed and said that we have to get over here fast."

Jim grabbed Dr. Marquand by the shoulders, searched his face. "Doctor, you found a cure, didn't you? You must have found a cure. Did you find a cure?"

"No. We've been studying the data."

Still gripping the doctor's shoulders, he turned to Jeff. "Then why'd he want us here?"

Jeff, who'd had his back to them, spun around to face Jim, his eyes deep, penetrating, and completely alien. He said in a sing-song cadence, "D'zeos, you have more friends than you realize."

"Vanqa?"

"More or less."

"What are you talking about?"

"I was referring to friends from six thousand years in the future. I know you remember that amazing, humane deed you and Zeleece did." He looked at Trina "The psychoprograms you installed in me? The ones that essentially gave us life?"

Jim's mouth dropped. "Ron? Ron the master robot? From Ektar? In the Delphi star system? Are you Vanqa?"

Jeff smiled and nodded slightly. "More or less. Yes and no."

Jim studied him, but it was not Jeff. Only his body. The eyes were controlling and penetrating. Metallic yet swarming with life, with depth, lit from within by nonhuman wavelengths. The entire body seemed to be shimmering with energy vibrating at frequencies above the observable. Beyond electromagnetic. Ethereal. Diaphanous. Aura-like.

"I am the one you named Ron." The Jeff-body tipped his head. "Now I can at last return the favor of life you and Zeleece bestowed upon us," he said as he turned and nodded toward Trina.

"I wanted to come back and do more," Jim said, "but was never able to return to Ektar. They put the whole planet off limits to protect those plant-beings. The Talal'a."

Trina was bewildered. "What are you talking about?"

Jim shook his head, confused himself. "I don't know."

"The Talal'a are a most gracious race, but they are content to remain as they are rather than evolve. We have left the entire continent to them, and they desire no more."

"But you," Jim said. "I guess we did enough after all."

"Yes, you did. Because you enhanced our social and empathetic tendencies, we quickly developed self-realization and became a cognizant, evolving, independent species. In your honor, we call ourselves zelaans." He nodded at Trina again.

"Now you're now a starfaring species."

"Not really. We only travel at sub-light speeds. It takes us centuries to go to the nearest star systems. On the other hand, such long travel times are not a concern for us, nor is atmosphere as long as it's not corrosive, or very hot or very cold. We have expanded to just three stellar systems, the planets of which are unsuitable for human life."

"But with your computer-centric brains, your abilities must be far beyond ours."

"As Vanqa told you, we do not have your most precious ability. Abstract or intuitive reasoning, you call it. We don't have your ability to leap nonlinearly to new concepts, to tap into some source of inspiration, to suddenly see a solution which does not follow a logical progression from previous knowledge. That human attribute allows you to imagine things that do not presently exist. We cannot do that. We can improve your inventions and ideas, and at mathematics we are far better, but we do not create. We understand the mathematics of your multiple universes but have no ability to exploit that for interstellar travel, as it seems to involve something intangible. We understand what you call your mind is involved, mind being of a higher order than brain."

"But you're here. You figured out how to do that."

"We zelaans did not figure out how to do this. A human team did, and ended up employing the part-human, part-zelaan construct you came to know as Vanqa. That human team, as well as much of the zelaan population, are linked to me right now. We could not do it without the human mind and human participation. There seems to be some higher order aspect to it which is uniquely human, and that is a crucial component. We are using Jeff to connect with you."

"So when I visited Vanqa it was you using his body."

"It was more complicated than that."

"Is this Ron occupying Jeff's body now?"

"No. Ron could not occupy a human body. Our physiologies are completely incompatible. Ron Zelaan First is not here physically."

"Then how..."

"I'm sorry, but time is limited. We must proceed. I will need a volunteer to act as an interface."

Trina and Abby stepped forward. "I will," they said almost in unison.

"It must be someone very familiar with using a computer. And," he said as he looked from one doctor to the next, "that person may not survive."

"I'll do it," said Sylvia as she stepped forward.

"Are you sure?"

"Absolutely. It's my dissertation."

"Any objections?" He looked at each of them.

"Yes," said Doctor Ebenstein. I don't want to lose her. Let me do it."

"I love you too, Morrie, but this is mine. I'm going to do it."

Doctor Ebenstein took her hands, pleading silently, then turned to the other two doctors. Doctor Fillmore shook his head ever so slightly, and Doctor Marquand looked aside. He turned to Sylvia, "Honey..."

She pulled his hands to her cheeks. "It'll be okay."

"We must proceed. Time is limited."

Doctor Ebenstein released her and took half a step toward Jeff. "Can we do it together?"

"No."

Sylvia said, "Go ahead, Ron or Jeff or whatever you're called."

Ron/Jeff looked at Maurice, who gave a just perceptible nod of ascent before turning away, then Ron/Jeff turned his attention to Sylvia. "Sit at the computer terminal."

Sylvia sat.

"Good." He came up with a device from somewhere that he put over his own and Sylvia's head. It looked like a linked pair of plastic headbands. He connected something to a port on the computer. Ron/Jeff turned to Peter. "I hope all your data are backed up elsewhere."

"They are."

Ron/Jeff pressed his hands together and a greenish energy enveloped them. He spread his hands and stretched the green field. His body seemed to glow. He passed his hands on either side of Sylvia's head, which became ghostlike, a flickering green x-ray photo. Ron/Jeff closed his eyes. The field gradually became steady, and he slowly drew his hands up to the top of her head, then pressed his palms together and pulled them up and away from her. "Established," he said. Ron/Jeff stepped back and said to Sylvia, "Who are you?"

"Ron Zelaan First over Sylvia Maynord." The voice was sing-song, not Sylvia's.

He placed his finger tips on Sylvia's shoulders. "Proceed."

Sylvia's hands fluttered, then became green ghosts spread over the keyboard. Code began streaming down the monitor screen in a blur, far too fast to see.

Ron/Jeff turned to the doctors, all three of whom were gaping. "Doctors, instructions for each of you is becoming available on those monitors." He nodded toward nearby workstations. "Everything is in terms you can understand. It will guide you to synthesize and administer a compound that will make Jim's mutation ineffectual."

Trina took a step forward. "Oh, thank you. Thank you!" Tears sprouted at the corners of her eyes. She took another step, unsure whether to embrace Ron/Jeff or not.

"It was not done for you. It was done for your progeny's progeny's progeny. For the human race."

"Our children? But I'm not... I can't..."

"You do. And without his suicide or this intervention, they would have inherited this same mutation, as would your grandchildren."

Doctor Marquand said, "Will this completely remove it?"

"No. That would not leave a functional Jim Drake. It will render it non-dominant and statistically almost impossible to recur from the residual mutations."

Trina reached toward Ron/Jeff, then pulled her hand back. "Will Jim be different?"

"Not so you could notice. The procedure will only undo the mutations in the germline cells while not bothering the somatic cells. That was important.

"Ron," Sylvia said weakly.

His head whirled around; his hands had never left her shoulders.

"I'm through," she said. "And I'm fading. Please help me transition."

Ron/Jeff moved his hands to either side of her head with a suddenly reactivated energy field, and he removed the headband. Sylvia slumped. He held her head as the green field glowed brightly and spread to envelop her entire head, then slowly died out.

Maurice rushed over, knelt down, and put his hand on her neck to check her pulse, his ear to her chest. "Sylvia, don't leave me. I love you. I love you."

"We were able to prevent her from scattering through timespace. She will return to you," said Ron/Jeff.

"Oh, thank God, thank God!" Maurice brushed her cheek with his hand, and her hair, and tears were running down his face. He kissed her lips softly.

Her eyes fluttered, and she smiled weakly as he put his arm around her neck. "We did it," she said softly. "We did it."

Ron/Jeff lost his balance, but caught himself on the computer table, and after a brief moment stood erect again. He said in the sing-song voice, "Ron Zelaan First had to leave. This is Vanqa, and I shan't be long. Nice old word, isn't it? Shan't."

Jim said, "Are you alright?"

Vanqa said, "The transition leaves one somewhat giddy, you might say. I'll be just dandy in a minute." He giggled. "Just dandy."

Jim helped him to a chair. After he was seated and seemed to have oriented himself, Jim said, "So you're Vanqa, not Ron now. Are you all right?"

"Yes. I'm quite sure. Thank you."

Everyone gathered around Vanqa/Jeff.

Abby's eyes roved over his face, "Will Jeff come back? Will he be all right? Will he be the same?"

"Yes. Soon. He is here now. But not. As am I and am not. But I do not have long. The laws of physics."

Doctor Marquand said, "Yes, the laws of physics. How are you here, and how did that robotic life-form get here? I can almost imagine mind transcending time and space for a brief time, but a robot? With a piece of hardware?"

"Not even mind can do that, doctor, at least not in the way you imagine. We exploited some high-order quantum networks of spacetime."

"I suppose that's completely beyond us to understand," he said.

"Actually," Vanqa said, "The genesis of the theory evolved from a foundation laid down in your time by the likes of a scientist named Roger Penrose. And others. Many others."

"But can we understand it?"

"Of course not. Not even Penrose could. After all, it took hundreds of centuries to develop this science from that little kernel. But it was a starting point."

"So the robot Ron wasn't here," said Peter.

"From your perspective, he was here for several minutes. From the perspective of his own timeplace, he was here for less than the Plank time."

"Plank time?" said Sylvia, who had almost completely recovered.

"What, ten to the minus forty-third power seconds?" said Doctor Marquand. He looked at Sylvia. "A decimal point followed by forty-three zeros."

"Yes. Vanqa said. "What we consider the normal constraints of physics do not apply over time intervals shorter than the Plank time. Due to quantum relativity and the higher dimensional manifolds of spacetime, the apparent time here was a number of minutes. In his timespace, it was less than the Plank time."

Sylvia said, "What about you? How is it you can stay?"

"I can't stay. I can only stay longer. There is another factor involved for humans that does not apply to non-human entities. It is called the Ineffable Factor. It applies only to consciousness, not to a tangible object like a robot or a human body, or Ron's coupling device. And you do not have the means to understand that."

Doctor Fillmore said, "That's why Ron, not you, brought the device. He said it was a human invention."

Jim said, "Why did you even need to come? How could you even come, since the mutation did not happen, or will not have, once the doctors fix it."

"Oh, but it did happen. You made the decision to commit suicide, and since the hammer was coming down, there's no way you could have changed your mind after that point. Had you not made that decision and done that, the human race would have perished. So our intervention did not change future history. You did. On the other hand, we knew you did not kill yourself unless Trina is already pregnant, because we know you had offspring."

Everyone looked at Trina. "No. I'm having my period now."

"But I didn't kill myself. So nothing changed until you came here and gave some instructions to the doctors."

"Everything changed. You made the decision and took the action, and the action was irrevocable so future history was set, right at that moment, and we from the future did not change it You did. You saved the race."

"But that doesn't add up. If..."

"Your universe, Jim, and therefore ours, has been altered. It will not be the one I am from. I may no longer exist, I don't know, but I do know the mutation does not propagate."

"If everything's already changed, how can you be here?"

"Ah, good. Excellent question. The answer is, hysteresis. So-called time travel has hysteresis, Jim. A lag between action and reaction on Plank scales of time, greatly exaggerated by relativistic and multiverse effects. On the other hand, within moments this entity will revert to Jeff Barton of your timeperspective. Vanqa from seven thousand years in the future will never be able to come here again. The only thing that will persist is your memory of me, and ours of you, D'zeos. The One. The Drake.

Jim said, "That, my friend, I have come to realize is not important. But I still don't understand how you stopped the gun."

Vanqa slumped and reached for the chair arm. "Time, the laws of physics are catching up, my friends." The sing-song voice quavered, "I love you, D'zeos. The Drake. The One who..."

He crumbled, but Abby was there to steady him. He seemed unconscious, his head hanging limply to one side. Abby was almost hysterical. "Honey! Come back to me. Baby! Wake up. Please." She looked up. "Doctors, do something!"

Doctor Fillmore took him by the shoulders to take the weight off Abby. "Give him a minute, Abby," he said calmly, although his pupils were huge. "Vanqa said he would recover." He had his fingers on his neck, feeling his pulse. "He's alive. I think he'll be okay."

Jeff began to revive. After several tries, he lifted his head.

"Oh, thank God!" said Abby. She kissed him all over the face. "Thank God."

Jeff looked groggily at Jim, and gradually brought him into focus. "Good God! You really are The One. That was no bullshit! I was... God damn! You weren't crazy!"

Doctor Ebenstein had his arm around Sylvia. He looked at her and said, "You realize you're not going to be able to use this as your dissertation, don't you? That you'll have to put the finishing touches on the one you had almost finished before?"

She nodded yes. "I'd be labeled a nutcase."

Doctor Fillmore said, "You'd never get hired anywhere."

Doctor Marquand said, "If you published this no one would give a second glance at another thing you said."

Doctor Ebenstein said, "She will get hired, though. I've been made Department Head, and I'm hiring her as soon as she gets a new Graduate Advisor and is awarded her Ph.D.

"Why does she need a new Advisor?" said Doctor Fillmore with a wide grin.

"You can see we're a couple. In fact, we're getting married. It would be unseemly, not to mention unethical for me to be her Advisor."

Jim laughed, "Once you're married, you won't be her advisor any more, that's for sure."

Trina elbowed him.

Jim said, "Me, I'm going to take up art and let you draw your own conclusions about what I'm trying to say."

"Sure."

"I'm serious. I'm going to enroll in some art and literature classes. I need an aesthetic balance in my life."

She said, "I should have thought of that years ago."

He shook his head no.

"Everything happens exactly on time. We just have to let it."

Epilog

In light of the events related in the preceding pages, it's time to repeat that Yogi Berra quip from the Prolog. As you now realize, it's not a quip. It's a statement of fact.

> "The future ain't what it used to be."

www.ingramcontent.com/pod-product-compliance
Lightning Source LLC
LaVergne TN
LVHW091110080826
845145LV00008B/1862

* 9 7 8 1 7 3 3 7 7 5 1 2 0 *